# PERMAFROST

# PERMAFROST

## A MYSTERY

## PETER

## ROBERTSON

GIBSON
HOUSE
PRESS

GIBSON HOUSE PRESS
Flossmoor, Illinois 60422
GibsonHousePress.com

Printed in the United States of America
20 19 18 17 16    5 4 3 2 1

ISBN-13 978-0-9855158-0-5 (paper)

COVER DESIGN: Christian Fuenfhausen

*for my family*

# ONE

I SAT IN MY CAR and read about Keith Pringle in a Chicago
newspaper article. His name shimmered above the page, like heat
above asphalt, and I shivered, with what was the only premonition I
had ever had in my life.

He was already dead, my premonition told me.

⁑

IT WAS A warm and hazy summer morning, already close to eighty
degrees with matching humidity, and not yet seven, by the digital
clock on the sleek wood dashboard of a black Mercedes SL600
convertible, or the thin gold Raymond Weil wristwatch beneath the
lightly starched white cuff of the cotton oxford shirt I had bought
one lunchtime on an impulse from Neiman Marcus.

The cellular phone was silent. The roof of the car was down in
an attempt to capture the best part of the day. In the trunk the CD-
changer located the fourth disc in sequence, and Rickie Lee Jones
sang "Rebel Rebel," by David Bowie, a song from my youth, with
which I would have liked to identify.

What had the day promised before I read the newspaper? I can
no longer remember. I am wealthy, I suppose I should mention, by
any conventional standards. I am white and male and European-
born and not yet old, and all I possess has come remarkably easily,
without stress or undue compromise, and is therefore largely
worthless, to my selfish eyes.

A large white car, perhaps a late-model Chevrolet, the kind of
car favored by older male drivers in passable off-the-rack suits, had

abandoned the road and stood, still hissing in some annoyance, on the parched and ill-tended grass on the shoulder. The car was empty and a bright red tow truck blocked two lanes of traffic in an effort to get at it.

Horns naturally honked, and the heat, and the promise of still more heat, made the good people angry and impatient. I just sat and waited and after a while unfolded my newspaper and skipped impatiently past the front page to the meatier sections inside.

I had no pressing engagements, and I don't have a boss with a scowling eye fixed permanently on a time clock or an evaluation slip.

I do find that people often mistake my complacency for contentment.

The article in question concerned the numerous hazards befalling European tourists in large American cities. I scrolled down through the fatal signs, the easy-to-identify rental cars and the shoddy maps, the dark streets on the wrong side of town. It appeared that virtually every state had at least one harrowing tale to tell.

Near the bottom of the page, Michigan's roll call of death was the smallest. Yes, an official agreed, they had their tourists, and yes, one was possibly missing. He was a British man, a Mr. Keith Pringle, who had been vacationing in the northern part of the state, where the population was sparse, but where tourism was quietly encouraged. Mr. Pringle was believed to be visiting a close relative, the article stated, but he was now also believed to be missing for close to two months. I noted that everything was only believed at this early stage. The British Consulate was naturally concerned, if essentially noncommittal, but the skilled woman journalist was able to hint darkly that this was indeed another hapless innocent, fallen to a rampant new crime wave.

The title of the article was "Innocents Abroad."

‡

KEITH'S NAME CAME at me from the page like a freak wave from a still sea, because he and I had been friends as teenagers. No, the term *friends* is perhaps too presumptive, and too intimate. We had known of each other, and we had met occasionally.

But he was preserved in a piece of memory I keep, and tend, if seldom access, from a hometown I have never managed to bring into any kind of emotional focus, but which is a memory, or catalog of memories, that, at times, resonates with more intensity than the present day.

⸸

NOW I WAS far from home. As was Keith Pringle. He was believed to be missing, whereas my position in the world is well documented.

I fed my premonition. It remained intact and had even blossomed some. I now knew for certain that Keith lay dead only six hours from me, from my expensive car, and my listless and shiny life.

But the six hours translated into thousands of miles, and almost twenty years distance, and a gently growing alienation, from the small and timid place where we had both started out.

But the distance wasn't that important, because I was going to find him.

# TWO

IT WAS HARD TO SPOT where one city ended and the other began, but somewhere in the crisscrossing suburban transition, the small Scottish town where Keith Pringle and I lived struggled to exist.

I grew up there, through my youth and the sullen years after my father, who I barely knew, died. Later, I still languished there, deep in an uncertain eternity of high school, handicapped by shyness and the chronic fear of physical contact with either sex, for whatever reason.

I lived there until I went to college at eighteen and blossomed into a demon lover and rugged sportsman who, in truth, existed only in my lurid imagination.

Our town had one bank and four pubs, it had council houses that looked in essence as pretty and as cared for as anything bought and paid for, or at least cheerfully brokered by the ever-willing building societies.

A betting shop owned by a minor sporting hero of a few years past was the older male's social focus in a high street that was a little too narrow for two lanes of traffic, while the co-op claimed the bulk of the elderly female allegiance. The four pubs duked it out for the loyalties of the rest of the adults.

⁜

THE TOWN SCHOOL was too small for the town children, so that some were farmed out to zealously progressive comprehensives in the two cities, and the rest were housed and educated in prefab huts intended for temporary use, but which were still standing and functional four years ago, when my wife and I took a more or less pointless emotional detour on a rare trip home to visit my mother.

⁂

IT WAS ONE of my few whimsical moments. It was one of my wife's few indulgences.

I remember stopping the car, getting out, expecting the warm jolt, some pleasing form of spiritual connection, the headlong thrust into reminiscence and reverie. But the huts all looked just as they had. There was no halo of nostalgia. They were just prefab huts.Old. And quite ugly.

My wife has less soul than I, I suspect, and was clearly uninterested, pausing politely, a slightly pained look on her smooth, sculptured face, reminding me that my mother was expecting us for dinner, and that she dealt badly with even a marginal disruption to her routine.

I got back into the rented car and we drove away slowly, moving like a lost tourist between the parked cars on the high street, which had never been widened, and never would now, because of the new bypass that catapulted the commuter traffic from city to city, without pausing to acknowledge our little town as it squatted, sulking, in the shadows of the concrete that stretched heavenward.

At a zebra crossing a lady guard with a huge orange lollipop of a sign took three children across the street quickly. One was crying. Two were laughing. An old man in a cloth cap and a Harris tweed jacket shiny at the elbows left the betting shop smiling like a fiend, and with a flourish entered the public bar door of the closest pub. Ill-gotten gains. He clearly felt flush, and would soon feel all the flusher.

Once the children had crossed, and left the sanctuary of the guard's domain, the crying one lashed out at one of the others and produced tears on a smudged cheek with his little hard fist. Now two cried, and the smiling boy was left out.

Why are children so relentlessly, callously horrible? Is it simply safety in numbers?

When I was fifteen I met Keith Pringle at a bad and otherwise uneventful party, where he chased after stupid, undeserving love, and got his nose bloodied for his trouble.

I don't now recall the name of the person who gave the party. It's very possible I never knew it. Doubtless a friend of a friend of a friend. Or else word of the event spread, and beer-fuelled teenage radar picked up the signal. You know how it is.

But I do recall the music, and the dark living room stripped of furniture by wise parents, the smell of cigarettes and spilt beer on carpets, and Brut aftershave applied a little too liberally.

Three delirious boys swayed like waves in the ocean in the center of the room, their arms spread across each other's shoulders like a Russian folk dance, drinking their warm beer from cans that never emptied.

They were loud, and they were drunk, or else they were pretending to be.

The song was "Jet" by Paul McCartney & Wings, and the year was perhaps 1974. I wore a navy brushed denim jacket and gray loon pants with a flare that fully covered my scuffed suede shoes, and I wore a leather thong around my neck and another around one wrist, and if it'd been a decade earlier I'd have been a real honest-to-God hippie. If my mother had let me grow my hair as long as I wanted.

Were there other people sitting on the floor in the corner of the room? In a just world there would be a lonely, pretty girl who was interesting once you got her to start talking and who would want to slow dance, and put her head on your shoulder when you took a chance and pulled her that little bit closer.

"My heart is like a wheel. Let me roll it to you."

A slow song. Jesus be praised.

But instead there was a drunken girl leaning against a wall, sullen between floods of tears, whose name was perhaps Jackie. She would dance with you if you asked, and she was undeniably pretty, but she would also try to kiss you with her dark red mouth all slack and wide open and her breath still smelling of sick.

You could kiss Jackie and feel her tits 'til they were raw and get as far as you could in the corner of the room, maybe get the finger up her in the forgiving darkness.

And the next day, if you had been unfortunate enough to have been seen by your friends you could always tell them you were drunk.

Near the end of the night Jackie would give you her phone number on a piece of paper as her sober friends finally would find her and drag her away. And by then one of your mates had seen you and the word had spread and you had some fast explaining to do later.

So you never called her, even though you'd liked her by the end of the night, and you'd stopped seeing how far you could get, and had started to talk instead.

You quickly left the living room in the small semi-detached and it didn't happen that way.

The kitchen was the talking room and the official sobering-up room. There, a girl in tight brown brushed denim flares and long straight brown-red hair and a milk-white complexion was making instant black coffee for some of the wasted boys, all pale and repentant and chastised under the bright fluorescent light.

A bedroom was reserved for necking couples. A single bed was piled high with winter coats for camouflage. But underneath the coats a tired, cocooned soul slept one off.

So the neckers were forced out onto the front porch, where their breath puffed in the bitter winter night, and they clinched on the steps, as the streetlights shone a pallid yellow that made the frost glitter on the ground. But they kissed furiously anyway, inept in their haste, their teeth clacking together, as they sought to generate a heat of their own.

The dining room was empty, except for Keith Pringle, who was huddled in the corner, cross-legged, crying into his hankie, which was wet and pale red with his blood and his tears.

We smiled at each other tentatively.

I knew him very slightly, no more than a face in the school corridor, either running or loitering between classes. A tall, gangly youth with a head full of curly brown hair, the palest blue eyes, all legs and trousers when he walked, like a pair of scissors standing upright.

His eyes looked horrible now. Just damp slits cut into snow.

"Do you by any chance have a Kleenex on you?" He spoke between sniffs, his speech muffled by lips that were bruised but uncut.

I didn't. I shook my head. He was a pitiful sight, but you had to admire the politeness of the question.

He touched his nose gingerly. There was something still damp and dark under one nostril.

"It really hurts." He let his hand run up through his hair so that it dragged a little of his blood with it.

"I wonder if it's broken." He spoke this last quietly, despite his misery; clearly he was bemused at the prospect.

"Jesus. What happened to you?" I asked him.

"Oh, nothing much," he said. "Jules Sweeney just gave me a kicking."

It should be mentioned that Jules Sweeney was known as something of a bastard, especially to those younger than him. He was one of the three rapturous singers in the living room, and his steady girlfriend was the brown/red haired girl in the kitchen, dispensing her coffee to the chastised paralytics.

I was fifteen years old. Jules was sixteen. Keith was only fourteen then and ripe for the sadistic attentions of Jules.

"He can be rather unpleasant," I helpfully offered.

Keith nodded in agreement. "Especially when he thought I was going after his Joyce."

Jules' girl was Joyce McKay.

"I tried to tell him that I wasn't, but the fucking bastard wouldn't listen to me."

His voice caught, and then Keith Pringle sobbed, and his pain and his anguish came gushing out and it made him forget that we were strangers, and that we lived in a country where this sort of cathartic emotional release wasn't the norm, wasn't considered proper, unless you were plastered beyond belief, and I suspected that Keith wasn't even close to that stage.

"I really fucking wasn't!" He was almost howling at me now. "Honest I wasn't. I wouldn't do a thing like that."

We weren't friends. A curt nod in the hallways. He lived close by. And his mother knew my mother and they talked about nothing things and the treachery of the weather as they waited at the bus stop.

Yet here he was unzipped, fully exposed in his anger and his despair, trapping me, uneasy now in a place between embarrassment and amazement.

I wanted to get away. I wanted to spare him his unguarded pain. But I was unable to, and in truth, I was unwilling to miss a single word or revelation.

"So he's just talking to me, like we're good mates, then he hits me in the face. He waits to do it in front of her, so I know it's just a game he's playing. And she's trying to pull him away from me as if she's shocked and concerned. But she's just playing too. She's really laughing and feeling like she's the damsel in distress getting her honor saved. The cow. The fucking cow. So I try to say something then. To try and explain to him that he's wrong about . . . but he wasn't going to listen. He's having a good time now. And his mates were there too now. Standing behind him. And they were laughing, taking the piss out of him about a second year kid necking with his girl. They were just making him go more mental."

He paused. Then his voice sunk to nearly a whisper. "When she told him about the tits I thought he'd kill me then." I must have looked confused. "Joyce was talking to him, telling him stuff like I was forcing her to kiss me. She said I wouldn't let her go. She said I tried to feel her tits."

He shouted. "I fucking didn't! I truly fucking didn't! I've fancied her all my fucking life. But I never would. I just couldn't do that. Not to her. Not the way I thought of her. Then his mates took me outside. In the back garden. They held me while Jules hit me. When

I fell he kicked me in the stomach and I was sick all over myself and he didn't want to hit me anymore then because he'd get it all over his good clothes."

I hadn't actually noticed the smell until then.

He asked me for a cigarette, which I didn't have. I went to the kitchen and scrounged one up and brought it back to him. He took it with a half-smile, lit it with a stainless steel Ronson lighter in a shaking hand that was smeared with mud and God knows what else, and took a deep draw.

"Thanks," he said shakily. And then he was silent for a moment, as he smoked hard.

I asked him. "Why did Joyce lie about you?"

He thought for a moment. "To make Jules jealous," he said finally. "And to save herself from getting found out for trying to get off with someone behind his back."

"Is that what really happened?"

He nodded. "She was here at the start of the party, before most folks got here. Jules was probably still in the pub with his mates. Getting himself pissed up. She came over to me and asked me for a fag. I had some then so I gave her one. She said a fag deserved a kiss and she kissed me then. It felt like it went on for hours and hours and she got most of her tongue down my throat."

"You didn't think to put up a fight."

"No." He smiled. "It never occurred to me."

I couldn't help asking. "So how does she kiss?"

He managed a rueful grin.

"Like a great big, perfumed Hoover. I was about an inch away from heaven. I've fancied that horrible woman forever and the awful thing is that I think I still do. I must be mental."

Once again Keith's words were loose, leading him like a lost dog, into the unacceptable, the heart-zones. Maybe he really was very drunk. But I doubted it. He was simply adrift, beyond a certain point, when all his inane utterances assumed an added weight, and a measure of resonance.

In the sober, sexually diminished light of day he'd come across as a drooling cretin, but that night he sounded like the last sensualist romantic on earth.

"She's a rare beauty," I said. I meant it too.

"You fancy her." He wisely divined.

"You'd have to be blind not to."

He nodded. "True." He said it wistfully.

"She's been with Jules for a while now."

He nodded again. "She has. Christ, I hurt all over."

"Love hurts." I said.

"Not like this. I spewed blood on the grass. Have you ever been in love?"

"Is it any of your business?"

"No." He hesitated. "But I can see that you haven't. It really does fuck you up." Was he talking about love or a beating?

"I can imagine," I said. "How's the nose now?"

"Sore. Since you asked."

"I have to go and piss very soon. I think."

"You really shouldn't drink so much."

"That's very good advice. Thank you so much."

"I'll see you later then," he said.

"You'll be okay?" I asked.

"My youth is forever gone," he intoned solemnly. "And I may have overrated her. Joyce. It's just possible. She might not be worth all this."

"You're a sick man. You should find someone else."

"An outstanding idea. Who did you get that cigarette from? Another would be just the ticket."

"Actually I got it from Jules," I said truthfully. "He's feeling very generous."

"I suppose you think that's funny."

In the bathroom there was a dry toothbrush in the medicine cabinet and an unopened tube of Macleans toothpaste. I brushed my teeth slowly and looked at my face in the mirror. The bathroom was decorated a deep blue, a nice enough color, but somewhat unflattering to anyone with a pale complexion brought on by a cold winter and too much beer. I washed my face in ice-cold water and dried it on a blue towel that perfectly matched the walls.

Did I look like someone who'd never been in love? I probably did. I wonder if I still do.

Keith was gone from the dining room when I returned and I was as much relieved as disappointed.

I gently rolled the drunk off my coat and left the party. I was late for the last bus home by fifteen minutes, but Umberto's Chip Shop was still open on the corner, so I went in. Vinegary steam poured out the door as I entered. As I was his last customer of the night, Umberto insisted on filling my bag to overflowing with chips he said he would only have to throw away if I didn't take them. I tried to protest.

"No. You take them." He said. "You not take them I have to eat them and I not need them." He patted a large but solid-looking midsection. "You nothing but skin and bones. Go. I shut up shop for the night now." And he waved me away.

⚡

I ATE MY way through about five pounds of chips as I walked home, in my head planning a series of complex and chivalrous strategies for winning girls away from posturing bullies.

I walked for almost an hour and I savored every cold second of it, taking the shortcut across a frozen mud path that ran between the public golf course and the school fence, then across the abandoned, graffiti-covered railway bridge against which I stopped to piss luxuriously, and onto a piece of wasteland that my mother's small house backed onto. I jumped the fence into our back garden, past the tiny greenhouse where my late father had puttered all the daylight hours he wasn't working, and in through the back door that my mother had foolishly, kindly, left unlocked.

⚡

TEN DAYS LATER the true story of Jules and Joyce was revealed to me in the back of a dull physics class. Joyce had apparently found out that Jules was going to pack her in and she didn't want to lose her man. So she decided to make him jealous, and poor smitten Keith got the job. He was the youngest boy at the party and, she rightly judged, the most likely to piss Jules off a lot. So Keith got the vacuum kiss and the snake-length tongue and it all worked out just fine when she told the drunken Jules that Keith had forced her into it. Jules lost his nut and laid into Keith. Joyce got Jules back and a quick shag on the coats in the necking room later that night. Jules got his shag and the chance to beat up a boy two years younger than himself as a nifty bonus. Keith got a peek at his own personal heaven for a minute, his conk battered, and then maybe he even lost his dreams too. That night.

But no. That wasn't quite right.

Because he was still fighting for love when I left him.

We smiled after that, Keith and I did, as we passed each other in the school corridors. And I watched his nose slowly get better. We were never to become best friends.

But we did smile.

And we would cross paths twice more.

# THREE

THE NOISE OF THE AIR conditioner in my office was distracting so I turned it off, sitting without moving in the warming silence, thinking about Keith, and constructing some kind of justification for what I planned to do.

The window shades were slit almost shut and the overhead light was turned off in the converted factory building where pencils were once manufactured.

The building now stands surrounded by converted lofts and art galleries and coffee houses and health clubs to work out in, in a rapidly gentrifying section of the city.

I called my place ArtWorks when I opened it. We custom frame pictures. The people who work for me are extremely competent, and I am at best extraneous to the day-to-day operation. Yet I come in early to work every day, and stay until we close, for reasons that have not been clear to me for a while, and try to look thoughtful, like the perfect boss, when I am asked a question by someone who already knows the answer.

⁜

THERE WAS A gentle knock and Cynthia came into my office. She brought coffee without my asking and I sipped at it after she left. I don't require any of my employees to fetch my coffee. If I want coffee I always ask if anyone else does, and if they do then I make them coffee, because, above all else, at ArtWorks we earnestly strive to maintain the illusion of equality.

⁜

In my first hour of silence I had arrived at a strategy. In my second hour, fortified by caffeine, I telephoned the British Consulate and the tourism board. Both calls were answered by harassed clerks with excellent manners and little authority, but I was promised prompt callbacks by more knowledgeable superiors.

A man from the tourism board clearly wishing to be nameless did call back very quickly, adamantly claiming to know nothing, and caring to divulge nothing, beyond the facts already presented in the newspaper article.

The police in several states had been notified, he did grudgingly allow. It was a police matter, he said curtly. I sensed he was constructing official barriers of denial beyond which I clearly wasn't welcome.

Was I *even* a relative? Did I *have* information? He wanted to know. His voice tended to naturally italicize.

I told him I wasn't. And I didn't.

‡

So I hung up, not terribly surprised at his reaction, which made Keith seem like a high priority police matter, even though I strongly suspected that he wasn't.

I looked at Sidekick on my computer screen and the time blinked at me in an ugly analog approximation. It would be six hours later in Britain. The middle of the afternoon.

I could call there. Who would I call there? And what would I say?

There was a gentle knock at my door, and before I could answer the door had opened and Nye had quietly entered.

ArtWorks does not make a profit, because that's how I choose to run it, and because I suspect I wouldn't like the place much if it did. But it also runs like clockwork and that's because Nigel Prior runs it that way.

An elderly, spinsterish twenty-seven, five years past his college graduation, where he majored in interpretive dance, of all things, Nye's rail-thin and tall and as always impeccable in an olive-green linen/cotton shirt and khaki cotton trousers, which I happen to know were purchased from Banana Republic.

Nye Prior is possibly the blackest person on the face of the planet, his face an imperious and inscrutable shadow that graced my door four years ago. Now he effectively runs things, powers us into the computer age with a vengeance, and leaves me free to squander the abundance of free time he has thrust my way.

Keith Pringle and I come from a land without people of color; pale inhabitants who tan easily cover the mossy hills and valleys, so quite often I err, making silly graceless remarks that Nye seems willing to forgive because I clearly don't know any better. But I never know how deep the hurt penetrates.

Nye is a gay man, albeit in an introverted, near-celibate manner that never seeks to advertise itself. Like many gay men he carries a list of the loved and the dead. He is very careful nowadays, and I suspect his sexuality has become a burden to him.

Below the imperious Nye are six girls and Titus, or Tye, as he has naturally become known. Tye is also black, but a paler shade of black, and he is very handsome, in a big, loutish, health-club manner, twenty-four, and also gay, but of a decidedly more hedonistic bent. In the face of Tye's slapdash sexuality, Nye quietly yet earnestly lectures. Yet Tye cruises on. Tye has been here two years. He's feckless and messy but he's beloved by my customers and mothered rather furiously by my girls, who fear Nye a little and, I think, consider me at best a wealthy dilettante and all-round loafer of little real consequence.

Tye has a gift for putting people at their ease and little talent in the art of picture-framing. He captures people, whereas Nye repels whenever possible. I fall somewhere between the two, finding myself constantly perceived as aloof, when I'm actually only uncomfortable.

The ArtWorks girls tend to be interchangeable. If one leaves, she invariably has a friend, or a roommate, or a sister, or a brother's girlfriend who happily steps in, and, guided by the proper, gently frowning, always diligent Nye, there is scarcely a ripple in our productivity. Two girls have, to my knowledge, fallen hard for Tye, and this he naturally finds hilarious.

If any have been smitten by the dictatorial charms of Nye he has kept it to himself.

These are my crew, along with the two elderly men who run the stockroom in the basement of the building, and the three elderly ladies who provide a stellar cleaning service in the wee night hours after we close.

This then is my ArtWorks, a small, tidy, much admired business that operates efficiently, without ever threatening to generate a profit.

A new and powerful computer sits on my desk and, in all honesty, merely takes up a lot of beige space. Nye keeps us firmly on the cutting edge, and, in his defense, it must be stated that he zealously ferrets out bargains. Nonetheless he is a fanatic, and I strongly suspect we have more ram and dram and megabytes and swap files than we really need. If Nye no longer has a sex life then he at least has an active and safe passion.

‡‡

TWO WEEKS AGO Nye put in an upgrade to our operating system. We techno-philistines can't actually tell the difference, but Nye was spotted humming to himself, which is always a sure sign of his overall well-being.

He told me about it, indicating that while he was more than satisfied with his purchase, he thought that one aspect of the system wasn't quite up to snuff. Could he find a solution? I innocently inquired. Yes, I was informed, there was a small northern Californian software company that manufactured just such a product, which would serve as a useful add-on.

Well, that sounds fine, I said.

Nye went to his computer to purchase ten copies of the supplementary product, while I faxed my broker and suggested buying shares in the smaller company. Our two deals were quickly done.

In the next few days I went online and monitored my new stock on the share index. As other companies upgraded their systems they too had found that they needed the add-on product and confidence in the small company rose. The share prices responded in kind. The company that manufactured the operating system, a juggernaut of a multinational organization, quickly saw their error, and bought a controlling interest in the small company, adding the program to future upgrades of their operating system. Confidence in the larger company rose, and the shares I had also bought in them, also rose steeply.

There are, I suspect, two truisms in investment. Firstly, consumer and industry confidence motivate the price of shares. And secondly, making more money when you already possess a lot of money is a relatively painless and simple endeavor, especially if you place little value on the money in the first place.

My two stock purchases had produced high short-term dividends. I brought up a calculator on the screen and came up with a profit of close to $150,000. I considered selling, but decided that the long-term prognosis for the parent company looked rosy. I bought more stock with my profits, and had my broker cut Nye a check for fifteen thousand dollars. A finder's fee if you will.

The subject of making money isn't a particularly fascinating one. It is an achievement neither brave nor noble, and has a level of satisfaction comparable with the solving of a tricky *New York Times* crossword puzzle in ink, by an experienced old hand.

Of course I speak from the position of a man unconcerned with shoehorning his meager salary into an adequate living for himself and a family.

Nye was holding the aforementioned check in his hand as he entered my office.

He spoke resignedly. "This really isn't necessary." He sat down, folding one leg carefully over the other.

"Perhaps not." I said. "But it's fair. It was your information after all, and without talking to you there would be nothing." I shrugged. "But if you like we can tear it up."

"No," there was the lightest imprint of a smile. "And thank you." He folded the check carefully in half, and slipped it into his shirt packet, checking to make sure the paper wasn't sticking out.

I pay Nye much more than he needs, as he has told me without qualms. If his exact life's motivation remains ethereal, it's clear that money certainly isn't a consideration, beyond food, and clothes, and software.

But I keep on doing it anyway. So he had put his unused money away in various sensible places, a few even suggested by me. And still he has too much left over to play with.

He sighed. "I suppose there are some things."

"Perhaps some computer things?" I inquired gently.

Nye nodded slowly.

He looked at his watch, a chunky digital affair manufactured by Timex and Microsoft that could read and store information from a computer screen. Nye had bought it the first day they were made available, ignoring the sad fact that it looked as if it should still have the residue of breakfast cereal stuck to it. But, for once in Nye's ordered life, style wasn't the central point here. Technology was.

"I should go back downstairs." He paused. "Tye's not in yet."

It was hardly an earth-shattering piece of news. "Has he called in?"

Nye didn't answer, but his mouth turned a shade lemony.

"Another of his sick relatives?" I inquired

He nodded. "At last count he's got four infirm sisters."

I smiled. "I think he's actually an only child."

"Thanks again for this." He touched his pocket.

"You're very welcome."

He turned when he got to the door.

"How's the machine working out?" He gestured toward the computer on my desk.

"Oh, very nice." I said. I was being a little less than completely honest. I couldn't tell the difference from the old one. "And we're still playing tonight?" I asked him.

"Of course," he said, and turned to leave.

‡

AS HE CLOSED the door my telephone rang, and a Ms. Chalmers from the British Consulate was breathless on the line and ever so sorry she'd not been there earlier to answer my query.

As I began to speak I deliberately let my native accent return; words were lifted up at the end of sentences so that everything spoken was transformed into a gentle question.

I told Ms. Chalmers I had read the paper, and that I had known Mr. Pringle, and I wondered perhaps if there was any other information? We were old friends you see? Had lost touch over the years? You know how it is?

She listened neutrally before she finally spoke, then she volleyed my requests back with excruciating politeness. For the British, being polite can be both salve and irritant and if I harbored strong suspicions, I still wasn't yet certain which was being applied.

She commented how kind it was of me to call and inquire. It really was awfully sad wasn't it? About poor Mr. Pringle.

I quickly realized that she had little to add to the text of the newspaper article, but she was determined to be positively effusive with what she had.

I lapsed into silence and waited. She was clearly a chatty person. And chatty people balk at the sound of silence, feeling the uncontrollable urge to keep on chatting.

It quickly transpired that Mr. Keith Pringle, a British citizen of no fixed abode, had been granted a tourist visa for three months. That was a short-term visa, which forbade him seeking employment. She made it sound slightly dubious, so I asked why it was so short. Well, she said primly, Mr. Pringle wasn't currently employed, wasn't a wealthy man of independent means, and wasn't married, or didn't appear to have dependents. He was, in a word, footloose, and might therefore be considered a prime candidate for slipping between the cracks, and entering the shadowy realms of becoming an illegal alien.

Yet he had been given a visa.

I decided to press her a little on this.

Well, yes, she agreed, he had a blood relative, an aunt, on his father's side, who had been married to an American citizen, but was now divorced. According to their records Mr. Pringle was supposed to be visiting her. Mr. Pringle had no criminal record, had never been convicted for drug trafficking offenses. And this was enough to clear his request for a visa.

Was there anything else unusual? I wondered.

Well, she'd replied, he'd not bought a return ticket, and he hadn't specified a length of stay. In the era of friendly relations between countries, visa restrictions were often waived with the good-faith purchase of a return ticket by a solid citizen from a reputable country. To Ms. Chalmers this blot on Keith's record clearly signaled a desire to stay in the country indefinitely.

He'd flown into the country on standby, thereby saving himself half the price of a one-way ticket.

But where Ms. Chalmers saw degenerate cunning I instead saw frugality. Keith had probably planned on flying standby back home. It was a first-come, first-served affair. He would show up at an American airport and keep his fingers crossed. In the meantime the length of his stay was indefinite, and that seemed to tie in rather nicely with the fact that Keith was clearly close to being a bum, or a hobo, or, as his native country had euphemistically decreed, a new-age traveler.

And so, as Ms. Chalmers continued her reserved character assassination, I closed my eyes and imagined him for the first time. Keith: sitting alone, tall and thin with his hair still an unruly shock of brown curls falling across his winter-sky blue eyes, slumped in a line of seats at a gate in the international terminal, drinking a cup of American coffee, furtively picking up someone's discarded newspaper, which could be from virtually any city in the world, buying a carton of American cigarettes, with the last of his American money.

Maybe he would buy Lucky Strikes. Maybe not. I was taking a romantic tack.

He would check his ticket repeatedly, and he would be nervous as he tried not to stare at the parade of reuniting families speaking in safety their own language, wrapped in a cocoon of blissful isolation, their words impossibly fast, their emotions scurrying all over the place, and all over each other, tears like the tributaries of lost rivers on the faces of the young and the old, especially on the old.

For the dysfunctional, the poorly loved, or the terminally alone, an airport, particularly one in the grip of the immigrant ebb and flow, was capable of producing an acute sense of despondency.

As yet I knew little about Keith, but I thought he might be alone. I returned to the kindly Ms. Chalmers.

"Do you have a recent photograph of Mr. Pringle?" I asked.

"Naturally," she said. Her tone grew colder. "We always keep one of the submitted passport photographs. For our own records." She paused. "But I thought you were good friends."

Oh we were, I quickly assured her. We surely were.

She spoke again, her tone harder and measured. "I think I need to know the precise nature of your interest in Mr. Pringle, Mr. . . . I don't believe you mentioned your name."

She was right. I hadn't. So I did.

⁂

THEN I TOOK a deep breath, and I told her what I had decided to do, the decision I had arrived at, as I sat in my car and read the newspaper in the early morning. An inexplicable decision, fueled by unfocused emotions that were noble and selfish.

But the oddest aspect was the spontaneity.

*That* was so unlike me.

"I'm going to try and find him," I told her.

And the amazing thing was that I believed it myself. I would take a few days, and I would track him down.

She was silent for a moment. Then she finally spoke.

"Isn't that usually a job for the police?"

"Well. Yes, I suppose it is. How are they doing so far?"

"Ah."

I waited.

"I suspect they haven't a bloody clue. And to be quite frank with you, they don't give a damn anyway. He's a destitute foreigner on an expired visa adrift in a great big country and they have plenty of nasty homegrown criminals of their own to deal with."

"I can understand their position."

"I can too," she said. "But tell me, what can you possibly do?"

It was a good question, and I didn't have an answer ready." Well. I have a lot of money."

It wasn't a terrific response. "That's very nice for you." She spoke coldly.

"And I have a lot of time."

"Mmm." Was I getting any warmer?

"So I can look."

"I see. And can your family spare you?"

I had to smile, because I have a wife, and I was very certain that she could spare me.

"Oh, I expect so," I said.

There was a silence, where I imagined she made up her mind.

"Well. Jolly good then," she said suddenly.

Did she really say that?

What was her first name? I wondered what she looked like. Was she pretty? Was she a battle-ax in fighting tweed? I managed to somehow juxtapose both into my imagination.

"Do you have a fax machine?" She asked.

I told her I did. Nye would have been outraged at the question.

"Oh, that's right," she said briskly. "I was quite forgetting you were rich. Well, give me the number then. I'll send you our complete file on Mr. Keith Pringle. I should warn you that it isn't terribly much."

I gave her the number.

"Thank you, Ms. Chalmers," I said.

"Phoebe," she said. "It's Phoebe Chalmers. I'll give you my number if you don't mind. Perhaps when you find anything you'll be good enough to call me and let me know. It's a little silly. But he's rather one of ours. Isn't he? And you won't tell anyone where you got your information, now, will you?"

"No I won't. And thank you, Phoebe." I said.

And there I hung up.

# FOUR

ON TWO OCCASIONS A WEEK, usually in the early evening
when our schedules permit, Nye and I play a competitive game of
racquetball in an expensive health club above a fashionable shopping
center on the near north side of the city,.

In truth, Nye and I are both antisocial and almost always free.
His is the modern monastic life, while my time tends to be more
quixotically arranged, as occasional social events come and go, and a
philanthropic façade has to be maintained.

Only one event in my week is rigidly allocated a specific day
and time; it's a charitable activity in a mildewy church basement
that, perhaps not so very surprisingly, isn't that far from the
health club.

‡

WHAT IS IT that I do?

And why do I find it so hard to talk about?

Perhaps a sense of modesty?

Once, a while ago, someone I knew very slightly asked me to
serve meals in a soup kitchen. It was, as I recall, at a black-tie affair,
and his request came out of the blue.

I was surprised by the question, to say the least, and found
myself blurting out a blunt, unthinking refusal, which, I'm sure,
must have sounded unbearably rude. Yet my slight friend smiled
wanly at me, a tolerant, practiced smile perhaps, and said that he
quite understood. I think now that it was the weariness and poorly
masked disappointment in his smile that did it.

We said no more, embarrassed, and quickly separated to find our respective spouses.

For a day and a half, I felt truly wretched. But I told myself that I really didn't have the time. I said it again and again. I really didn't have the time. I really didn't have the time. I called my friend the following day and pledged to help out when I could.

This happened a long time ago and I've missed few nights. In truth I'm not much of a cook, but I know how to lay out a mismatched knife and fork, and I possess the necessary skills to scrub and dry the chipped dishes that wallow first in the huge stainless steel tubs that are filled with scalding hot soapy water.

At the soup kitchen, I've passed many hours without knowing it, and I've listened to and occasionally participated in conversations I can never ever forget.

It occurs to me that I've told no one up till now about my secret philanthropic life. I expect we modern saints are by nature a circumspect lot.

⁂

NYE'S RACQUETBALL TECHNIQUE follows a predictably robotic inclination. Each shot is an angled equation. If the blue ball drops beneath a certain height he kills it, if it bounces high he drives it into the ceiling and regroups. He seldom varies, and each movement is measured, evaluated as a possible winning option, or else an injurious risk. I spot him a decade and I often win because my game ebbs and flows, and he is quite unable to modify his calculations to include the random elements. He knows all this of course, but knowing it is one thing. He's quite powerless to change his mode.

I suspect that people often think me a cold fish, but I'm a seething emotional caldron beside Nye Prior. Tonight he won, and I responded, uncharacteristically, by smashing my oversize Ektelon Catalyst hand-laid graphite racquet against the glass wall at the rear of the court. Both racquet and wall survived without a scratch, although I did draw an alarmed spectator or two.

Nye looked at me in slight dismay and confusion, as I clearly was, at that moment, an unfathomable jungle of mental disarray.

"Thanks for the game," he said quietly.

I huffed off the court. Wordless. A graceless lump. Livid for reasons I was totally unable to prioritize.

Thirty minutes later, and close to my sunny self again, we sat in the whirlpool, just the two of us, the soft enveloping steam rising from the smooth water.

I spoke, the movement of my chest disturbing the water. "I'm leaving you in charge for a while."

"Is this a business trip?" He asked.

"No." I paused then, unsure how far to go in explanation. "I need to get away. I'm heading up north I think. Perhaps to simply drive around for a bit. It would be best if you didn't try and pretend you need me at the store."

Nye failed to react to my news. He simply asked, "Can I reach you if I have to?"

We both knew the likelihood of him needing me to be extremely remote, but I also understood the importance of technological lifelines to my associate and victorious racquetball partner.

"You'd better give me one of the laptops," I sighed.

⚼

INSIDE THE TWO company 60 Meg Pentium laptop computers were 28.8 fax/modems running WinFax PRO software, which ensured us the fastest bps transmission speeds currently available, so that, if necessary, Nye could reach me in a nanosecond or less.

My sudden leaving was unusual and gossip around the store would be rife. Was I engaged in a torrid affair? In the throes of a hostile takeover? Surrounded by exotic courtesans and oily vicelords in an opium den? Nye would take no interest in the speculation and thus flame the speculation.

"How long will you be away?" He asked.

I hesitated. "I think perhaps a week. Possibly even ten days. Certainly no more. Can you handle things? Tye?"

"No," he said drily. "But then who can?"

"Quite. Well. Do your best. Fire him if you have to."

"And have all the girls walk out?"

"Mmm." I nodded. "I see your point."

He hesitated. "Can I ask . . . I wondered . . . are you all right? Is everything all right?"

I smiled. "I'm fine," I said. "Just tired. A little tired. That's all."

"You aren't in the habit of taking vacations. Sudden or otherwise."

"I know. Call it a change of habit?"

"You aren't in the habit of changing habits."

"No," I said a little sadly. "I'm not, am I?"

After Nye had spent a few more uncomfortable moments tiptoeing through the booby-trapped regions of my personal life, he abruptly gave up, and lapsed instead into silence, and a steely-eyed contemplation of the water surface.

I said good-bye then and left Nye to soak in his solitary, self-imposed silence. Was he plotting my overthrow? Considering a slew of hideous chores for Tye? Dreaming about a safe man? Or just letting the water splash over a young, beautiful body that housed a quick mind, that had turned both timid and a little trivial before its time?

I parked the Mercedes in a tight space close to the house, on a quiet residential street two blocks from the lake, a mile north of the business loop of the city. The street has permit parking and a discreet security force on constant patrol, retired police officers, unwilling to tolerate smart-mouthed teens in suburban malls, and paid for by a number of concerned residents.

When we married, I bought two adjacent townhouses on the street and immediately tore the dividing wall down, commencing the widespread gutting and rehabbing only newlyweds would attempt. The result was a house that didn't actually gain more rooms, but which instead boasts several oppressively large rooms, all track-lit, bare-bricked, pale-wooded, earth-toned, and impersonal in their sterile designer starkness.

I sat for a moment in my car as a neighbor hurried past with his German Shepherd dragging him determinedly toward the park. I didn't know him or his dog, even though they live in a house three doors down from mine. A lawyer or a commodities trader, he lived alone, but was reputed to entertain blonde-haired prostitutes, who arrived by taxi late at night, and departed in the morning, pale faced and smudged, blinking in the sunlight like vampires.

He was a mover and shaker.

He was a complete stranger.

⚓

THE LIGHTS WERE on in the living room, and her newly washed cream-colored Lexus was parked directly in front of the house. The obvious deduction to be made from these observations was that Patricia, my wife, was home.

Was there ever a time when Patricia and I loved in the conventional way, the misty-eyed way, in the myopic intensity of a newlywed vision that excludes all others in its blinding focus?

It seems impossible now, as the entrenched stasis of our existence holds fast. I think I know why she married me, although I'm altogether less sure why she's still married to me, or why I'm still married to her. We do share in a complacency. Or at least, we did.

At the end of my second year, in a not very impressive red-brick English college in a pretty market town not so very far from London I instigated a first small act of rebellion.

My coursework up until then had been doggedly acceptable, and I was perhaps on course for a sound, if unspectacular, second class degree in American literature. The seminars I attended were certainly pleasant enough, even if the subject matter was at times weightier than I was willing, or equipped, to appreciate. After two tortured readings of Thomas Pynchon's *Gravity's Rainbow*, I had yet to form even the most embryonic of opinions, and I had positively squirmed through the snide and clearly envious sexual detailing of *Couples*, by John Updike. This painful experience would be alleviated years later, as I discovered his quartet of Rabbit books all by myself, quietly marveling at the erudite brutality with which the author rendered his constantly evolving main character.

After the sniveling physical fear that characterized my early adolescence I found sports with a vengeance in my university years. Tennis and beer in the summer. Squash and beer in the winter, earning a place on the college teams in both sports, and only amateur status as a beer drinker.

By the end of my first year I had managed to sleep with two plain girls in a very tight timeframe in my very narrow bed, and relished the thought of each one somehow finding out about the other. The juicy vision of a to-the-death catfight, with long painted fingernails and a lot of intense hair-pulling got firmly anchored in my fevered head.

I can assure you that it never happened.

An exchange program had been set up with an American college in Chicago. The name of the institution was meaningless at the time, but the location triggered images of machine guns in cases and slick hoods in dark pinstripe suits and truthfully not much else. I applied for a place on the program on impulse, secured the requisite student aid, and asked a tennis friend to housesit my punk rock 45s in the old farmhouse his wealthy parents had rented year-round for him.

Miraculously my applications were accepted, and an interview and a joint with an extremely laid-back professor/advisor went smoothly. My place in the program was assured.

⁂

I WAS BOUND for the States, a year's worth of pleasant assimilation and light study ahead of me. And there I would meet and quickly marry Patricia, never to return to college for a final year in the august company of John Irving and Saul Bellow.

It was referred to as a "kegger."

She was sitting on the edge of a loud group, on the edge of a beige plastic chair, in a shambolic yard filled with wildflowers and weeds and blissed-out students. We had drifted downstairs en masse, from the spacious loft apartment on the fourth floor, where I had sat on a windowsill, and looked out across the abandoned factory buildings spot-welded to the contrary course of the brown snaking river. That I was drinking an icy Budweiser beer from a long-necked bottle in a room filled with plastic cups was a sure sign that I was the guest of honor, even if I was being unintentionally ignored by the bulk of the sundry raucous collegiate types.

Patricia was a tall and willowy beanpole of a girl, her severely pissed off and fashionably distanced looks seemingly precast in the supermodel deathly anorexic mold. Her long thin hair fell somewhere between blonde and brown and descended in an odd assortment of strands and groups of strands, fanning patterns and misty tangled tendrils reaching down almost to her narrow waist. Her hair would edge closer to blonde in the summer months, even though she was dangerously fair skinned, and hid out from the sunlight as a rule.

We were attending the same college and the same party. She was in her freshman year, indifferently pursuing an indefinite variety of liberal arts degree.

When the party descended to ground level, I was frog-marched downstairs and presented with a bacchanalian flourish by the hosts. There was thin applause, but seconds later, left once again to myself, I turned to the girl on the edge of the chair.

Somehow we were introduced and she took my hand. As she did this she turned away and smiled at what I took to be a private joke. It was a mannerism, I would learn later, and one that would invariably elicit either irritation or the near deranged desire to impress. When she spoke it was with the unnerving confidence I was initially inclined to attribute to all Americans.

She was eager to tell me that she was wealthy, or rather her people were. Her wealth was clearly an odious subject to be quickly dispensed with. She told me how much the party sucked, how much she hated domestic beer, how much she liked my accent, how much her father would love it because he loved all things British, especially the food and *Upstairs Downstairs* and *Benny Hill*. She told me how much she thought *Benny Hill* sucked and from all this I was forced to conclude that sucking was clearly a bad thing.

On the plus side she told me she liked pancakes and maple syrup and I must have looked confused.

We found a diner three blocks away and she said she'd pay.

We sat at the counter of the empty restaurant and put our four elbows on the cherry-red Formica and she talked about her family, and her plans, and the rest of the world, which shrunk with her words into something fierce yet tamable, a small yapping dog, a world she would make her own in a few short years, a world she would fill up with a career and children and love and charity and enterprise and whatnot.

This is how we are at nineteen.

I noticed that she wore no makeup, or none that fell under the usual garish classifications, that her nose was an unexpectedly button one, doubtless left over, like a keepsake, from a pampered childhood. It was, I thought, a pretty aberration on a face that in general bespoke a far more serious intent.

I listened to her plans and watched her delectable nose and her fine thin hair as it fell onto her forehead and as she swept it back, at first as affectation, and eventually with impatience, and I thought that it was all a very fine dream.

It will be perhaps less than earth-shattering when I reveal that virtually nothing Patricia wanted for herself would come to fruition. She was and is neither dishonest nor deluded. She simply talked a hell of a good game. As many of us do. As I doubtless did. In truth, much of what she wanted I would take away from her, or else simply neglect to provide her with. She has been admirably silent throughout this extended period of denial and outright theft, and my failure has been an unnamed one.

For our own reasons we chose each other that first night, over proud boasts, weak coffee, and soggy pancakes. We have stayed together ever since.

Faithful to each other. Spineless in our fidelity.

She showed me her doomed longing which I took then for steely determination. I showed her my guile, my gift for easy accomplishment, and an insipid gracefulness, all wrapped up in an adorable accent and surface manners.

All this she mistook for charm and acumen.

I wonder which of us is ultimately the more disillusioned now.

But perhaps I can pretend that my catalog of emotional crimes can be sanitized by the holy grail of Keith Pringle. Does that somehow assume too much? Of course it does. But, no. I stand by it. Keith will avenge me.

I am chanting this mindless yet comforting inner mantra as I turn the key in my front door. Keith will avenge me. Keith will avenge me. Keith will avenge me.

I entered my house.

The living room was still as if the air itself feared to move. András Schiff was playing Bach's "Well Tempered Clavier" on piano. It was precise. Mathematical.

Patricia sat motionless. A drink rested on a table beside her. Her thin, ringless hand was poised an inch above it. Perhaps it was a test of will. Perhaps she had forgotten to move it. Perhaps she was holding the air motionless. More likely a test of will.

She read *The New Yorker*, turning a page with a sudden snap, then sipping from the glass without looking away from the magazine. The level of the liquid looked to be the same. The glass was cold. The wine was chilled. Probably a good dry white wine. The room was cooled by central air conditioning, which was efficient and soundless.

Her hair was perhaps two inches shorter than it was when we first met. It was still fine. It was still the first thing you would notice about Patricia although she is no longer strictly a natural blonde, even in the summer months. Her blouse was a brown linen that her flat leather shoes exactly matched. Her slacks were a light tan, also linen, and close to white. Her wedding ring is fashioned from white gold inlaid with small, expensive diamonds. Her watch was a silver ladies Rolex that her father, Ben, now departed, gave her as a wedding present. Her earrings are discreet diamond studs that she is seldom without. They were a birthday present from me, and bought under strict supervision.

This is the sum total of her jewelry. Her clothes are mostly beige and brown. Her underwear is uniformly modest and ivory colored. Her skin is white and when she smiles her teeth are small and even.

As I moved across the room she looked up at me.

Then she spoke. "I was wondering who Keith Pringle was?"

I must have looked surprised.

She spoke again. "You received a fax earlier this evening. I think it was perhaps two hours ago. I'm not absolutely certain of the time. But I did hear the printer running in your room as I passed in the hallway."

I remembered I had given Phoebe Chalmers my home fax number. The computer was in my office. Patricia was very seldom in my office. Naturally the door to my office wasn't locked. Equally naturally, I have no secrets from Patricia.

"Did you read it?" I asked her, amazed at my sudden irritation.

There was as always no hesitation from Patricia. "Yes," she said, as if answering a drooling idiot's question. "I did read it. Was it something I shouldn't have read? Something private?"

"No, of course not. It's not even especially important. He's someone from my hometown, a missing tourist. It was in the newspaper this morning. Did you happen to see it by any chance?"

She shook her head slowly. "No, I didn't," she said. Then she spoke again. "Was this someone you knew well?"

"Why do you think I knew him?"

"Well." She spoke slowly in a voice I imagined her using to lecture a small and bad child. "His picture's now in our house, and I just assumed that you . . ."

I cut her off. "Yes. I did know him. But only very slightly."

She raised her eyebrows, pretending to be puzzled. "Then why the sudden fascination? The mysterious fax in the night?"

"Why are you quizzing me?"

She sighed softly.

I tried to smile soothingly. "He's just a person I once knew. He's simply gone missing."

"Yes . . . I see."

"And he might very well be dead."

"I do understand," she said. But she clearly didn't.

"I thought I might try and find him."

It came out dreadfully wrong, like a teasing schoolboy. All it required now was for me to stick my tongue out and pull her pigtail. This was not the urbane conversation I had rehearsed driving home from the health club.

"Where exactly are you going to be doing your hunting?" Her voice flattened out, to one long emotional line, like a fading heart rate on a hospital monitor.

"I think I'll start up north. In Michigan." I hesitated. "I'll be away for a day or two. No longer."

"How many days exactly?" There was a tension.

"I don't really know. It's hard to say." I hesitated again. "I'll call you often of course."

"Yes. Well. I shall worry about you." There was a pause. "When will you leave?" It was spoken casually, an intended afterthought.

"I thought perhaps tomorrow."

And then she snapped. The next words exploded. "You have to be . . ." But she stopped. She grabbed the reins. "You'll need clothes and things of course."

"Yes." We were going to be brutally civil about this. "Of course. I thought I'd shop for the things I need first thing in the morning. And try to be on my way by late lunchtime."

"Is Nye aware of your plans?"

"I've already spoken to him. He can look after the store. And, as I say, I won't be gone so very long." I wanted to explain. "It's . . . you see . . ." But I faltered hopelessly.

She gazed at me thoughtfully. Then she closed her magazine slowly, purposefully. Then she smiled. "We can have a nice breakfast together in the morning. Before you leave."

"Patricia, I need to . . ."

She stood up. "Do you, Tom?" She tilted her head. Musing. "I wonder what it is you really need. But perhaps you'll come back to me, a kinder, gentler man. Or perhaps not. If you do find your friend, please say hello for me."

She left the room.

I thought about throwing her wine glass against the wall but I didn't, instead I took it to the kitchen, carefully rinsed it out, and left it to dry on the wooden rack by the side of the sink. The glass was crystal and fragile and it would never survive the rigors of the dishwasher.

It was a house filled with fragile things like that.

⁑

I PUT ENOUGH water in the Braun coffeemaker for two cups, mixed two types of Starbucks coffee beans together, ground them until they were a fine brown dust, and switched the machine on.

In a house of large rooms the smallest room had become my home office, a place as comfortable as it was possible to be, in a place filled with tasteful empty space that defied all the natural instincts of a vacuum.

The twin bay windows face out onto a well-ordered play park where preschool children play in a giant sandbox made into the image of a bright red diesel train, while their diligent nannies watch one-eyed, and converse in an assortment of eastern European languages.

It was dark now.

The park was empty and locked up for the night.

I turned on my computer. A lowly specimen; a Gateway 66mhz/486DX2—salvaged from the store during Nye's recent

Pentium purge—with 8 meg of RAM and a double-spaced 420 MB hard drive, running Windows, Quicken, CompuServe, Quattro Pro, Word Pro, Approach, and Sidekick.

While I connected to CompuServe I scanned the paper copy of the fax from Phoebe Chalmers. It was a scant three pages long: a copy of the passport photo, a copy of the passport application, and a copy of the visa application.

"Was there more?" I wondered. Perhaps some information that the British Consulate clearly considered not meant for public consumption.

I would probably never know but I did have what I wanted: his parents' names and their address back home, his aunt's name, which was Bridget Cassidy, her current address, and her phone number in northern Michigan.

Nerves like the beating of a small bird's wing touched me, as I picked up the last piece of paper, which was a recent likeness of Keith Pringle.

It was a small, grainy image, which made him look like a petrified petty criminal.

I put the papers aside, loaded WinFax and located the fax document in the mail inbox. When l loaded Keith's image onto the screen the resolution was terrible. I fiddled with the magnification settings until his face filled an 8-1/2- x 11-inch piece of paper, then I sent the file to the printer and crossed my fingers.

As I waited for the laser printer to run off thirty copies, I faxed my thanks to Ms. Chalmers and gave her the number for the laptop I was taking with me. I left a message in CompuServe for Nye, telling him my plans in slightly greater detail, and also letting him know I'd swing by the store to pick up the laptop in the morning. I faxed my bank and informed them that Nye was holding the fort. I realized I'd need to make a sizable withdrawal before leaving town. I faxed my broker and told her I'd be traveling for a while.

I gave them all the laptop number.

There is virtually no escape in the modern world and I am as addicted to the enforced security as anyone else.

After this flurry of keyboard-mouse interplay, I stood up, put a CD of Mary Chapin Carpenter on the player and got my coffee from the kitchen. When I returned the last page had escaped from the printer, and the machine had turned itself off.

I don't know what I had expected him to look like.

But Keith Pringle looked an awful lot like Jesus, or whoever it is on the famous fake Shroud of Turin, or on all these oil-painted Eurocentric renditions. His face was bone thin, his chin coming to a sharp point. Deep, pained lines exploded out from the corners of his eyes, which were smaller than I remembered. His hair was long and stringy, where I remembered a halo of boyish curls.

In his present guise he would make a fine serial killer, a stranded hitchhiker, or else an impoverished and therefore sinless televangelist.

He looked like a tramp.

He looked like a total stranger.

I sat at my desk and stared at his image, as my carefully prepared coffee grew cold, and Mary Chapin sung about a foolish man, who decides to keep his wife, and his wise wife, who decides she'd rather not be kept after all.

I would leave town tomorrow.

# FIVE

THE VOICE ON THE TELEPHONE was made old and timid with
years. Querulous and slightly unsure, it was rendered still more
hesitant by a slight transatlantic electrical echo as he spoke.

"Is that . . . is that you, Tommy?"

I looked at my watch. It was close to nine in the morning, which
translated into three in the afternoon where he was.

Where was he?

He was where misty rain was carried by the teeth of a wind from
the North Sea, outside the window of a tiny council house on a
cloudy afternoon; the drizzle so insubstantial, so slight you could
never fully see it as it seeped, all the way to the marrow. This was if
you were silly enough to venture out without an umbrella or a plastic
jacket, to the wee store at the corner of the street perhaps, where the
ever-polite Pakistani man in the starched white shirt who never slept
would sell you a packet of tea, or twenty fags, or a loaf of thin-sliced
white bread, when the co-op in the town was either long closed, or
else too far away.

"That's right. It's me, Mr. Pringle. It's been a long time. How are
you doing?"

There was a slight pause. While the phone clearly made him
suspicious, I hoped that my voice and the fiber optic lifeline to the
safety of the past would soothe him.

"Och . . . as well as can be expected. Jeez . . . It's been an age
Tommy . . . yer Ma . . . she tells us all about ye when we see her at
the shops . . . ye're doin' very well I hear. I cannae believe it's you. I
just cannae . . . Jeez . . . an age an' a half."

His verbal powers were scattershot at best; his accent thick and warm enough to wrap yourself up in. Was he just the way I remembered him when he came once a month to our house? An essentially good man? Uncomplicated and benevolent and determinedly dour on the surface?

His teenage son had been a mystery to him. But in fairness, anything more complicated than a pint of heavy beer when he asked for it, or the pink sports paper on a Saturday night on the bus home from the match would have been beyond the myopic vision of Jimmy Pringle, a simple man in a simple land.

He would be retired by now, or very close to it, forty odd years door-to-door for the Gas Board, one of the walking legions of traditionally hangdog, dark-uniformed souls, who showed up to tip their hat and read the meter.

Stripped of his soul as a prerequisite, Jimmy Pringle was the gas man on our street, a fixture, like the bright red postbox angrily spray painted, or the streetlight on the corner that blinked a cold yellow as the first of the night blustered in.

"Ma. The gas man's here again." The emotionless shout echoed in the corridors of prefab concrete long before he reached the door in question.

⁂

THE TOWN. OUR town. I have to keep reminding myself that the town as I remember it isn't there, existing only in an imagination fueled by nostalgia, and made sentimental, tarted up by present-day uncertainty.

"Ye'll have heard all about our Keith then?"

"Yes. It was in the local paper. I'm very sorry Mr. Pringle."

"Oh yes . . . dear me . . . that's a big place ye're in now, is it no? Not like the old town. Jeez. . . . A big place it must be right enough."

"The papers didn't say very much about Keith, Mr. Pringle." I noticed that my accent was creeping ever so slightly homeward. Would Keith's father think I was making fun of him? I somehow doubted it.

"No? Did they no? Well . . . he's aye been a good lad Tommy. A good lad. But. Well, it's no been easy. I'll tell ye that. No easy at all."

"When did you last see him?"

"Well. There's the thing, Tommy. The thing is . . . I . . . well . . . his mother and I havnae seen the lad in three long year."

"I'm sorry to hear that Mr. Pringle."

He sounded suddenly suspicious. "Aye . . . well . . . But why all the questions Tommy. Whit's the game?"

"I'm sorry. I should have said. I want to help find him, Mr. Pringle. The place where he was. The last place they think he was. It's not so far from me. A couple of hours drive and I could be there."

"Aye? Is that so? I always thought of yon place as being huge. Well. . .that's very nice o' you Tommy. . .He could aye use the help. Keith could. That's no lie. But listen Tommy . . . this phone call . . . it must be costin' you . . . it cannae be cheap for you to call all this way."

"That's all right." I suddenly didn't want to tell him I could easily afford it.

"Oh? Well . . . like I was saying . . . yer ma must be right proud. Yer a credit tae her. So ye are. Well . . . maybe ye can help us. The polis here are worse than useless, and thae folks at the immigration dinnae seem tae have a clue either."

His voice coalesced then with his anger and frustration. "Nae wun cares whither he's alive or deid. Nae wun's bothered. His Ma's close tae tears all the time. She cannae sleep nights. We need tae know, Tommy. Whit's happened tae oor Keith? Nae wun's telt us shite here. We need tae know one way or another." His voice grew softer. "He's been a worry tae us fir years now. But his Ma, she cannae stop lovin' him. Cannae just let it go. At least we always kent he was alive. Now we dinnae even ken that. We need tae know whit the hell's happening!"

So I took a deep breath. And then I spoke.

"Can you tell me about him, Mr. Pringle?"

As I listened in the indistinct haze of the early morning, a summer sun peeked like a truant over the edge of the willow tree in the small courtyard at the front of our townhouse.

I sat barefoot at my desk, in a faded Ralph Lauren denim shirt and loose khaki trousers, sipping at my Starbucks coffee, fiddling with my burgundy Mont Blanc pen, every once in a while writing on a notepad, mostly a list of the things I would need for my trip: a new Gillette Sensor Excel shaver—would it come with a small container of shave gel and enough blades for the trip? Clinique soap, Colgate toothpaste—what size made sense? Whatever anti-perspirant was on sale, because, in my experience, they all tend to work the same.

At the rosy-hued beginning of our marriage, my wife Patricia would smilingly regale her lunch friends with my countless little eccentricities. This kind of snippy behavior is expected of newlyweds, and Patricia, in truth, had ample fields of opportunity to draw from, notably my supreme indifference in some areas and my dogged, persnickety insistence on minutiae in many others. As Patricia would testify, the juxtapositions were fleet and baffling, and the accompanying logic often markedly suspect.

For example, I write only with black ink, and try to use only expensive pens when possible. I buy cheap white sports socks from drugstores. Watchbands must be leather at all times except for sports activities. Clothes must be made of cotton. Shirts must fit very loosely. Underwear shall be white and full-cut and boxers are strictly for exposure on low-grade sitcoms. All shoes will be expensive. Yet haircuts can be economical. Cars must be exorbitant, but must also be proven to be worth every penny.

I have endeavored to explain much of this more than once. Cheap shoes are quite obviously no bargain, and expensive haircuts only mean the application of more styling mousse.

As I say, all this used to amuse her, but I suspect that the cumulative effect has been as grains of sand in shoes; a gentle hinting at sunny beach pleasure at first, then a mild irritant, and ultimately a discomfort that finally necessitates the removal of said footwear.

So I wrote in black ink, with a costly writing instrument, and I picked up my watch by the camel skin watchstrap and glanced at the time, before realizing that the calm I usually find in the cocoon of the familiar wasn't there this time.

But I did have a fallback.

There was a loud howl through the open bay window. Was it hurt or happiness? I couldn't really tell. But it did signify the arrival, in nannie-tow, of the first unruly infant at the play park.

And I could watch them play.

Then I remembered Jimmy Pringle.

Jimmy spoke in a more deliberate manner now, his bitter, inarticulate, unfocused rage choking him up on occasion, and masking his meaning. But he dearly wanted to be understood, to lead me through fifteen years in the life of his missing son Keith.

Keith left school at eighteen, which was an achievement only half the children in our town high school were able to manage. There existed a large whisky distillery nearby, which claimed most of the early leavers at sixteen, to bottle, pack, and blend, and to stand curve-backed before a long rattling conveyor belt eight hours a day, in silent deference to a product that ironically was denied the legal enjoyment of for two more years.

For those able to resist the insidious lure of time-and-a-half on Saturdays and Sundays, there were universities located in the two nearby cities. There was also a lowly polytechnic sulking in red brick and glass, offering courses of a less academic but conceivably greater practical application.

Keith Pringle went there to study at eighteen.

His parents were less than affluent, but the noble Labour government of the time saw fit to provide him with a full grant.

This was in the gentle years, before the reign of the Iron Lady, when the chronic wasters were ruthlessly weeded out, and education was strong-armed into becoming a privilege instead of a right.

Keith studied journalism at the poly for close to a year then dropped out to roadie for a punk band I had vaguely heard of on a

tour of continental Europe. He abandoned the road soon after, to
live with a Greek girl on a white-sand beach near the town of Oporto
in Portugal. He lived rough by all accounts, but happily, if his few
brief postcards home were any indication. He was young and the
nomadic life sits especially well on the young. The sand was bleached
and warm during the long days, and it was forgiving to pliable bones
at night.

Keith and his girl fished from the harbor walls and cooked their
catch over a fire at dusk, surrounded by friends. Someone had a
guitar. Someone else had a jug of cheap red wine, and someone
else doubtless had a joint to share. The water was still at twilight, an
unreal mirror of relentless blue, and his girl was soft, dark, and very
pretty.

That she was also a small-time drug dealer, or else her possessive
former boyfriend was, only became clear later. Maybe she was just
mean-spiritedly set up by him. Keith wasn't very sure.

But either way, she had come to the attention of the local police,
and although Keith wasn't convicted or even charged, he was no
longer welcome in Portugal.

Once he was back home he spent an indeterminate amount of
time squatting in one of the big cities in the south. He moved from
house to house. Ahead of authorities, and contractors, and property
owners, and, sometimes, the wrecking ball.

The squatting periods were broken up by stints on well-meaning
friends' floors or house-sitting during university vacations. These
interludes often ended badly as charity is almost impossible to give
and to receive without tearing decent friendships apart. He would
stay too long, or eat too much, or clean up too infrequently. It was
an endless list, that really only functions as emotional longhand
for: we no longer like you because the nature of our friendship has
forever been altered.

He was a house guest for a college professor one summer, in a pretty
thatched home on a famous river with a tall willow tree at the bottom of
the garden that dipped arthritically into the slow flowing waters.

The professor, an art historian, liked to host parties where he could provide the lion's share of the bold and witty talk, and where the presence of at least one genuinely dissolute bohemian was required to titillate his callow, well-heeled students.

This gig came with a supply of drugs, and required only the very occasional night in the professor's bed, with the professor's tired wife, while the professor watched the one-sided bout from the safety of the sidelines.

For long spells, Keith seemed to exist in some counter-cultural demimonde. His dole money kept him after a fashion. He attended folk festivals all over the country, hitching on the side roads, occasionally working in farms as seasonal labor, berry-picking in the summer months. He even managed a hard stint in a northern fishing town on the lobster boats.

There were women rather often, but they tended to tire of him quickly, and almost every coupling managed, like his house-guesting, to end on a sour note.

One girl even went as far as to change the locks on her cottage. Afterward Keith sat in silent protest on the grass outside her front door for two days and nights, cross-legged, lost in some passionate inner mantra of unrequited love. When a complaint was eventually filed, poor Keith was moved on.

The last time Jimmy Pringle saw his son was three years ago, in the dull heart of the winter. Even at first glance it was clear that Keith had lost a lot of weight.

He came home for a week and stayed for seven, and as he silently, without any outward show of gratitude, ate his way through the family fridge, his mother washed every piece of clothing he possessed and hung it on the line outside on the few fine drying days.

At the end of the seven weeks, after a bitter and senseless argument in which both men inexplicably took things very personally, Jimmy Pringle gave Keith fifty pounds he could barely afford and, crying like a child who had broken a new bicycle on Boxing Day, threw his only son out of the house.

He was deeply sorry now, he told me, and I had no reason to doubt him.

When he had finished, I told Mr. Pringle my intentions. I told him I would keep in touch. He mumbled something in reply but I wasn't sure what. He had talked and talked and now he was quite tired, and he was suddenly aware that I was little more than a stranger, and he perceived that in recapping his son's life he had exposed his failures, or what he imagined were his failures, to an unknown and unsympathetic light, one that could conceivably damage him.

When he at last hung up the telephone, I was certain it was to cry, because his pain was a lost thing that, once he had found it, would hurt him again and again.

Even this early, Patricia wasn't home, but she had left a note taped to the laser printer in my office.

She was to be shopping at a mall north of the city with a friend who she didn't bother to name. Then to a concert. Then to dinner. She might sleep over at the friend's or she might return later tonight. She had thought to cancel a dentist's appointment, one I had doubtless forgotten.

She closed her note by hoping I had a nice time.

I folded the note and put it in the inside pocket of the jacket. I folded the paper so that it was flat. So that it didn't wrinkle the material of the jacket.

For the rest of the morning I shopped, pausing at the store for the laptop, and picking up money at the bank. I bought gasoline and mints and a map of Michigan at an Amoco station that offered a cheap car wash with a fill-up. They promised soft cloths and mild soap, so I took a chance.

I had packed my bag with mostly new clothes, a pair of jeans, some shorts, khaki trousers with cuffs, three cotton shirts with long sleeves, a faded denim shirt, some white underwear from Bloomingdales, T-shirts, an older pair of Reebok cross trainers and an even older pair of Timberland boots.

I bought a box of floppy disks and CDs by Shawn Colvin, Patty Larkin, Patty Loveless and Trisha Yearwood.

In the drugstore, the ingredients listed on the back of the store-brand shampoo were the same as the expensive brand.

Standing at the checkout counter I bought a thick spiral notepad on sale and a three-pack of Snickers bars on impulse, and felt absurdly happy with myself for the indulgence.

Hovering close to outright giddiness, I had to keep reminding myself about Keith Pringle, telling myself that this was not an adventure.

At a traffic light I sat in the car and once again succumbed to stupid, inappropriate happiness.

Keith. I said sternly to myself. Keith. For God's sake just think about Keith. But the novelty of my predicament was intoxicating; I had no definite plans, other than to nose around and try and pick up his trail. I always have a definite plan. I had no hotel reservation. I always make a reservation. There would be places to stay along the highways. I felt sure there would be. Doubtless they would be rank places. I never stay in rank places. But they would do in a pinch. Was I in a pinch? What exactly was a pinch?

Had I packed spare batteries for the laptop? I had.

I should have called Keith's aunt today. That was simply lazy. Or outright cowardly. But Jimmy Pringle had been hard enough. He was a lost man. I would call the aunt tomorrow from wherever I was staying. What was her name again? I never forget names. Bridget? Yes, that was it. Bridget. I would call her tomorrow.

Did I have my phone card?

I did.

It was tucked inside my wallet. I carry very few cards inside my wallet. A driver's license. Two credit cards. And money. I don't require a lot of paper, notes to myself, reminders, receipts for things, things I will forget that I bought, things I might not realistically be able to afford to buy in the first place, and should very probably take back for a refund.

I don't need reminders.

I don't forget things like that.

It just isn't something I do.

And, when you get right down to it, I can afford almost anything.

Then the traffic light changed.

# SIX

IN THE SUMMER MONTHS, the Interstate highways are plagued by construction work, and I made painfully slow time as I headed north. It took close to two hours to clear the southern edge of the city and the state, heading east along the industrially smudged tip of the lake, and another restless, finger-tapping, station-to-station hour to cut across the anonymous corner of Indiana that stands spoiled by and subservient to the nearby big city.

At the first rest stop in welcoming Michigan, I pulled in beside a dark-blue Ford LTD with no hubcaps and mud-splattered Mississippi plates.

I bought an orange juice from a vending machine, and ate one of my three Snickers bars with the windows of the Mercedes all the way down and the map spread out across my lap.

The gentle shifting of three tall trees and lightly spinning litter—a Burger King bag—suggested a slight breeze.

With a splutter of static I lost the last respectable radio station just as Sheryl Crow was leaving Las Vegas.

In another hour I planned to turn north and follow the edge of the lake, with perhaps three more hours driving after that, although it was difficult to tell, as the roads grew smaller, two-laned, plagued by upstart small towns, and paper distances became dishonest.

A Latino man, close to my age—perhaps a little younger but cheated out of his youth by deep lines and pain—sat on a blanket with two small children, both girls, no older than six or seven, and ate what looked like fast-food chicken from a paper bucket. The children were sharing a huge soda with a cartoon character I didn't recognize, on the side.

The man himself had nothing to drink. He ate his food sparingly. His jeans and polo shirt were of some vintage designer label no longer desired.

They were obviously poor.

They belonged to the tired bulk of the LTD that sat rusted out and uneven on nearly dead shocks and bald tires.

When the man lifted a small piece of chicken to his mouth his hand shook violently. Instinctively I found myself looking away. The older child did likewise. But the younger one, maybe she was three years old, stared at the man, who was undoubtedly her father, with eyes that were dark and bold and ageless, and an expression that was impossible to read.

I got out of the car and walked over to them. I handed the man my remaining two Snickers bars. Before he could say anything I walked back to my car, climbed in, turned the ignition, gunned the engine savagely and drove quickly away, carefully resisting the urge to glance back in the rearview mirror.

A rich man impulsively gives away a dollar's worth of melting chocolate and the world goes on much as it did before. The Latino man hasn't won the state lottery, and his car is still a thin inch away from the metal graveyard reserved for Detroit's once shiny chromed-up dream-stealing machines.

Would it surprise you very much to know that I desperately want children of my own?

Patricia and I had been as selfish as any other newlyweds as we began our marriage in the deliberate isolation of our first home—a stark white condo filled with good light and very little else—and laughingly declared the darling little monsters to be quite incompatible with our self-centered life plan. Kids were for the drudges, we sagely opined, for those inching ever closer to their dotage, stained and harassed in their station wagons, driving from cold, shiny malls to swim team practice to costly orthodontists.

We were giddy in our arrogance, and complacent, knowing that we could so easily change, given the time that stretched expansively out before us, and the hormonal disturbances of which we had heard tell. So, like the wise new marrieds that we were, we were more than happy to wait, and perhaps reevaluate at a later time.

And now there was no later time, because I knew, without asking, that Patricia felt no different today. She didn't want a child. Or, at least, didn't want a child with me.

I thought of the two children on the blanket, their fast-food-slicked fingers holding the melting chocolate bars, eating as fast as they could, in the cheating summer heat.

*I wiped their cheeks with a used tissue and took the crushed wrappers from their hands and dutifully found a trashcan. I ushered them into the car as they sweetly protested, still intent on playing, on prolonging our little picnic. I strapped them carefully into the back seat of the sensible car, a sturdy four-door Volvo or Saab saloon, before pulling slowly, gently away.*

And a single wet, worthless tear slid down the length of my cheek.

The children run and fall and run again in the play park outside my bay window in the summer months. Made boisterous in the sunshine, they play without any of the restraints my life has assumed, and they make a mess, spraying their sand, bloodying their knees, and howling like little banshees for the short time it takes a grown-up to administer a kiss, or apply a miraculous Big Bird Band-Aid.

I watch from my window.

I suspect that they could teach me to be messy, and I suspect I would like that.

As I headed north I passed the edge of a small town.

There was a phone that worked by the side of the road, with a directory intact, outside a shiny pizza place that was hiring delivery drivers at a full dollar over minimum wage plus good tips.

I reached the booth before an elderly gentleman in pressed jeans and a baseball cap. I hadn't noticed him, and, realizing my eminent rudeness, I made to offer him the booth first. But he shook his head, and smiled at me, and gestured for me to use the phone, making an obsolete turning motion with his finger to signify dialing a number.

He turned away from me, spying a waitress inside the window of the restaurant. He waves at her, a tinkly-handed kind of wave and she waves back. Then she points to me and laughs. He laughs too. Heartily. For a second I imagine his laugh is going to evolve into a hands-on-knees then head-thrown-back hale fellow kind of performance. But it doesn't.

His small moment of bad luck is somehow hilarious to both of them and I wonder if they are deeply blessed, or else stupefied by rudimentary rural notions of contentment.

Either way, I knew now that I was a long way from the city.

I dialed the number for Keith's aunt from memory. Her name, I remembered, was Bridget Cassidy, and she answered on the third ring. When I told her that I was looking for Keith she sounded pleased. When I asked if we could meet she sounded surprised but also perfectly willing. With no urging she gave me directions to her house, which was located close to the lake, in a small town called Harmony, a little more than a two-hour drive from where I was.

Harmony was a summer resort town, the kind that all but vanishes during the winter months. The main drag was narrow, relentlessly crafty, and teeming with shivering souls in shorts and T-shirts and spotless sneakers, skin raw-red in the middle of the afternoon. There was a Harmony Fashions. And a Harmony Realty. There was a gas station, one old crappy diner, one garishly tarted-up one, a liquor-drugstore with a reassuring fifties exterior, and countless small shops selling rough and crafty gift items.

The street dissolved into a parking lot, beyond which a breakwater of large, angular gray stones gave way to the white-sand beach, which in turn surrendered to the lake. That day a thick, insistent mist insulated the beach and shaved a good twenty degrees off the temperature.

A large brown dog of indeterminate breed was swimming in the water. A pre-teen intently manipulated a Nintendo Game Boy and sat all but motionless on one of the breakwater rocks. Three seagulls were picking listlessly at a bun from an old hot dog in the parking lot, and on a green painted bench facing out across the still water, Bridget Cassidy sat in faded denim shorts that showed lengthy tanned legs with goose bumps and waited for me with a slightly smiling face that I was certain had very little to do with my arrival.

She wore no shoes on her feet and her shirt was denim, large and loose, washed less, or else newer than the paler material of her shorts. The sleeves were loosely rolled up, her arms were a carelessly tanned brown. She was long-fingered, and her ringless, precise hands refuted the common wisdom of defining their owner's exact age. A solid silver bracelet hung on her wrist. Her hair was dark red, thick and straight and reached down to her shoulders. Her nose was improbably long and pointed and she was made more beautiful by the imperfection.

She stood up as I approached her and I noticed that she was tall. Then she held out her hand, changed her mind, and very tentatively hugged me to her instead.

When she spoke, her accent was stripped down to the kind of transatlantic netherspeak many people accuse me of using.

"I'm awfully glad you're here," she said. "You made such good time. The road can be so slow in summer. With the repairs and the tourists. But today has been an odd kind of day hasn't it? I could feel the temperature falling like a stone just walking down the road from my house. It's the mist from the lake that's doing that. I thought about going back and finding some warmer trousers to put on but I didn't want to keep you waiting, and to tell the truth the chill is rather welcome. But poor you. You look positively freezing. Let's go back to my house instead, shall we? This is really much too cold for summer. It makes rather a lie of the season."

So we walked to her house.

"I tend to prattle on when I first meet people," she said, and I smiled. "Living in a small town does that. My mouth doesn't get enough practice."

The street was sprinkled with sand, the ground beneath the grass in the front yards closer to sand than to earth.

"How do you like our Harmony?" She asked. She had taken my arm as we walked.

"It's very quiet," I replied.

"Yes," she said laughing. It was an easy laugh. "It certainly is that. A place best suited for people who have retired or opted out in some fashion, I always used to think."

"You seem a little young for retirement."

She laughed again. "A lot young. Thank you very much. But I did retire I suppose." She looked thoughtful then. "Well . . . perhaps it was more of a spiritual sabbatical. My husband chose to divorce me a few years ago. It all came out of the blue, and it was all rather unpleasant. Are you married? There I go again. That's an abrupt and insufferably rude question to ask. But I can't help it. Do you mind my asking?" She shook her head in playful befuddlement. "Oh why am I asking you that? Of course you're married. You have a wedding ring. And you look so married." She paused and looked sheepish. "I should try to be much quieter," she said quietly.

"I am so married," I said then, "I suspect it's evident even without the ring."

She gazed at me quizzically. "Oh dear, I managed to stumble into that one, didn't I? Well, I'm just going to keep on talking. Where was I? Oh yes. Well, we had this place but we so very seldom used it. He hated it. My husband, that is. It had been in his family and he'd never got around to selling it. We lived in New York, but he was from here originally. So I took it as the settlement. I must say I surprised myself. It just suddenly seemed the right thing for me. It was really all I wanted from him." She smiled. "God, I don't think he could quite believe his luck. Anyway I licked my wounds here after our divorce was final. And after that I grew to like living here very much. My rash moment of intuition proved correct. The winters are long and beastly cold, but the isolation can be beneficial and the summers are truly a tonic. It was for me then, certainly, and now I'm happy to say I'm as well as can be, and considered something of a local by the genuine locals."

"How do you live?" I asked her. "The upkeep. And things like that." I realized I was being inquisitive.

She seemed happy to answer. "Oh I live very cheaply. I find myself dieting much more than I eat, as I get a little older. I like to swim and walk in the woods nearby, and these things are free. Before I married, I worked in New York for a publishing house as a copy editor. I still get work from them occasionally. I proofread the local rag. There are a few writers in this neck of the woods, good ones actually, though a little backwoods macho, and I edit their work for them and make sure they sound as tough as they want to be." She smiled proudly. "I'm really rather productive. I'd starve to death in New York, of course, but here I do manage to get by."

"It sounds like a pleasant life," I said.

"Oh, I daresay. For some people at least. Confirmed hermits like me, I suspect. But it's certainly not for everyone." She paused before adding. "A citified soul would go stark raving mad here in winter."

We waded through a tiny screened porch full of clutter—old walking shoes and winter coats, a box filled with cook books, another filled with old newspapers, a lamp with its shade shapeless and askew—to the door that led into the house proper.

It was a small and comfortable place, all on one level, a white cottage of freshly painted wood, with a garden far wilder and prettier than the ones on either side. The living room was warm and fussed over. There were bleached logs in the fireplace and well-read books packed tightly into two fitted bookcases, an antique desk with a Compaq computer that Nye would frown upon, an external modem, and a dot matrix printer nearby. Two armchairs and a small couch circled a coffee table, a portable television was pushed into the far corner of the room, and framed posters showed painted flowers from a gallery exhibition in Los Angeles that had taken place more than twenty years ago.

I couldn't help thinking that they were very nice frames, my chosen profession seemingly reluctant to cast me loose.

There was also a bathroom, two small bedrooms, and a kitchen. All were tidy without being obsessive; all contained vases of cut flowers, either fresh or else dried, all were painted a pale yellow-white, like the color of aging sunlight.

She offered me beer or coffee and I said a beer would be nice. She returned with two bottles of Rolling Rock. I wasn't offered a glass. After a moment's hesitation, we sat together on the couch and drank for a while, engulfed in a pleasant silence.

I found it impossible to believe that Bridget Cassidy was James Pringle's younger sister but that was what Keith's passport application had stated. If James was close to sixty, then Bridget Cassidy, who had obviously chosen to keep the name of the husband from whom she was now divorced, could only be in her middle to late forties, and was fighting the aging process with spectacular success.

I wanted to ask her but she beat me to it. "I should probably tell you that I'm not actually related to Keith."

I must have looked puzzled. "But on the passport application . . ."

She nodded slowly. "Yes. I know. I'm afraid that document is very much inaccurate in that particular regard. Keith wrote to me a while ago and he said he wanted to come to America to visit. He was a little vague about dates, about everything actually. He's mostly a boy you know, much younger than his years. His job history and such were spotty and he needed a relative to vouch for him in order to obtain an entry visa. I was the obvious choice, probably the only choice. But I was very happy to do it. It seemed like a formality. I never even expected to see him."

I was confused. "Then how did you . . . did you even know Keith?"

She shook her head. "I didn't actually. No. Oh, I did know of him. You see I went to teacher training college with Tony, Antonia I should say, Jimmy's younger sister. She was older than me and decided on teaching late. I trained but then I packed it in. We've kept in touch over the years though, and she must have given Keith my address."

"You lied to the immigration people."

She raised her eyebrows. "Oh gosh yes. And the British Consulate too." Then she smiled. "I used to be a right little

Bolshevik when I was younger, and little people in positions of authority still manage to bring out my worst side. I'm afraid I've lied before and I rather expect I'll lie again. Can't be helped I'm afraid. Thankfully no one ever bothered to check Keith's statement, and lo and behold, he suddenly had an aunt in America. But I think that's enough of my sordid side for now. I want to know something about you. You're doing a good thing you know. Looking for him. I have to admit I'm slightly curious."

"Why am I doing this? Why am I looking for him, you mean?"

"Well, yes. I did rather wonder."

"Mostly for my own small and selfish reasons."

"You don't accept praise very well, do you?"

"*You* helped him."

She shrugged. "It was easy. A little lie on a piece of triplicate paper in all likelihood filed away and forgotten. I remember Tony talking about him in her letters. He was the proverbial black sheep of their family. But I got the impression that they were all much too fond of him for their own good. He would grow to hurt them with his charm and his helplessness."

"Why did you help him?"

She smiled as if recalling a cherished secret. "For much the same reasons. Because he was charming and because he was helpless."

I said nothing then. But I did wonder if perhaps he had hurt her also.

Her legs were on the coffee table, and when she crossed them I noticed that the balls of her feet were hard-skinned and smooth, the result, I imagined, of spending much of the summer barefoot, walking fearlessly over sharp grass and soft sand. The largely nonsexual urge to touch her legs was an incredibly insistent one.

"What can you tell me about Keith?" I asked her. "What do you know that will help me find him?"

"Oh, I can tell you lots about Keith," she said. "I assume he's still missing."

I nodded.

With an effort, I stopped looking at her legs.

"He came here to see me at the beginning of the summer. He was going to stay for a week and ended up staying for almost three. A cynic would assume he planned it that way. I'm not so inclined. He's a disorganized boy, I feel, but not a disingenuous one. Oh and I'm not complaining about that. I do like to have company. He certainly wasn't any trouble. Keith's a timid soul. He phoned early one evening and said he was close. He wondered if it would be okay if he dropped by, to pay me a visit, to just say hello. He wanted to thank me for the passport. I asked him how he was. He said he was okay but he didn't especially sound it. I told him it was nonsense just dropping by like that. He could stay for a few days if he liked. He said thank you and I could hear the relief in his voice. He showed up later that same night. It was almost dark. I'd made a beef stew which he shoveled away in silence. To look at him you couldn't imagine where it all went. A racing metabolism he must have, perhaps. As I said he stayed for almost three weeks. We walked in the woods a lot. It was still a little colder than the locals like for their outdoor activities, but us hardy foreigners are used to the cold. He so loved to walk. We even swam in the lake. Brrr." She pretended to shiver. "Can you imagine the temperature of the water that early in the season? But he was an excellent swimmer." She stopped suddenly.

"Dear me. I notice I've relegated him to the past tense. That is always made ominous in mystery stories. Is he really dead, do you think?"

I shrugged, which instantly seemed a cruelly glib gesture. "I really have no way of knowing for sure."

She looked hard at me. "But you do have a strong suspicion."

I nodded slowly. "I somehow can't help thinking that he's dead. When I saw his name in the newspaper all I could think . . ."

"Yes?"

"Was that I was reading the name of a person already dead."

"It was an intuition, was it?"

"Don't you believe?"

She hesitated. "No," she said slowly, "not especially."

"I don't either. Or I didn't. I think this was my first."

"And you are inclined to believe it?"

"I don't know."

"And then you came all this way. Despite your intuition."

"It's not so very far. And anyway it's not . . . it's something I can very easily do."

"You do seem to insist on making light of it."

"You seem intent on interrogating me and trying to make me confess to being on a holy crusade."

"I'm very sorry." She spoke quietly, and I knew I had offended her.

I spoke quickly, "Did you know we grew up in the same town?"

"No, I didn't." She looked hard at me. "You'd never know to look at you. You're a very different species from Keith."

"I left there a long time ago. I've lived here for a long time. Maybe having come into some money . . . perhaps that makes a difference." But I knew as soon as I said it that that wasn't right, that that wasn't what made us different.

She hesitated. "No . . . I don't think that's quite it." She spoke carefully. "He's a young man still. Keith's a wide open soul. . . he's haphazard . . . nervous . . . utterly passionate."

"I'm not terribly passionate by nature," I admitted.

She smiled a little maternally then. "Don't reprimand yourself. As a nation, we're a soulless, callous bunch. Keith must have had some swarthy infidels' blood somewhere inside him."

We drank for a while without speaking. Then she put her bottle down and turned to me. "There's something I'm going to tell you now." She raked her hair with her hands. And then she turned away, for the first time suddenly unwilling to look into my eyes as she spoke. "I told myself before you came that I wouldn't say anything about this. But now that you're here I find I do want to tell you. I slept with Keith. It was the very first night he was here."

I said nothing.

"It was close to midnight when he arrived. I remember letting him in. God, he was a sorry sight. Covered in dirt. He said he'd hitchhiked and walked."

I tried to touch her shoulder. "You don't have to tell me this," I said softly. "It isn't necessary."

"No. It is though, for me. I want to, anyway. Please let me finish. After we ate, I made up the bed and showed him where the spare towels were because he said he wanted to shower; he was so filthy dirty. I went to bed and fell asleep listening to the water falling. Later in the night I woke up and he was in the bed with me, sound asleep, his hair still wet on the pillow. I just watched him for a while. Watched him breathe and shiver from time to time. And then I fell asleep again. I really couldn't think what else to do. In the morning we both woke up very early, and we made love then. And after we made love he cried like a baby and I held him in my arms, and I remember I felt very maternal and very foolish all at the same time."

She was crying now, a rush of tears, perhaps for her foolishness, perhaps for the lost Keith, perhaps for both.

"Please don't cry," I said, inanely, in time-honored stupidity.

She wiped at her cheek with her hand. "It never happened again. I can't imagine why it happened at all."

I couldn't think of a thing to say.

And then I said the first thing that came into my mind.

"I wonder if it made him happy?"

She smiled a little. "It would be lovely to think so," she said. "Wouldn't it?"

She put her head on my shoulder.

"Is it all right if I do this for a little while?" she asked.

I stroked the end of her hair and said nothing, enjoying her closeness and tricking myself into believing that it somehow mattered who I was. We sat like that for a long time, until it had grown dark outside.

She got up and lit the small lamp on the desk beside the computer. I would have to leave her soon. I had noticed a motel on the road out of town and I had planned to stay there for the night. There was the sudden ugly thought that if I pushed I could stay here, with her, and render up more insubstantial lust disguised as tender compassion, as she took hold of my shoulder, an anonymous source of marginal comfort.

She asked me then, "Did you know that Keith has a child?"

I said I didn't.

"It happened," she said, "about a year ago. He has a baby girl named Lilly. And like the great soft romantic he is, he even offered to marry the poor mother. She wisely turned him down. Clearly a sensible girl. Oh, Keith had . . . has a good heart behind a dazed mind and a dilapidated body. The girl's family naturally wasn't terribly amused. They threatened to bring the law down on poor Keith. So, as seems often to be the case, he was swiftly given his marching orders. Another nail in the coffin of the psyche, I'm very much afraid."

"I saw his passport picture. He looks like death warmed over."

"Yes," she said. "That's quite accurate. I gather he's lived rough for a good while. He's not in the greatest of health. His teeth could use some work. There's some kind of rot working on his feet. He limps a little, and he badly needs glasses. His skin is a weathered shade of red. As if he's been sandpapered." She paused. Then her voice grew a shade softer. "And mentally. I'm afraid he's starting to lose the place . . . to slowly unravel. And this," her voice rose theatrically, "this is the person I chose to sleep with. Hardly a conquest."

"You had other reasons."

She nodded slowly. "Perhaps."

"Is he dangerous?" I asked. "To himself, or to others, do you think?"

She smiled as if my suggestion was the most foolish thing she had ever heard.

"Don't be silly. He's the softest soul I've ever met."

There was another silence as I finished my beer.

"I wonder why he turned out this way," I asked, not really expecting an answer.

It was as if she were waiting for just that question.

"I'm of the opinion that love screwed him stupid. It tends to do that, you know."

It was in truth a decent enough theory.

I got up to leave.

It took a while longer. I stood foolishly. She sat.

The mist still lingered and the night promised to be an unseasonably chill one. She began to light the fire and I watched her as she knelt and lit the bundle of dry twigs and newspaper she was using as kindling. I sensed that I was, for all intents and purposes, no longer there.

It would be harmless and fun to imagine the havoc she could wreak on my stupid excuse for a life. Would the plight of a missing man be the unwitting impetus for me to fall in love with a woman a decade older than I was? The emotional flow would be all one way. But perhaps I would have my passion.

Was I really and truly thinking all this?

I had the sense that my real life was ticking over, marking time, in an orderly limbo several states away.

Against all my impulses I did leave her house a half hour later. We stood on her porch and said our goodbyes.

"I was nervous about meeting you," I said, "about upsetting you somehow." I held out my hand against the side of her face. She turned her head so that her lips brushed against my fingers for a split-second.

"Why was that?" She spoke very softly, her words dampened by the mist.

"I spoke to his father this morning," I said. "On the telephone. It wasn't easy."

She nodded. "And you thought I would be another distraught relative?"

"Yes."

She smiled. "My loss is . . ." she searched for the word, "different. Did James Pringle love his son, do you think?" she asked me.

"I don't think he quite understood him. But I think perhaps he did."

She thought for a moment. "The failure to understand must have made him love him all the more."

I was sure she was right. Her street was quiet except for a plaintive dog far away, clearly anxious to either eat or walk.

"So where do I go from here?" I asked her. The question was addressed as much to myself as it was to her.

"When Keith left me, he headed north," she said, "and he took the rural route that winds through the forest preserve, then curves around the edge of Paddle Lake. When I left him at the edge of town, he was riding off on a green bicycle."

I smiled. "A bike?" It seemed an odd notion.

"Yes, a bike," she grinned back." A green one. An old wreck of mine. I made him a present of it. It's metallic green. An old Schwinn ladies number. No gears. Nothing fancy. A handy basket on the front for messages and whatnot. It's a solid enough machine. He was amazingly grateful. I thought he would cry. But then, that's what he tends to do doesn't he? He cries. If you thank him for washing the dishes, he cries. If you ask him to close the bedroom door, he bloody well cries. The walls in the house are paper-thin. At night I heard him, as he cried himself to sleep a few times. Yet on other occasions he stayed up late and laughed fit to burst at nothing at all. He's strange. He was strange. Whatever. His emotions aren't really functioning on normal levels. He's either euphoric or else downright bloody miserable."

"Does he have a plan?"

"Of course not," she said, "he's drifted halfway across Europe and now he's doing the same thing here."

I was curious. "But why did he come here? Why did he come to see you?"

"I'm not altogether sure." She thought for a moment. "He tends to do things impulsively. America may have simply caught his fancy. But coming to see me. Well, he had to fly to this part of the country because the authorities are under the impression that he's staying here with me for a time. And I think he maybe just got lonely and afraid and needed a safe place to hide out for a while. Have you ever lived rough?"

"No."

"Neither have I," she said. "It must be terrifying."

And I suddenly thought of the men I had met in the soup kitchen each week. And the fear that never lets them go.

There was something else I was curious about. "Why is it that the police aren't looking very hard for him?"

"Oh they are. I think. Not especially vigorously mind you. But they did show up here a while ago. And I . . . well . . ." She faltered.

"You what?"

"I sent them on a wild goose chase of sorts. I told them Keith had mentioned going to Detroit to look up an old friend."

"And he never actually mentioned Detroit."

"Not once."

I asked. "So why did you lie?"

She looked rueful. "This was early on. Very soon after he left. I wasn't especially worried about him then. I just thought that he'd naturally want the police kept at a safe distance. He's had very little luck with authority in the past. He's a chronic paranoid, but perhaps he's justified in this instance. Anyway, that was what I told them. And they went away quite satisfied."

"You could tell them the truth now?"

"Yes. I suppose I could. And maybe they'll find him in a ditch somewhere with his throat cut. But I still like to think that he's safe somewhere. And if he is, then he still may not want to be found. He has vanished for long spells before." She thought for a moment. "I'll tell you what. If you don't have any luck finding him I'll go to the coppers like a good little girl and tell them the truth."

I smiled at her.

So I was searching for him alone. The thought managed to both scare and excite me.

"Do you think he might be suicidal?" I spoke my thought quietly.

She spoke quickly. "No, of course not!" Then she pondered the question some more. "I mean, I really rather doubt it. He loves life far too much. It's just that life tends to get the better of him on occasion."

I wanted to tell Bridget that life gets the better of us all on occasion, but I thought at that moment that she was looking to me for strength, and I didn't want to become less in her eyes. And anyway I didn't want to tell her something of which she was already well aware.

Before I left she kissed me on the cheek. It was light, tentative, a kiss between friends. I spoke of coming back to see her, whatever happened. And she nodded absently and said yes, it would be very nice if I did.

⁂

I WALKED RELUCTANTLY back to my car. The beach was dark and empty and the mist lay like a gentle shroud on the mirror-smooth water. A car pulled away from the parking lot with its headlights turned off and the engine sound muffled, as if wrapped tightly in gauze.

The windows of my car were wet from the mist.

I started the engine and let the fan run. When the windshield was clear I drove slowly through Harmony. By now, the mist had taken the whole town hostage, and when I turned on the radio, Pam Tillis was singing about a woman losing her man, gaining a horse, and feeling reckless and young.

I turned the volume up and peered uncertainly through the mist for the motel lights, welcoming the chance to concentrate on something other than Bridget Cassidy.

The Getaway Inn was the kind of motel where your car is always parked close to your room, and they write your license number at the top of the form they run your credit card over when you first register.

I sat on the overly soft queen size bed and looked at a vague painting of Mount Fuji on the wall. I powered up the laptop, logged onto CompuServe, and checked my mail. There was none. I stared for a while at share prices and contemplated a bold financial strategy. I found a weather forecast for Michigan for tomorrow, and I scanned a "Conference Room" for bored people supposedly in their early thirties. There were six people in the electronic room, and a woman named Cheryl was lamenting the lack of good babysitters in the Denver metropolitan area. She had four young children and a husband to mourn, recently killed in a motorcycle crash. The other people in the "room" were superficially sympathetic to her plight, but they were doubtless just teenage interlopers from some sci-fi role-playing forum, and were clearly anxious to trade crude witticisms and talk longingly about good sex instead.

There were too many lonely travelers on the information highway, and with a self-righteous click or two I logged off.

The room was cold and much too bright from a streetlight that lit up the parking lot and shot a harsh yellow light through the gaps in the curtains. When I had taken all my clothes off, I got into bed and pulled the white cotton-blend sheets free from under the spongy mattress.

As I fell asleep, my last conscious thoughts were of Bridget Cassidy holding a skinny blubbering boy in her strong, tanned arms, walking through thick celluloid mist, barefoot and bold.

The thought became a hope-dream and I became the boy in her arms. The dream ended there, unfulfilling, as all good dreams do, and I was awake again.

When I fell asleep again it lasted till the morning, and I dreamed instead of Ben Wise, the late father of my increasingly indifferent wife.

‡

I ONLY KNEW Ben for three short years, from the day I first met him, to the day he died. From the first, he struck me as the all-American businessman, tough and pragmatic. I would never waver from that view, although the man did manage to deeply shock me on several occasions.

He always claimed that he took instantly to me on our very first meeting. It wasn't evident, as his affection was displayed in a less than effusive manner. That first meeting was at a suitably tense family dinner, where I was brusquely shanghaied into his study afterward, and subjected to a ruthless interrogation punctuated by stiff drinks that I dared not refuse. What were my views? And what were my prospects? Did I think college was to be a springboard to business success? I wasn't at all sure how to answer as my financial views and prospects were a nebulous, ethereal concern at that point, and I truthfully was far from decided on the vexing question of academic worth. He listened to me as I wallowed pitifully for a few long minutes, then he pulled his chair closer, fixed his eyes on mine, and told me my life plan in a handful of short unequivocal sentences.

I never did return to my hometown or to my university. I never finished my studies. Instead I married his daughter, and exactly half of his artist's supply company, which comprised three retail stores and a highly lucrative mail-order business, became mine, after I had apprenticed myself to his philosophy, and after his large and contrary heart had suddenly hemorrhaged in an out-of-the-way bar one very strange winter night.

Patricia and I would subsequently sell the three store properties to a video chain, a bookstore chain, and an auto parts chain, respectively. A small part of the money would go to an abandoned northside warehouse, where I chose to locate ArtWorks, my framing store.

The ArtWorks site, I reasoned, was close to perfect, as the young and well-heeled were making the trek northward, gobbling up overpriced loft space, creating a vacuum to be filled by frozen yogurt stores, art galleries, health food markets, and gourmet coffee outlets. It was the gallery migration that first alerted me. The upscale clientele would need new frames for their hastily bought overpriced artifacts, and I would be on hand. The galleries would need their works mounted and framed and once again I would be happy to oblige. ArtWorks did a steady business thank you, right from the start.

But the mail order business was the crown jewel in the Ben Wise empire and we prudently hung on to it. He serviced schools and artists and libraries and talentless housewives enrolled in art classes all across the Midwest. He seldom advertised. He produced four cheaply manufactured catalogs a year and leased inexpensive storage space near the airport. And he made a killing as his three retail stores ticked over at best, languishing in their prime locations, selling the occasional box of ten drafting pencils to a woolly-haired art student.

We were wise to sell the stores. We even gave the woolly students and the other regular store customers a nice discount on their very first catalog order.

Although Patricia's mother was initially reluctant to see the stores go, she softened her position some when we paid off the mortgage on the large house Ben always claimed not to be able to afford.

But all this happened later. After Ben Wise died.

The fourth time I met Ben we sat on the outdoor patio of his large house in the northern suburbs of the city, the house he told me cheerfully he could ill afford. He said that wasn't important, the high price he paid. As a businessman his image was his most prized asset. He had to inspire confidence. In his workers. In his investors. In his customers. I told him that sounded like good advice. I thought he was right then. I truthfully still do. Although I do sometimes wonder about the price he paid.

After we had eaten the choice, well-done cuts of beef that Ben insisted on grilling himself, he told Patricia and her mother that he and I were going out for the rest of the evening. There was no audible argument from the women.

We drove east and south for a long time, into Chicago, to a part of the city with which I was unfamiliar. He said nothing as he drove his steel-gray Volvo, always within the speed limit, coming to a complete halt at every four-way stop sign, always slowing for an amber light.

Eventually he parked the car on a dimly lit side street and entered a bar with no name visible above the door.

In the near darkness, I saw other men sitting at small round tables lit by white candles placed inside smoked glass jars. They were older, all close to Ben's age, drinking and talking together quietly. The tables were waited on by four young men, twenty-two- or twenty-three-years-old perhaps, in puffy white shirts, skin tight jeans, cowboy boots with heels and short carefully styled hair. As the young men served drinks they were touched often by the men at the tables, their thick hair stroked, their hard thighs grasped. Hands seemed to follow then, tangling them like webs, but they smiled at the attention and the tips.

The realization that I was sitting in a bar that catered exclusively to older gay gentlemen slowly dawned on me. Ben sat in silence and studied my candlelit face. Then he spoke, his words escaping slowly, a long-rehearsed speech, or else one he had given before.

I thought then that it couldn't have been easy for him. But Ben Wise was above all an honest man, as prepared to admit his failings as he was to proclaim his successes.

Occasionally, he told me, he found himself subject to attacks of homosexuality. This was the phrase he chose. Attacks of homosexuality. Was I supposed to imagine something like a virus, a bug, a cold, or perhaps a case of the flu? They came. These attacks. He continued. Without any warning. He indulged them. His word again. Indulged. Then they subsided. And left him alone.

He paused there to ask if I, too, suffered from the same malady.

I told him I strongly doubted it. He seemed visibly relieved. I thought at the time that was a strange reaction, that he would want the sympathy of a fellow sufferer. But I was wrong. He considered himself in the grip of an occasional illness, a curse, one that he could have clearly done without.

He told me he was discreet. That he didn't indulge in teenage boys. Underage boys. He sadly acknowledged that a few men in the bar did on occasion. That was wrong, he thought. They were weak men. He had no patience for weakness.

He professed to have no interest in propagating his illness. He would endure it, in the company of his fellow sufferers. He liked to hope that it would someday pass. But he had begun to doubt that it would because, if anything, he told me sadly, his attacks were occurring more and more frequently.

I asked if Patricia's mother was aware.

He said that she was, but that it wasn't a subject to be discussed.

And what about Patricia? I asked him.

No. He was quite adamant there, his policy of honesty apparently hitting a solid wall. She didn't know. And she wasn't to know—ever. She wouldn't understand.

I thought he was right about that.

Later that night another man joined us at the table for a few minutes. He was introduced as Andrew, and we studiously shook hands. His face was instantly familiar to me.

Andrew Coburn was a prominent lawyer in the city, with a blonde socialite wife who was younger than he was. Alyson Coburn was conspicuously active in charity work, particularly for one of the city zoos, where she had gone so far as to pose in a tiny fake leopard-skin bikini, behind the bars of a monkey cage, for a recent promotion. On the next day, she had made the front page of the two city newspapers.

Andrew and Ben talked for a while. Without meaning to, they largely ignored me. Later Andrew ordered a fresh round of drinks from one of the young men, who let him run his hand softly over the bulging front of his blue jeans as he slowly made change for a fifty-dollar bill.

I looked at the aging hand. I looked at the smooth features of the young man, expecting to see disguised pity, or disdain, or a stolid acceptance. But I saw none of these things.

Ben Wise's stout heart burst open like a ripe cantaloupe one winter night. He died quickly and painlessly in the office above one of his three retail stores, working late, his nose pressed hard to the grindstone.

Or so the official story went.

And so we solemnly intoned, to each other, at the well-attended funeral service, where I searched in vain for at least one of the candlelit faces I had seen that night in the nameless bar.

I remember wondering to myself if they might be mourning elsewhere.

Several months after the funeral, I did run into Andrew Coburn again. Inevitably it was at a charity function where, at five hundred dollars a plate we were eating dry chicken, and helping a bold young theater group to purchase a newer and much larger venue.

Later we slunk off together, to a nearby wine bar, with a secluded table in the back of the room, where, over two good glasses of the house Chardonnay, Andrew told me the real story of Ben's death.

He had died in the bar. *Their* bar. On Leather Night.

Once a month, the young men dressed up in small leather G-strings that promised to hide very little. The older men tended to drink more on these occasions, and the place was subsequently louder and rowdier. The tips were much larger, and the expectations of the paying customers that much greater.

Ben Wise had died on his knees, kneeling on the bar floor in a good suit, licking the leather-clad crotch of a young man named Steven, clutching a thick roll of twenty dollar bills in one hand and a smooth, firm barely post-teenage buttock in the other.

Andrew told me that Ben had suddenly pulled away, a surprised look on his face, before doubling over and falling to the floor, thick blood suddenly erupting from his mouth and nose, his body twitching for the shortest time.

Then he lay still. The music stopped. Steven knelt down in the blood and searched for a pulse. And the bar became still more silent as Steven held Ben's hand and began to cry softly, keening like a repentant siren. And the crying was taken up by the others in the dark and otherwise silent room.

Half an hour later, Andrew and another man cleaned up the body as best they could and drove to Ben's store, where they left him hunched over an open ledger book, with a cold cup of coffee sitting beside his white bone-chilled hand.

The police weren't completely convinced. But the collective clout of the old men was too much for them, and the book on Ben Wise's death was quickly and quietly closed.

I had been right.

Ben had been mourned elsewhere.

In a chilled, bright motel room in a town called Harmony, I sat up wide awake on a soft bed, and imagined again the whole strange saga of Ben's death. There was something in his tragedy of Thomas Mann's *Death in Venice*, and something else, the sleazoid lure of amphetamined gay leather imagery perhaps. Yet despite the surface weirdness, Ben Wise had surely managed to die the best way possible, enveloped in friendship, even love, and mourned by beauty.

# SEVEN

WHEN I WOKE NEXT MORNING, the sun had burned away
yesterday's mist, and the rest of the day promised still more heat.
Less than refreshed, I showered under gentle, tepid water and
quickly dressed, sipping a complimentary cup of instant coffee.

At the front desk, I attempted to strike a blow for the luddites.

"You registered with a credit card, sir." The girl behind the front
desk was quick to tell me.

"Yes," I said, "but I would like to pay the bill with cash." I spoke
pleasantly.

"We're really set up for plastic," she primly informed me.

I essayed mild surprise. "And you can't take actual money?" I
asked evenly.

"No. We can. It's no problem. Really." There was a slight
pause. "Plastic is much easier for our records though." She smiled
tightlipped.

I said nothing as she picked up my odious money.

On the way out of town, I stopped at an office. The outside of
the one-level building was largely plate-glass, and, inside, the knotty
wood of late-sixties rec room vintage was aging rather badly. The
marquee sign above the four-car parking lot read Harmony Realty.
Inside I met the sole proprietors, Tom and Marcie Younger, partners
in life and residential real estate sales.

Both were large, loud, and shockingly friendly people, but
happily the volume fell as Marcie headed for the door and a "real hot
prospect." Her pudgy fingers trilled a goodbye, and I noticed that
her nail polish was shiny and violet.

I was left all alone with her husband, Tom, who slapped a seat with the palm of his hand, sat down on the edge of a desk next to it, and asked me in a booming voice how in the heck he could help me.

I lied to him.

I began brazenly waxing lyrical on the joys of a summer house in the area. Nothing too remote. Somewhere near here perhaps. I naturally wanted a pretty location. Near a lake would be perfect. I was keen to look at a few properties. Could he help me?

Managing not to lick his lips, he asked me about my price range.

I told him the right place was more important than the price, and it was all he could do not to whoop out loud with glee.

In an instant Tom Younger became a blur of industry and enterprise. Copying and stapling. Did I want coffee? That would be nice. Where was I originally from? Marcie just loved foreign accents. What kind of mileage does the Merc get? Did I have kids? I lied again then and told him yes. Kids were some kind of magic weren't they? He said. I assured him that they surely were.

In what seemed like seconds Tom had a thick folder and my second cup of instant coffee of the day placed in front of me. He had twenty listings inside the folder, all in what he liked to refer to as the "upper bracket."

On the outside of the folder was a map and his business card, which listed a home phone number, a car phone number, a work phone number, and a fax number. Tom even wrote a fifth number on the folder with a pen and a flourish.

"The golf club," he explained with an attempt at a sheepish grin. "It's the only other place I'm ever at."

As I gingerly opened the folder Tom Younger got up from the desk, stood, leaned over my shoulder, inhaled deeply, and leveled his sights for the hard-sell.

"Four of the best listings are all brand new ones," Tom Younger said. "'Bout thirty miles north of here is Paddle Lake. Right here." He stabbed at the map with his pen. "Named after the shape of the lake. Yeah. I know. It looks more like a bat. Heck, what do I know?

Maybe someone thought Bat Lake sounded kinda dumb. What the hell. It's a choice location is what it is. Here." He pointed again. "This is the town of Paddle Lake, population nearly 9,000. Hell of a nice place. Quiet. Slow kinda. Couple of nice shops. A big supermarket that pretty much services the whole county. I can show you places in town. No problem there. But what I think you might like more is further out of town. More exclusive. More vacation-oriented. This here," he pointed again, "is a quiet road that runs 'round the edge of the lake. Beautiful piece of water. Maybe eight miles long and three across. Crystal-clear water. Sand for the kiddies to dig. The four new properties are all at what the locals refer to as the Handle. Five miles from town, at the southernmost point of the lake. Eleven pretty houses there all told. Ranch style mostly. All on the side of the road facing the lake. All with access to the private beach, a dock, even a tennis court. White sand beach naturally. Real nice bunch of residents. A few are year-round, retirees and families with young kids. School system here's the pride of the state, let me tell you. But the year-rounders, that's good for security. Shallow water for the kids to swim in. No rocks. Dock's close to brand new. Not too many jet-skiers there yet." He hesitated. "You don't, do you?"

I assured him that I didn't.

He looked relieved. "Excellent. Wise decision. Expensive pieces of Japanese crap that make a hell of a noise and piss most of the locals off.

"Anyway," he continued. "It's a short drive to the town. Nice little town. A few good places to eat. Nothing fancy. But decent sized portions and a discount if you get there before six. Deep woodland all around the houses. Huge rural lots. A couple of the places I have are set back a ways from the road for privacy." He seemed to run out of steam for a moment so I cut him off.

"I'd like to drive around a bit, Tom." I said. "Perhaps take a day or two and look for myself. The listings look extremely promising, and the map will be a lot of help. I'll call you and let you know."

He'd clearly had a lot more to say. But he wasn't about to blow a prospective deal with a show of pique.

"That's real good thinking, Tom. My advice to you? Drive real slow. Stop and look around. Talk to the natives. Get a feel for the place. A friendlier bunch you'll never find. Breathe in the air. Then you find a place that catches your eye? You call me or Mar. We'll be there in a flash and show you around." He paused. "Now tell me this. Where are you gonna stay up there?"

"I hadn't really thought . . ."

Tom had a ready answer. "I thought not. Listen. Your best bet's Sandy Weller's place. She has a huge barn of a house up there. It's really a glorified B and B, Brit style, so you'll feel right at home. And Sandy will give you a meal at night if you sweet-talk her right. Tell you what. I'll call her right now. Tell her you're on your way. Tennis pal of Mar's. Before she had to give it up. Sandy'll see you all right."

"There's really no need."

Tom waved my objections aside. "My pleasure. Actually Sandy can be a bitch on wheels. If she feels like it. She's a hell of a looker though. Not that I'm in the market, you understand? The original one-woman man. That's Tom Younger here. Mar would have my nuts on a platter anyway." He laughed loudly.

With a lot more gusto and persuasion Tom Younger steered me to the door with my folder full of "shit-hot properties." He crushed my hand in farewell before holding the door of my car open. Before I could get in, he stuck his head inside and whistled softly.

"Is this the 500?"

"No," I said. "The 600."

He sniffed deeply at the leather. "She's a hell of a machine, Tom. What did you say you did?"

I hadn't. I told him then.

"Goddam!" he shouted good naturedly, "I'm in the wrong racket."

I drove away from Bridget Cassidy, Tom Younger, and the town of Harmony. I had two cups of acidic coffee inside me, and

I was suddenly very hungry. The first two places I passed looked unappealing, and before I knew it I had left the town behind. It clearly didn't pay to be too picky. My stomach grumbled, and I almost looked for the two Snickers bars before I remembered.

The radio delivered either loud static or stations terminally locked in the seventies, so I turned on the CD changer and listened to Lucinda Williams instead.

The folder was on the seat and I glanced at the front, at the map of the misnamed Paddle Lake, the town and the body of water, and the Handle, where the real estate market was jumping. Four properties for sale out of a total of eleven. Was that odd? If Tom Younger thought so he'd have been crazy to mention it.

If I were Keith . . .

It was a seriously flawed notion.

It was a lake.

And Keith apparently loved to swim.

There were woods.

And Keith loved to walk in woods.

It was on the road that Keith had taken out of Harmony. Thirty miles or so by old bicycle.

It was a quiet place.

And if I thought Keith Pringle wanted anything in this world that had thus far conspired to royally screw him over, I thought he must surely want solitude.

But the Handle was an upper-middle class place.

And Keith Pringle wasn't even classified.

It was a place for families.

And Keith was conspicuously all alone.

But I had no other places in mind, and I sensed that I wouldn't be getting any more intuitions. It was now a question of playing percentages.

As Bridget had promised, the two-lane highway first cut through the middle of a forest preserve. The road wound some, usually attaching itself to the wayward shoreline of several small lakes, but just as often shifting randomly, or else adhering to rules defined long ago, for farmland no longer tilled, and fields no longer fenced.

Close to the lakes, I passed innumerable bait shops, and places renting the much-loathed jet skis. I noticed cherry stands outside tumble-down houses with their siding falling away, the finned wrecks of Detroit history rotting metallically outside more than a few of them.

The preserve was green and lush from the summer, which had been an unseasonably wet one. Three wild turkeys stood pencil-legged and scrawny at the side of the road and watched me pass.

I purposely drove the Mercedes slowly. Not slow enough to approximate the speed of a man in poor health on an old bicycle, but slow enough to notice the places where he might have stopped. I reasoned that Keith Pringle had taken this road. It was the one he had started out on. It boasted few exits. It was a minor road heading north. It appeared to be the most scenic route, and, unlike the major state highways, it allowed cyclists.

I passed a gas station bereft of the usual convenience store attachment. I assumed he would have had little need of gasoline. But he might have needed air for his tires. Or directions. Or a restroom. Or a drink of tepid water from a tap that poured into a grease-stained sink.

But I wasn't sure. And all I was really doing was hazarding wild guesses about a person I once knew slightly, who had surely changed beyond all emotional, mental or spiritual recognition, and who meant little to me, until a few days ago, when he reentered my life on a baffling and possibly tragic tangent.

A waitress in a small diner wiped off the top of the cash register with a bottle of generic glass cleaner and a piece of paper towel. She wore a pale blue uniform that was stretched tight around her hips and gaped loose at her chest, where a nametag said *Ginnie* in curly script letters. I ordered some coffee and blueberry pancakes with maple syrup, silently wondering if the syrup would be real maple.

Ginnie read my mind. "The syrup ain't real," she informed me with an incongruously bright smile.

"It's not real syrup?" I said blankly.

"It's real syrup. It's not real maple." She was clearly dealing with an urban simpleton. "He's too cheap to buy real." She jerked her head toward some imaginary cheapskate. "He really ought to buy the real stuff, don'tcha think?"

"Absolutely."

"If it says maple on the menu, it should be maple. I always tell folks when they order. Just seems like the right thing to do. Tell 'em up front. Anyway. You still want 'em?"

I pondered this. "I think so," I said finally.

She shook a chubby finger. "I warned you."

"And I do thank you for the warning." I smiled brightly at her.

I pulled out one of the fax reprints of Keith's passport photo, placed it on the counter, and I asked her if he looked at all familiar. I did momentarily feel like a complete idiot as I did this.

"Are you one of these private dicks on a case?" She grinned, steeply compounding my moment of acute embarrassment.

I told her I wasn't. I told her he was a friend who was missing.

"I'm real sorry." She stopped smiling. "I've got me a smart mouth." She looked closely at the picture and shook her head. "I've gotta say he looks kinda shitty, doesn't he?" Ginnie picked up a carafe and poured stewed black coffee into a cup as a large cat with red hair close to the color of hers traced a figure-eight pattern between and around her feet, which were encased in the white, sensible kind of shoes nurses often choose to wear.

She was a woman in the netherworld between girlhood and middle age, with no ring on her wedding finger, no makeup on, and hair that was teased and tortured to an unnatural texture.

"Yes he does," I said, "he's been living rough for a while. Traveling around. I think he might have passed through this way a while back."

She looked at the picture once again.

"Can't say he looks familiar, because he doesn't. Wish I could help ya," she said.

"It would have been a couple of months ago," I persevered. "When he was through here. Are you alone? The only waitress working here I mean?"

"Yup." She smiled at me wistfully. "Just little ol' me. It's a small place. Small town. Just locals living here. Off the tourist track since we're a ways from water. Mostly old guys come into the diner." She waved a hand to take in the six or so men sitting alone, at the counter, or in the booths that lined the window that faced the road. "Just after coffee and some talk and a place to cool off in during the dog days. A guy like that, like your friend, would surely have stood out. Not just cause he looks so gamey but 'cause, well, to tell the truth, he's really pretty good looking. Maybe you cleaned him up some. Wash that hair. Looks like a New York kind of actor guy. I'd have surely remembered him. Mind me askin'? Was he a good friend of yours? This guy?"

"No. Not really."

She said nothing. "I don't really know. I'd just like to find him if I can."

She nodded slowly. "That's a nice notion. This day and age. Friends looking out for friends. I have to say I kinda like that. Good luck to you then. Hell, clean him up some and send him down here when you do." She laughed out loud.

I said I would.

Three old men sat at the counter. Two wore baseball caps and read the local newspaper without looking up. One wore a real hat in an ancient style I couldn't quite identify. He turned and stared hard at me.

Six Formica booths stood clean and empty, except for sugar shakers, plastic menus with bright pictures, red plastic ketchup bottles, and salt and pepper shakers in a metallic holder with napkin dispensers. Everything looked to be meticulously clean, rather than just hastily wiped down between carloads of hungry families, and I was forced to concede that this was not a thriving business concern.

The old man in the hat spoke up then.

"That's some fancy car you got there, Mister." It didn't sound anything like a compliment.

"Thank you," I said stiffly.

He looked hard at me. "Folks 'round these parts, we don't have a lot of use for imports."

I said nothing.

"We don't see too many goddam yuppies either. What's in the picture?" He wanted to know.

"I'm looking for someone."

"Show it here." He stretched his hand out.

I hesitated. He wasn't planning on being helpful. But he may have seen Keith. I slid it over.

He sneered at it. "Looks like a goddam bum."

"Have you seen him?"

He sneered again. "We used to call them hobos. Made it sound more romantic that way I guess. Like they jumped on boxcars late at night and sang cowboy songs to the moon. Bunch of goddam horseshit. Bums they were then. Bums they are now. Pissing away my tax money."

Ginnie spoke up then. "Shut up, Don. You're too cheap to pay tax anyway."

She took the photo back and handed it to me.

"Don's not exactly known for his warm personality," she explained, "or for his generous tipping."

"Thank you for your help," I said.

"You're very welcome," she said. "And be sure to bring him in here for a meal when you do find him. I'll make Don pay for it." She laughed hard and loud.

A minute later she put my pancakes down in front of me, and I ate them quickly, bogus maple syrup and all. They were hot and I was very hungry.

Don chose to say nothing more, but he stared hard at me as I ate, with his face eloquent in its silence. Don had been cheaply betrayed at some point, and his bitter little eyes followed me even as I left the diner.

As I drove away from the place, I listened to Paula Cole sing, and my mind fast-scanned backwards, to a previous place, and a previous time, when Keith and I met, face to face, one winter afternoon, under a glittering deluge of shattered glass, of tiny shards of cold light.

Near the edge of the town where Keith and I grew up stood a red shale playing field, with two sets of rickety goalposts and a wooden hut that smelled of dog piss and served as changing rooms for the amateur soccer team who played there regularly, keen as all outdoors, but terminally hopeless.

Our town wasn't large enough to support its own professional soccer team. But since it stood sandwiched between two larger cites that did, the faithful were free to choose between two very good teams, and partake of the long-established and fierce rivalry between the two that was by and large good-spirited, rather than violent.

The soccer-playing season is a long one, which limps doggedly through the winter months of cold and rain and severely truncated daylight hours. Yet fans are loyal creatures, uncomplaining, stoic souls for the most part, standing on muddy terraces, drinking cold tea or lukewarm beefy beverages, eating greasy meat pies, watching their cherished heroes win or lose, the diehard fan always finding solitary moments to justify this neo-Calvinist self-abuse: a surprise win, a singsong on the bus home after an away match, walking home victorious in the crispness of an early winter's night, a warm scarf in team colors tied snug and tight, a bag of chips at the corner shop, a hot bath at home, a pint or two with the lads later that night, a chance to relive the goals and the saves and the near-misses.

On a bitter January afternoon, I stood on the packed terraces and watched the teams from the two nearby cities clash in a tense game that ended in the ultimate of cathartic teases, a goalless draw.

We left the grounds numb, with both groups of supporters plainly less than pleased with the result. Only the sporting dilettantes like me, who watched the occasional game, perhaps to remind myself from time to time of our nation's true character, could have been content with the inconclusiveness of the outcome.

Perhaps the local police were wise. Doubtless they were trained to nose out trouble. The two opposing sets of fans had been separated as they entered the grounds, those wearing red were placed on one side of a barbed-wire fence, those wearing blue on the other. Police with trained Alsatian dogs manned the narrow strip of no man's land in the center, and on the busy streets outside the grounds, young bored constables rode tall horses and scanned the multitudes for signs of impending violence.

But thus far things had been quiet.

On occasion a prominent drunk was pulled by the hair from the terraces for throwing a bottle or dart onto the playing field. Local legend had it that the coppers took the offender to a secluded room somewhere in the heart of the grandstand and beat the living shit out of him, always being careful to inflict damage only to body parts well hidden by clothing. Whatever the case, the police had my sympathy; they were brave souls who could doubtless have found better ways to spend their Saturday afternoons, and were therefore entitled to play for keeps.

At the final whistle that afternoon, only one set of terrace gates were opened. The police plan clearly was to maintain the strict segregation and have each set of fans exit the premises separately. The crew I had attached myself to were the first to be released. We were the home team followers, and only a few of us had to catch a train to the other city, one that passed through my town.

We were jeered and hissed at as we left, a few chunks of cold meat pie and nearly empty paper cups flew across the barbed-wire fence as we began to pour out. We responded spunkily enough with volleys of obscene gestures. Someone even dropped his trousers, and exposed a white spotty behind to the unamused red-clad masses, who instantly locked salvos of spit on the pale, fleshy target.

For the few heading for my town, the station was a ten-minute walk, and the train was due to arrive at the station in ten minutes. It was that tight because no one in authority had factored in the extra time: the fifteen more minutes played after the game was tied at the end of regulation time. I had a good chance of making the train. The other team's supporters, who were all taking the train, were being held back in the stadium by the conscientious coppers. They were cutting it very fine. The next train after that was four hours later.

Turning a final corner, the train station was visible, and at that point several things happened very quickly and in a strictly observed sequence. There was the sound of the train approaching and our group began to run for the station, our blue scarves streaming like vapor trails. Close behind, the other team's supporters had narrowed the distance between us to about one hundred yards. They too had heard the train, and they too were making a dash for it.

Except for the runners, the street was empty. A flurry of feet echoed on the cobbles. The police were still at the stadium. Shops were sensibly closed early, locked safe and tight. A solitary betting shop stood bravely open, and an off-license was barricaded up more securely than a maximum-security cell. An old man riding a bicycle turned around in the face of the charge and pedaled sheepishly away.

In a matter of seconds, close to four hundred people had formed a bottleneck at the top of the narrow stairs down to the railway platform.

The stairs descended perhaps twenty steps to the glass front of a newsagent's shop, then they right-angled down twenty more steps to the platform. The train was there. Waiting. Empty. Swing doors wide open.

The crowd in the back of the bottleneck pushed all the harder.

I was close to the front when the inevitable happened.

The shove came from behind, sending me stumbling down three or four stairs. I grabbed at the jacket of the man in front who turned for a split second to face me. His face was scared and angry.

And it was Keith Pringle.

I don't know if he recognized me as he began to stumble himself. The swell caught me and I rushed forward again. I held on to Keith. But as he began to pitch forward I noticed the small figure directly in front of him. A young boy. Seven or eight. Crying. I couldn't hear his voice, but his mouth was wide open, and tears streamed down his cheeks.

I tried to pull Keith to me as another swell caught us.

And then Keith grabbed hold of the boy with both hands, pulled him into his chest and then spun himself around. It was a graceful movement. Balletic. Keith and I were suddenly, implausibly, face to face and being driven forward, irresistibly. Then time stopped. I threw myself at Keith, grabbed him around the shoulders, and held on tight.

Then our world exploded.

The doctor who tended to us in the hospital emergency room was a well-spoken Indian gentleman who said we were brave and very lucky. He said Keith's back took the brunt of the glass. If he had gone through the window face-first he would have done much more damage to himself. He also told us we were mindless yobbos, who made his life a bloody misery on game afternoons when he liked to potter in the garden with his wife. He reckoned we had passed through the glass window so fast we had cleared the worst of the spray of broken glass that had injured a few people behind us, although thankfully no one had been cut too seriously. The hospital was busy treating the numerous injured. Keith had a few superficial marks on the back of his head, some cuts on his neck and a splitting headache. They plucked a lot of glass from my hair but almost none had drawn any blood, although one ear was nicked. A nurse had tenderly combed my hair, searching for stray shards.

The little boy cocooned between us was unscathed and his frantic father searched us out in the emergency room.

"Yer both good lads. So ye are." He kept on saying this and it became his personal mantra. His head was tightly bandaged. He had been right behind us and had caught much more of the flying glass than we had.

"I telt him to keep holdin' onto my hand. But the wee bugger widnae hold on." He began to cry then. His son took his hand. I was glad they were both okay. He shook our hands, still crying, as his son led him away. At the end of the corridor, the boy turned and waved.

When they had gone, Keith and I sat in silence for a while. We were in a long white corridor, waiting to be discharged.

He spoke first. "Boring game."

I nodded.

"Got any fags?"

I shook my head. It hurt a little to do that.

"The wee kid was okay then?"

"Yes."

"Good," he said.

We were silent once again.

Then he spoke again. "You're at the university now?"

"Yes. First year."

"Any good?"

"It's better than school."

"That wouldn't be very hard. How come you're here?"

"Christmas holidays."

"When do you go back?"

"Next week."

He was silent for a while. Then he spoke.

"Remember that party?"

I smiled. "Oh yes."

"I was truly guttered. It's also just possible I might have made a right arse out of myself that night."

"You were in a highly emotional state of mind."

"But was I an arse?"

"No," I had to admit, "not particularly."

"That's a relief. Do you know kissing Joyce MacKay was almost worth all the aggravation?"

"You're still a great romantic," I told him.

"True," he admitted. "But sometimes it's a curse. I find myself thinking about her often. She's going to be my one big regret I fancy. She's at the hospital now. A trainee nurse, she is. Can you believe it?"

"This hospital?"

He nodded. "This very one. Imagine if she'd seen to us."

"It fairly boggles the mind," I said.

With little more than a few Band-Aids and a handful of aspirin between us, Keith and I were back at the station two hours later. All the glass had been swept away as two youths chewed gum and applied the final touches to the cardboard and wood that now covered up where the window had been. When they slouched away there was little left to mark the incident.

We stood on the platform and waited for the last train home. When it came it was busy and we could only find single seats in two separate compartments.

Several years would pass before Keith and I would meet again.

Suzanne Vega sang about wounded men with missing limbs and nerves raw and strangely intact, while I sat at a rest stop ten miles past the diner and tentatively sipped the jumbo coffee refill Ginnie had kindly provided me with, possibly as recompense for listening to the doltish Don.

With nothing else to do I powered up the laptop and got online, where a message from Nye waited. I possess a car phone but Nye doesn't much like to call me on it.

I was informed that the store hadn't yet burned to the ground and that he was coping. Tye had even showed up for work that morning. He asked me how my vacation was going. I replied, being careful to express my gratitude that the store was functioning, and telling him that my trip was going very well. I sent the message, then I called up the weather forecast and discovered heat and rain promised for the next two days. I loaded Word Pro and composed a short note for my broker, asking her to broadly outline the extent of my finances. I called up WinFax and faxed the note to her.

Nye opts for the medium of electronic mail, while my broker hungers for a fax-driven relationship.

She is a pretty woman, around my age, who works from a home office and has been confined to a wheelchair for eight years, after her legs were crushed flat in a car accident. She had been intoxicated, and there had thankfully been no other victims. Not surprisingly, she doesn't drink any more.

She would, I'm sure, object strongly to the word *confined*. Two summers ago she bungee jumped during a scuba-diving vacation in the British Virgin Islands. We have never actually met face to face, my broker and I, yet our fax modems screech at each other several times a week. The bungee jumping was reported in a city magazine article, which also ran her picture.

I stared out of the car window and considered calling Patricia.

Our house is paid for, worth close to two million dollars, and is in Patricia's name. ArtWorks turns only a small profit. Perhaps because of the nature of the business, but I suspect more so because I refuse to elevate it beyond the status of hobby to full-blown going concern. ArtWorks belongs in total to me, the land and the building and the business. My most tangible asset. The Lexus is paid for. The Mercedes too. Their combined value is close to one hundred thousand dollars. The mail-order business belongs wholly to Patricia. Even she isn't aware of that. And it earned her three million dollars in clear profit last year.

My own assets aren't quite so simple. I carry two million in life insurance, as does Patricia. I have numerous stocks and shares, but have set aside woefully little for my golden years of retirement. Individual Retirement Accounts had been set up but not added to sufficiently, although I have always meant to. Perhaps five hundred thousand is earmarked in total to safeguard me in my period of dotage.

Patricia is well provided for, as much by her father as by me. She is and will always be an extremely rich woman, her mother likewise.

The laptop beeped with an incoming fax message, and I loaded the fax viewer. As of the close of business yesterday my accumulated shares added up to a net worth of close to nine million dollars.

My broker had attached a brief note, Why the sudden concern? Was I ill? Was it terminal? Was I depressed? Was I thinking of early retirement? Was I considering a new broker?

I laughed at her last question. Then I thought of my answers.
I don't know. No. No. Perhaps. No. And of course not.

I turned the laptop off and sipped at my now lukewarm coffee.
A rich man with little else vital in his life pulls the glass bottle full of
pennies from beneath his bed, and begins to count, soothing himself
as he does.

Suzanne Vega was still singing about mental health.

It seemed to me that I had created a secure world for myself,
without touching anyone else in the process.

Sitting by the side of a road it didn't seem like much of an
accomplishment.

I started the engine.

A nameless gas station stood sulking at a curve in the road. The
sign overhead said simply GAS, but it was old, and the light above it had
burned out. Another sign was peeling from an exposed brick wall. It
touted a brand of gasoline no longer in existence, but the price marked
on peeling cardboard on the two pumps still working was almost half a
dollar less than what was generally charged back in the city.

And gasoline, I frugally reasoned, was gasoline.

The tank was still a quarter full.

Unlike the other place I had passed after leaving Harmony, this
one came with some kind of convenience store attached.

"Try Our Freshly Made Sandwiches. Choose From A Variety of
Fillings," the sign on the window said.

I pulled in.

Self-serve was the only option offered, and I pumped twenty
dollars worth of gas.

Inside the place stood two people clearly related. My first thought
was that they were father and daughter. At a stretch they might even
have been husband and wife. Both were meaty, overweight. Both
were sullen. Both were silent as I entered.

At the nearest of two cash registers, I handed the man a twenty
dollar bill. He pulled a thick bundle of notes from the top pocket
of his stained overalls and placed the crisp twenty somewhere in

the middle of the soggy wad. I couldn't help noticing that his roll contained notes of all denominations, and probably added up to more than a thousand dollars. A lot of money. I wondered why he bothered with the register.

He said nothing during the transaction.

Then I turned and walked from one world to another, from engine dirt and man-sweat to a pristine cleanliness. The food counter positively shone, the glass in front and over the assembled sandwiches sparkled. I glanced down at the floor, which had metamorphosed from lubricated filth to well-scrubbed squeaky industriousness in a matter of a foot.

I had stepped from one person's domain into another's.

The same family. Wildly opposing work ethics.

Behind the food counter the woman became a girl as I got closer. I smiled at her and her face did something similar in return.

"What do you recommend?" I asked her.

As I spoke, she looked at me with an odd, unreadable expression. She took a long while to answer me.

"They all pretty good," she finally, grudgingly, allowed.

"Do you have any roast beef?"

"Surely do." I had offered a mild insult.

"What does that come with?"

She took a deep breath. "Why don't you just tell me what it is you want?" She was throwing down the challenge.

"Well. Let's see . . . lettuce, tomato . . . Swiss cheese if you have it . . . potato chips. Not too many. No mayo on that if you please."

"Drink?"

"Coke . . . Pepsi . . . whatever you have. It doesn't matter."

"Some people got a preference."

"I can't tell the difference."

"Coke's got a syrupy taste to it."

"What do you have?"

"We got RC."

I very nearly laughed. "That'll be just fine."

"Diet?"

"Why not?"

I pulled out Keith's picture and placed it on the counter in front of her.

She nodded at it slowly. "Yup. That's him. That's who I was just this instant thinking of," she said mysteriously.

I was confused. "That's him? What do you mean?"

"He spoke just like you. When you spoke just now. I thought of him. Then you showed me his picture. Pretty weird, huh?" she said.

"He was here?"

"Sure was."

"Long ago?"

"Mmm . . . two months . . . maybe longer . . . no . . . it was two months. Sliced turkey was on sale. He had the turkey. On a Kaiser roll. Chips and a soda. Three dollar plus tax. He wanted water. I told him it came with soda. He wanted water. I told him the price was just the same. Three dollar. Soda or no soda." She shrugged. "But he wanted water. I gave him water."

"For the three dollars?" Why was I getting into this?

"Nah . . ." she smiled ruefully. "Gave it him for two fifty."

"You're sure it was him?"

Her eyes widened to take in the whole place. "Many customers do you think we get? Strangers? Lookin' just like tramps? Ridin' a bike. Talkin' with a strange voice?" She paused. "No offense," she quickly mumbled.

"That's okay. Not many, I'd imagine."

"Right. It was him. He was here." She hesitated. "Your friend?" It was becoming a very common guess.

"Yes."

"Lookin' for him?"

"Yes."

She nodded sagely. "He was headin' up north. Paddle Lake's a few miles further up the road. Maybe headin' there. Pretty enough place." Her tone said she didn't care much for it, pretty or otherwise.

"Yes . . . maybe he is." I said absently.

She nodded and walked away.

I stood in a daze and waited.

I had myself a lead.

Keith had been here.

She returned with a brown paper bag, three large napkins, and a paper cup with a straw sticking up from the clear plastic top.

"Didn't say which size you wanted for your soda," she said, "I guessed you for a medium."

"You'd have been dead right," I said.

She looked pleased with herself. "Good. Three sixty-nine. Comes to. With tax."

I gave her a five and told her to keep the change.

"This ain't no restaurant."

"I know."

"So keep your money. I done nothin' fancy for it."

"You helped me out."

"Just told the truth. Nothin' special. Keep your money."

"I've offended you."

"No." She held up her hand. "You meant it okay. But it ain't right. You go on an' keep it."

I took my change back. I opened the bag. I sniffed at it.

"It smells very good," I said.

"Darn right," she said, casting a superior look toward the dirt-soaked figure on the other side of the room.

"Did he say anything else?" I asked.

"What about?"

"Where he was going? Anything?"

"Just asked for his food. Paid. Left. Got on his bicycle. Headed north, like I said. If he'd have said more I would have told you. I don't lie. I don't keep things back from folks." Once again the oily figure on the other side of the room received a sour, cryptic look.

I decided to leave before a familial squall blew in.

# EIGHT

BY THE CLOSE OF THE AFTERNOON the humidity had transformed air into liquid. The Mercedes crested a gently rolling hill, and descended into the Handle, the collection of single-story ranch houses situated at the southernmost point of Paddle Lake, ten miles from the town of the same name.

The two-lane road curved around the lake in a loose, looping semicircle. On the right, the beach sloped softly down to the water, which as Tom Younger had attested, was as clear as cut glass and inviting in the moist heat.

The houses were uniform, all windowed to face out over the water, with dense scrub behind for privacy, and severely manicured lawns spread out like dropcloths over the sandy soil and low fern cover in the front. Lawn met road. Road met beach. Beach met water. And water stretched three miles across, to a mirror image of trees and houses.

Past the last of the houses the beach came to an abrupt end. There a rugged and pristine dock extended out into shallow water, where a dozen boats, mostly the flat pontoon type, were moored. Past the dock there was an empty asphalt parking lot, and a single tennis court, partly hidden behind a green practice board. A basketball hoop hung over the far corner of the lot, and a small children's playlot stood nearby, the pieces of pale wood bolted firmly together and left standing in a stretch of cut grassland that also housed a communal barbecue area, four long wood tables, with a well-used gas grill sitting squat in a circle of worn mud in the middle of the grass.

On a notice board nailed to a tree, families reserved the barbecue at weekends, signed their guests' boats into the empty dock berths kept vacant for that very purpose, and politely petitioned that a water curfew of ten o'clock be observed, especially during school nights.

It was an oasis of order.

An old Richard Thompson song was being sonically assaulted by Bob Mould on the CD changer. I sat in the car with the engine turned off, eating my sandwich and potato chips, sipping my medium Diet RC Cola.

The first house I had passed belonged to the Tait family. This wasn't exactly a difficult fact to ascertain, as a sign fashioned out of smooth, thickly lacquered wood at the end of a newly sealed driveway proudly bore their name. There were smaller wood pieces underneath, all linked together by tiny chains. George and Sylvie, Chip and Greg, and Tammi.

I reasoned that when one child left for college their name would doubtless come down. When they returned in the summer months they would naturally be reinstated. It was meant to be cute. I idly wondered whether Sylvie was George Tait's first wife, whether her nameplate had replaced someone else's.

The Tait family garage was almost as big as the house and it stood boastfully open. Inside were three mountain bikes, a relic of a red Toro snow blower and matching lawnmower, a set of golf clubs, a white Corvette and a mid-sixties Ford Mustang in a lurid yellow, and an empty space, where another car obviously stood. My guess was Sylvie's, possibly a more practical vehicle, a nondescript late model Buick or Oldsmobile perhaps.

The other houses on the road displayed a similarly cavalier disregard for security. Names were always prominent. Garage doors all stood wide open. Even house doors were unlocked, their screen doors the only flimsy defense against the outside world.

As Tom Younger had promised, eleven houses followed the curve of the beach road, and four orange Harmony Realty signs were visible.

A diagrammatic listing of the berths on the dock hung on the tree by the picnic tables and five minutes of study yielded the names of every inhabitant of the Handle, another minute and the names could be matched to the boats. A stroll along the road would enable the easy identification and cross-referencing of family, house, boat, car, golf clubs, tennis rackets, power mower, and child.

Did they possess no secrets in the Handle? Were they that safe or indifferent to outside danger? Or just that supremely overconfident?

With a whittled stick I pulled a child's gym shoe from the water underneath the dock. I kicked at a smooth pale stone, and it rolled into the water without making a sound. At the furthest point on the dock I looked out across the smoothness of the water to a small tightly wooded island that lay low in the water, as if playing dead.

My first glance from the road hadn't made out the island, which was difficult to spot against the uniform tree cover on the other side of the lake. But now I saw that the island had a beacon; one solitary tree had turned to a fall color already, rushing the next season, its leaves all aflame, an angry, cheated red, as autumn slyly, surreptitiously stalked the last days of summer.

When I turned and walked back, an old muddy Jeep Wrangler was parked in the lot and a tall older man in well-worn khaki shorts with deeply tanned, bony legs was gazing thoughtfully at the Mercedes. We met halfway across the sand.

His shirt was plaid, faded from what had once been a vivid red to shades of dirty muted pink. His hair was gray and thinning. He was late fifties, perhaps older, but whipcord fit, more from daily rigor than enforced exercise. It wasn't by any means a friendly face, eagle-eyed, a chin like an arrowhead pointing downward, his hands knotted around a piece of rope.

"Never have owned an import," he spoke quietly.

I was clearly in a land governed by Detroit rules, and I couldn't come up with a good way to answer him.

"Dumbass boat always needs something." He gestured toward the dock with the rope.

I nodded my sympathetic understanding.

"Name's Bill Kraft."

I told him my name, and we shook hands. His grip was softer than I had expected. I had stupidly guessed him for a blusterer. He quite clearly wasn't.

"Interested in buying a boat?" he asked me immediately.

I told him I was looking for a house.

He nodded. "They got four nice ones 'round here up for grabs."

I said I knew.

He remarked that it was a swell spot for kids.

I couldn't argue with that.

"They play on the beach all the day long in the summer months," he told me. "When the schools let out. They row out into the lake in the old rowboat that's pulled up on the sand, and they love it. Mine are way too old for that now. Both got kids of their own. Living miles away. They bring them here sometimes. Not as often as they should. I miss them." His voice grew soft. "Do you know I hear the kids' voices from the house? And for a moment I sometimes think they're mine?" He shook his head as if to clear it. "Gotta be about the stupidest thing you've ever heard, right? Like I was some vegged-out relic? Dumb, right?"

I tried to smile.

"I gotta fix that dumb buoy. Wife's been after me to do it."

I smiled again. There wasn't any space in the conversation for me.

"I'm pretty sure all the houses up for sale come with boats as part of the deal." I must have looked mystified. He explained. "Folks tend to sell 'em with. Often as not. All four got pontoons. Good boats, these pontoons are. Maybe not much to look at. Nothin' pretty or sleek but you put a big enough engine on, maybe 350 or so, and they'll drag a couple of fat-assed skiers behind 'em a ways." I must have looked skeptical. "That's no lie," he added.

I told him I was sure it wasn't.

"Well. Like I say. Gotta fix that dumb buoy. Hangs too high. Boat hits the dock. Used to be I could take her in and hardly need the buoys at all. Gettin' sloppy with old age." He held up the piece of rope. "Nearly a foot longer than the old one. Gotta make all the difference, I figure."

He walked away from me looking thoughtfully at his rope.

On an impulse, I pulled my shoes off and walked across the rest of the sand toward my car. The sand was bleached white and warm beneath my pale feet. There were beach chairs stacked tidily behind a giant oak tree. A rope was attached to another tree, and towels and swimsuits hung in the sun to dry. There were toys piled up in colored crates: plastic shovels, buckets, floatation devices of bright colors and various shapes.

I didn't notice an old rowboat anywhere.

⁂

BACK AT THE car, I opened the folder and looked at Tom Younger's extensive property listings. According to Tom, the Claytons, the Blacks, the Sanders, and the Alexanders were all anxious to sell.

I quickly scanned the listings. There was little biographical detail on either the Alexander or Sanders families, but amazingly Younger had appended the other two listings with a sizeable portion of gossip, which was a remarkably unprofessional act.

While each of the four houses looked very similar in layout, the inside of each property showed a notable disparity.

First there were the inhabitants. Will Sanders was a semi-retired lawyer in his late forties, whose name was reasonably well known to people like me who followed the legal machinations of the big four automakers. Mr. Sanders had represented one of these companies in headline cases, where two burning deaths had been blamed on gas tank placement, a manufacturing defect of which the company had been all too well aware. Each case had been a victory for Sanders and the car company. No one had ever accused the lawyer of illegality or deceit, but he had willingly placed himself in the unpopular position of defending big business against grieving families who nevertheless had been able to put a price on their suffering, and a high price at that.

Younger noted that he had a wife named Chloe and a nine-year-old daughter named Beth. His house was priced to sell, the tenacious Younger noted in the margins of the listing.

Connie Alexander lived alone in a house that, if the photograph was accurate, was the most charmingly featured, and boasted the prettiest interior by far. She was a petite woman, with elfin features and dark hair, in her mid-fifties perhaps, sitting primly in an ornate high-backed chair, surrounded by massed antiques. There was no mention of other family, dead, elsewhere, or just absent. She essayed the slightest of smiles in the photo. Younger clearly thought including her in the photograph provided a nice touch. He also reckoned she'd drive a harder bargain but, like the Sanders, would take a decent offer, if she got one.

It wasn't mentioned anywhere in Younger's notes that Connie Alexander was an artist, a painter of rural watercolors that were rather good, that tended to sell for fair if unspectacular prices, and which ArtWorks had, on occasion, been called upon to frame.

It was a small world.

I actually liked her art very much. But as always, those who make a profession out of what many consider a vocation seldom manage a truly aesthetic appreciation of the subject. We are simply too close. Or else too fixated on profits and bottom lines.

I live in an art world, yet I can as much judge art as I can compose a symphony, or fire a handgun with any degree of accuracy.

Cindy Clayton had three small children to raise on a considerably more meager divorce settlement than she thought she would receive from her regularly unfaithful golf pro husband, Mike. The inside of her house was aggressively strewn with Barneys and Lamb Chops and Power Rangers and every other overpriced kid fad she had purchased to keep her three infants happy, as a very ugly divorce proceeding unfolded.

This house was an absolute steal. Younger made heavy use of his highlighting pencil here. Priced way below market price. Needed minimal cosmetic work. Should sell very fast. Cindy was desperate.

Younger's scrawl on the front of the folder mentioned that all three of these properties had come onto the market very recently, almost simultaneously. He drew no conclusion from this fact. At the bottom of the page he expressed the hope that this background info on the selling families was helpful. He asked me to keep it to myself as he prided himself on his professional discretion.

I almost laughed, and for the first time I wondered whether Tom Younger was much of a salesman.

The last property for sale belonged to Curtis Black who, coincidentally, lived year-round eight blocks west of ArtWorks. He was a man close to my age. He seldom used his house in the Handle. Unlike the other three, his place had been on the market for six months.

In Younger's view, he was asking way too much.

It had been his father's summer home until his father had died. The local people had liked the late Mel Black. These same local people clearly thought Curt was a faggot dickhead yuppie asshole. Younger never quite said that. He just very delicately inferred it.

Curt Black traded in grain options in the city and Tom reckoned he was less successful than he pretended to be. Either that, or he spooned most of his profits up his prissy little faggot dickhead yuppie asshole nose. Again this was hinted at with sledgehammer sensibility.

I was more than a little surprised that Younger made me privy to all this information and speculation.

But we men of the world like to stick together.

The photo of the Black interior showed a few pieces of very good but old and very neglected furniture. Younger hoped that eventually Curt would get smart, or else go broke, and the house would then sell for a fairer price.

I closed the folder and started the car.

Two miles beyond the last house in the Handle I passed yet another jet-ski sales and rental store. Just beyond that, the road separated from the lakefront and I turned left down an unmarked road, away from the lake.

Two miles beyond that turn, on a empty road that had dissolved into dirt track without my noticing, I found Sandy Weller's huge, ugly, gone-to-seed but undeniably impressive Victorian house, an ornate example of bygone architecture, all the more striking for being miles from anything else manmade.

I parked the car outside and sat for a moment.

On a porch swing, on a porch that needed painting, an athletically short-haired woman in a loose white T-shirt and black spandex leggings swung listlessly, pushing herself with one black Reebok-clad foot.

A ground floor window was open and music was playing.

Lyle Lovett had been to Memphis.

I had been there also.

In my car, Emmylou Harris was singing, and I waited politely until she was finished.

She was going back to the Crescent City.

I hadn't been there.

But I still thought Emmylou was perhaps luckier than Lyle.

Everyone was getting to travel nowadays.

⁜

SANDY WELLER WAS a beautiful woman from a distance and equally striking up close. Her legs were shaped and tan where her leggings ended and her eyes were a dark brown. Her watch was a man's antique model, self-winding, and hanging loosely on her thin dark wrist. There was a small tattoo of a winged horse on the inside of her other wrist.

She waved a tall drink at me as I approached her.

"Hi," she said, "you have to be the guy that fat, slimy fuck Tom Younger said was coming."

"I am that very guy."

"Did Tom call me a bitch?"

"I'm afraid he did."

"If I had a dollar for every time his pudgy hand landed on my ass, I'd never need to rent rooms in this place."

"He seems all right," I remarked mildly.

"If I let him actually do what he keeps on pretending he'd like to do he'd probably shit himself."

"You know his wife." I was feeling a little lost.

"Yup. Mar's a real nice lady. She's a very good realtor too. Easily the brains of the team. Tom couldn't get himself a fuck in a whorehouse."

I had to laugh.

She smiled back. "You're laughing at me, aren't you, you citified prick? Oh I know. I'm one of these rural characters you hear about. You swear there's just no way we can really exist. The one-time homecoming queen, whose life got weird, and she ends up living in the ass end of nowheresville, drinking gin and renting out rooms in her big stupid empty house to people who have to be truly fucking lost to be here in the first place, and all the time being foul-mouthed and quaint and too fucking colorful for words." She took a deep breath.

I thought that she believed in everything she said, but that she also saw the funny side of everything she said. She had hoped to shock me a little. Now she saw she wasn't going to.

I liked her a lot already.

"You do look like you could have been a homecoming queen."

"Spare me," she said. "So. Will you be joining me in an aperitif on the ver-annn-duh?" With the last word her voice turned all Southern and teasing.

"That would be nice." I spoke politely, a little overwhelmed.

"For a moment I thought you'd say something coy about it being a little early in the day for you."

"No. A drink sounds fine," I said. "Do you like Lyle Lovett?"

"I do," she smiled wickedly. "Very much."

"He's no longer a married man, I understand."

"She was damn lucky to have him. If he came near here, he'd never get away."

I surely believed her.

I followed Sandy Weller through the main floor of the house
to the kitchen. The rooms were white and sparsely furnished.
Her windows were all wide open behind ivory lace curtains that
shimmered, filtering the fading light into white layers formed
through a prism of summer dust.

The memory of a breeze caught tree branches hanging close
to the house, grass grown long in the back yard, and wind chimes
shaped like jumping horses that tinkled above the back porch.

In the kitchen, she pulled open the door of the oven and looked
dubiously in. Slightly reassured, she added two thick fingers of
Gordon's gin to her glass and a splash of diet tonic.

I asked for red wine. She didn't have any. She produced a tall
bottle of Stroh's beer from the back of the fridge and I said that
would be fine.

She spoke as she twisted open the top. "Don't even think about
saying you don't like lasagna."

"I won't," I said, "I do like lasagna."

"This is the best thing I make." She admitted. "I can't really cook
for shit."

"Tom Younger didn't tell me too much about the arrangements."

"I rent out rooms. If I feel like it you get dinner, but you get a
greasy cooked breakfast either way. There is a hotel in town but it's
a boring place where they have non-smoking rooms and an all-you-
can-eat salad bar and neat stuff like that. You get a dry muffin that'll
block your anal sphincter and a cup of truly shitty coffee for breakfast
there. I charge a lot less than they do, but you drive a fancy car so you
probably don't give a fuck about that part, and I do exude a lot more
class and charm. They have big TVs in the rooms there. But I've
rented a movie, and after dinner you can sit in your room and be an
unsociable prick, or you can stay down here and watch it with me. I
might even let you cuddle up if you're especially good."

"What's the movie?"

"*Short Cuts.*"

"With Lyle Lovett."

"You've got it. I was just getting myself in the mood when you got here. If I start drooling, for fuck's sake wipe me up."

"That's a lovely image. Please tell me why I'm staying here."

"Shitloads of ambiance," she answered me quickly. "And I'm much better looking than the girl at the front desk of the hotel, even if she is younger. Did I mention fresh ground Starbucks coffee at breakfast time?"

"Ah," I said, "that must be it."

We sipped our drinks on the porch as Lyle sang, doubtless unaware of the effect he was having on Sandy.

She talked about herself. She was single. She always had been. For some reason that surprised me. She noted my surprise.

"You pictured me in the gold digger mold I bet?" She smiled. "Jumping from worn out husband to husband? Gathering all them big divorce settlements?" She laughed out loud. "Nope. Sorry to disappoint. It never happened that way. I've lived here for a while now. This was my family's place. My dad left us when I was young. I went to a big college in the east after graduating high school. I was a real star in high school, track star, wiggling my little ass in a short skirt at football games, and then I went on to become pretty much a nobody at college. It took me a long while to adjust to that. I came home soon after college. Right after that my mom died. That was a horrible time. I was young, only four, when my Dad left. Losing Mom was much harder. It's twelve years now but it still feels like her place to me sometimes. Like she's waiting round a corner for me. Picking up after me. I've been hammered sometimes. Real late at night. Can't find a bra I swear I left on the floor. I swear she's there. And she picked it up and threw it in the hamper behind the bathroom door just like she always did when I was a kid. That's a really strange feeling. Haunted by a neatnik ghost for Christ's sake. Your folks still alive?"

I told her my mother was still alive, that my father was dead. She nodded sympathetically at that. I told her that I seldom saw my mother, that I went home only rarely, and she seemed to understand all about love and distance.

We stood in the kitchen and talked for a while. She would interrupt to look in the oven, answer the phone just once, and add some diet tonic to her glass.

When dinner was ready, we took our plates out to the front porch and ate lasagna and garlic bread and chocolate flavored frozen yogurt in big plastic bowls and watched the sun sink behind the woods on the other side of the dirt track that was her private road. She hadn't played anything after Lyle Lovett. Perhaps she hadn't wanted to break the mood.

She made a nasty face as she dug into her frozen yogurt.

"Only a moron could confuse this shit for ice cream," she said, "but it's tolerable and you don't get fat eating it."

She didn't look in eminent danger of getting fat. I told her so.

She snorted. "I eat like a goddam bird most of the time, and teach aerobics classes in town five days a week," she said. "And with any luck I might just get to be rich and famous any day now."

She explained. "I got the aerobics job after the first teacher, who was a purebred cunt ten years younger than me, and too thin for fucking words, got herself married and pregnant and left to be the, now how the fuck did she put it, the 'primary childcare provider' for the fat little porker she and her asswipe husband created." I tried not to smile. "I sound like a real shit, don't I? She really didn't want me to get her job. She wanted it held open for a year or so until young Tristan, I kid you not, got older and she could return. But I wanted that job and I got it." She grew reflective. "The first thing I wanted real badly for a while. Even though I had no goddam experience, beyond attending the silly bitch's class, which I hate to admit was a pretty good class. So anyway." She took a deep breath. She clearly loved to shock and talk. "I started to teach. And I liked it a lot. And I got to be pretty good. I do mostly step stuff, and the ladies, we get a few guys but not many, they like me. I think they do. They better. The fat slugs. Maybe. Maybe not. Where was I? So anyway, more ladies sign up, including this one ginormous blimp of a chick who shows up, sweats like a pregnant sow, gets herself into Weight Watchers at the same time, and transforms herself into a fucking stick insect in nine short months. And her delighted husband, who's now porking her again, and saving himself a fortune on hookers, is a video director, and he rewards me with a video shoot for an aerobics video. So it's shot, and edited, and all that technical and financial stuff and he's right now off looking for whatever you're supposed to look for, backers or something, to make us both a veritable shitload of money. And if everything goes right I'll be the next Kathy Smith, and you won't be able to turn around in Blockbuster without seeing my skinny well-toned ass staring you in the face."

Kathy Smith? I must have looked blank.

"Oh never mind," she said. "It's a good thing. Trust me."

After we had eaten, the rural night had pulled itself across the house and the road and the yard and the woods like a blanket. The last of the summer's insects finally drove us indoors. I had offered to help with the dishes.

"Don't be a cretin," she said. "You're being charged for this. You're a guest here, remember?"

I asked her, "Well? Which parts am I paying for, exactly?"

She replied, "Does it really matter?"

I said no, it truthfully didn't.

After that exchange, we settled down to watch Lyle and the rest of a large cast in a very good if very long movie. We ate popcorn and didn't cuddle, after which I said goodnight, and from the couch she too said goodnight and offered hazy directions to my room and the bathroom, which was next to my room, and which were both on the second floor.

I walked out to the car to get my bag and the laptop from the trunk. On an impulse I speed-dialed Patricia at home. The phone rang twice before the machine kicked in. Two rings meant there were other messages. I could have retrieved them. But I didn't.

When the recording stopped I spoke. I said hi. I said I would call in a few days. I said I was okay. I said I missed her. I said goodbye.

In the enveloping blackness I lay on my bed and struggled to fall asleep. I generally sleep very well. It isn't usually a problem.

Waiting for my eyes to find a shape to focus on, I began to question the sense of this trip. Was I wasting my time following a near stranger who didn't want to be followed? It wasn't any kind of great mystery. He was stone-dead in a ditch somewhere. I had no authorization. If I found him, then what? I could call his family and tell them something that, in their hearts, they must surely already know. I could call a woman at the British Consulate and she could close a minor file, complete some piece of insubstantial paperwork, and move quietly on.

I could stop pretending that this was all because of Keith Pringle.

Because it wasn't for Keith.

It was for me.

It began the day I read about him.

No it didn't. That too was a lie.

My sad essence: I was a hapless straight man in a pampered, compartmentalized joke of an existence that skirted the norms of everyday life. I made little jokes and displayed impeccable manners and looked earnestly concerned when I had to. I generated a paper trail of words and money and investments and business dealings. But that was all. There was little of flesh and blood and mind and matter behind these superficially impressive numbers at the bottom of corporate columns, in business reports, a mention occasionally to be found near the foot of the city society pages.

I had never killed. I had never knowingly cheated anyone. I had never told a woman that I loved her. Or a man. I had never said the things I truly believed because I had never believed enough in anything of any importance, believed enough in it to shout it out impetuously, and to then be damned and ridiculed in the aftermath.

I had tinkered and fine-tuned and finessed my way into a gray-hued demimonde of conformity and compliance dressed up as mobility and a modest competence. I had taken no chances. Except with money, but it was money I had never honestly earned.

And that was me in my sad essence.

My only possible gift was the ability to assess my flaws perfectly.

So now I was taking a little leave from the ease and the smug innocence. Coming up for air. Seeking after some purpose. And if I couldn't quite summon the gusto to grab it with both hands, I could at least view it from a safe distance.

It wasn't to be a purpose especially romantic or dangerous. I wasn't a lover or a detective. You would have to care a great deal more deeply about life than I clearly did for that kind of sacrificial derring-do to be possible.

It would be, at best, a narrow victory, a marginal yearning, a brief respite. A barely perceptible thaw in the emotional permafrost.

I did eventually fall asleep.

And I woke much later. Slightly confused. The dark was impenetrable, defying the usual modes of time-place calculation. I fumbled for my watch before I felt Sandy's hand take mine. And I sensed rather than saw her, that she was naked, standing over me, and smiling. I felt sure she was smiling.

"Don't you dare say a single word," she whispered in my ear.

I didn't.

She pulled the sheet back and climbed in beside me. She smelt a little of soap and gin and garlic.

Her hand slid between my legs, and in an unbelievably short time I was snugly encased in a condom.

"I might be a craven slut but I'm not suicidal," she said, as she climbed on top of me.

I lay there afterward as she kissed me once and got up to leave.

"You won't get all romantic on me will you?" She asked in a girlish voice.

I promised her I wouldn't.

She bent over me. "I'm a damn fine lay," she said with a laugh. Then she found a piece of flesh on the inside of my thigh and squeezed it between two fingernails. "Admit it."

I admitted it between yelps.

"It was that goddam Lyle. He made me do it," she said. As she opened the bedroom door a dim light from the hallway showed the lithe outline of her body.

"In the future, I'm only going to fuck men with bakers' hats on," she said.

The door closed gently and her feet padded softly across the bare wood floor outside my room.

Then it was quiet and I slept once again. This time until the early morning.

# NINE

WHEN I WOKE, sunlight enveloped the room. A large window stood open, and ivory lace curtains billowed in the slight breeze. The room stood empty except for the bed, a pale wood dresser, and a matching bedside table, on which dried sunflowers stood in a tall vase. Were the flowers chosen as dried, or else long abandoned?

I turned to the bedside table, picked up my wristwatch, and looked hard at it. It was just before six. Early. I put the watch gently down and sat up, blinking in the brightness.

I hadn't really noticed the elevation of Sandy Weller's house during the drive up, but now, as I looked out the window, I saw that it stood on the highest point for several miles around. All of Paddle Lake lay visible beneath a light dusting of morning mist that swept across the water like soft gauze, which the sun would strip off as the day progressed.

I remembered the forecasted heat and rain and I thought that the latter seemed unlikely, as the morning sky was a perfect, cloudless blue.

Inside my bag, I found a pale gray T-shirt, underwear, baggy blue shorts, and Adidas cross-trainers. I put everything on but the shoes and went downstairs gingerly, feeling with my toes for loose floorboards, trying to be as silent as humanly possible.

There was a note on the kitchen table. There was a cup beside a coffeemaker. The carafe was half full, and a plate of blueberry muffins sat beside a toaster.

The coffee and the note were, I suspected, already a half-hour old.

She had gone for a run.

I should pull the door shut behind me if I went out.

French toast and sausage would be served at nine.

*Drink the damn coffee because I made it especially for you.*

*Love and kisses, Sandy.*

*P.S. Last night was fun. I hope I haven't spoiled you for other women.*

I found skim milk in the refrigerator and drank a half cup of coffee standing at the screen door and gazed without thought over the backyard wilderness of uncut grass and scrub that gave way to the thicker woodland, which effectively shut out the world.

I had planned to run but instead walked the four miles back to the Handle. When I came at the houses from the other direction, they produced an effect oddly symmetrical to my arrival yesterday. The road still curved, the houses were similar, and the very first house, like the Taits' on the other end, had a wide-open garage door that flaunted the family machinery stored inside.

A large and prominent sign proclaimed the identity of the inhabitants, in this case Calvin and Joan Mitchell, who were, if the wording was to be believed, "retired and lovin' it."

Calvin was pushing open his screen door as I passed the house.

"Fine morning." He bellowed at me. He was wearing short running shorts and a local college sweatshirt. He was clearly preparing for a jog. He looked fit enough. He also looked close to seventy.

"It sure is." I shouted back.

"You staying up there with Sandy?"

"Yup."

"She's a pistol, that one."

"That she is."

"Heart of gold though. This a business trip?"

"I'm looking for a house 'round here."

"That so? Four for sale right here in town."

"I know. Tell me, have you lived here long?"

"Close to five years. Place has changed some even in that short a time."

"All for the good?"

He shook his head. "I wouldn't exactly say that."

"How do you mean?"

His eyes grew colder. "Oh. I don't know." He tried to smile. "Just me talking foolish talk." Then he turned away. "Good talkin' to you." I wasn't sure if he meant it. He grinned at me. "You give that Sandy one for me."

With that he took off across a well-tended front lawn at a respectable speed for a man half his age. I decided there and then I didn't care much for the happily retired Calvin Mitchell.

The parking lot beside the beach was empty. At the tennis court, a listless male youth of indeterminate age hit balls against the practice wall with a fluid style and very little enthusiasm.

He favored topspin forehands, which he hit with an expensive Wilson oversized graphite racquet. He had two more racquets leaning against the fence. He was very good. He looked bored to tears.

"Would you like a partner?" I asked.

He shrugged in that universal teenspeak for gushing enthusiasm.

We played one set. He served aces followed by double faults. His forehand was ferocious, but he hit long, faulting as often as he landed the reluctant ball inside the lines. I served and volleyed like the old timer he obviously had me pegged for and wore him down with consistently mediocre tennis. I'm a decent enough player. He would soon be a great one.

I won six games to four.

"You kicked my ass," he said sullenly.

"Don't worry. In a couple of years you'll be far out of my class."

He shrugged, but didn't actually deny it. "Maybe," he said. "Depends on a lot of things. Like scholarships and stuff. They're a bitch to get."

"How old are you?" I asked.

"Sixteen."

"Do you need a scholarship?"

He looked at me. "Are you for real? My grades suck."

I held out my hand and told him my name. He obviously found the concept droll but he consented to shake my hand limply. His name, he told me, was Greg Tait.

I told him I was looking 'round the Handle for a place to live. I'd seen his house. I'd seen the Corvette in the garage. Was that his? I hit a vein there.

"That's my brother Chip's 'vette," he said, the jealousy oozing from every pore, "at least it is until Dad takes it away from him for flunking out of college, like he said he would. I don't get to drive yet. Dad wants better grades before he'll spring for lessons. If I get the grades and pass the test he'll let me drive the Mustang." This was clearly an effective motivational tool.

"Does your mother drive the Mustang?"

He laughed. "When her nerves aren't totally fucked up, she drives a piece of shit Plymouth Horizon." He sneered. "And only a total doofus would drive that."

He clearly liked cars. "What do you drive?" He asked me suddenly. I told him.

He was plainly skeptical. "Bullshit," he said.

I showed him the keys.

He shook his head. "Any asswipe can have keys."

Did all the inhabitants of the Handle have such graceful vocabularies?

I said, "We can walk up to Sandy Weller's house and you can take a look."

"That's miles," he protested.

"I'll let you drive it back."

He was incredulous for a moment. "Are you shitting me? Without a license?"

I threw him the keys and he started to walk very fast.

Greg Tait gunned the poor Mercedes mercilessly for the four miles, made me put the top down, and found a radio station playing Van Halen. He turned the volume way up. He was clearly very happy.

Outside his house he sat in the driver's seat and squirmed luxuriously in the soft leather. When Eddie Van Halen had finished his solo he turned to me.

"You're not real old."

"Thank you very much," I replied.

"How'd you get the money for this?" He stroked the dashboard affectionately.

"Mostly luck," I replied. It was an answer he could understand. It wasn't especially inaccurate. He nodded sagely.

As we sat like old friends his mother came out. This was Sylvie Tait, the high-strung driver of the piece-of-shit Plymouth. She opened the driver's side door.

"Come inside Greg. Oh, please come now." She spoke softly, nervous and tired at the same time.

Sylvie Tait was attractive and close to forty. She wore a denim skirt and brown leather sandals, a black shirt with no sleeves and a high neck. There was a wet stain on the side of her skirt. Her hair was mid-length and very dark with a few gray hairs carelessly noticeable. Her eyes were deep-set and slightly puffy, hidden deep in a face that either turned away when she spoke or else sought safety in a far distance. I took these both to be habitual gestures.

Her breath smelled very faintly of bourbon.

"This guy kicked my ass six games to four." Greg spoke loudly.

"That's good, Greg." She addressed this to the beach beyond the roof of the car, through tightly pressed lips, as she shepherded her son toward the house.

"Thanks for bringing Greg home. He has to get ready for school now." She was almost running away from me.

"You're very welcome," I said after her. "Greg wanted to see my car. I'm staying up at Sandy Weller's for a few days."

She stopped and turned and looked at me with an odd, unreadable expression that turned to disbelief. "What for?" She forgot her shyness for a moment.

"Cause he wants to. The Weller woman's a babe."

"Shut up, Greg."

"I'm house-hunting around here," I said pleasantly.

"Why here?" She sounded appalled, almost amused at the idea.

"It seems like a nice spot."

"Mom thinks it's full of weirdos." Greg said.

Her voice grew soft again. "I would like you to go inside now Greg, please."

There was a blur of activity. A girl of twelve or so ran across the yard toward Greg. He grabbed her and they both fell to the ground laughing and fighting. A moment later Greg was sitting on her face. She mumbled something inaudible but he only laughed more and pressed down harder.

"Get off Tammi's face, Greg," his mother said. He did. Tammi Tait got up. She was dressed much like her mother, but wore denim shorts rather than a skirt. She was paler, fleshier, and considerably less inhibited. She struck me as fearless.

She scrunched up her pale face and spoke. "His ass smells gross," she said with a solemn dignity.

He cuffed her on the back of the head gently. "What do you expect you little mutant. It's an ass."

"Stop it! Both of you!" Sylvie Tait was suddenly shrill. Then she anxiously tried to backpedal. "It was good to meet you. We have to go now. They have to . . ." Tammi swung her foot and a Doc Marten boot connected with Greg's shin. He yelped, mostly for effect.

"Stop it! For God's sake!" Sylvie Tait shouted at her children. They laughed at her.

She tried to smile at me. A kids-will-be-kids smile. But the warmth of the gesture never reached beyond her mouth. She steered her children toward the front door of the house.

I watched them go.

Sylvie Tait was an extremely nervous woman, even allowing for the sensory brutalizing of which two teenage children were quite easily capable.

She was also the second person on my trip to react strangely when she first heard me speak.

And I was curious about that.

There was a noise, a masculine shout muffled. I looked back at the Tait house. The blinds were partly open as Sylvie Tait stood with her back toward the large front window. She raised her arm and slapped her son as hard as she could. His hands went up around his ears as he easily fended off his mother's tightly clenched fists. To one side the younger girl watched, howling with laughter.

Child abuse is of course a serious matter, but Greg Tait was much too big and strong for his mother to do any physical damage. He stood his ground as a succession of her feeble blows rained down on him, and when she had exhausted herself, he lowered his arms, and I saw that he too was laughing.

Perhaps she saw me as she turned toward the window, in the split second before the blinds became tightly closed slits. Did her wet eyes gaze out toward me, and beyond me, out across the lake, to the island?

I started the car and quickly silenced Bon Jovi.

But as I began to pull away a movement caught my eye. Two houses past the Taits' a man opened his screen door, strode across his lawn, and approached my car with an air of importance.

I glanced at the number of the house, at the Harmony Realty sign sticking out of the grass and realized that this was Will Sanders, onetime special counsel to the faceless might of the Detroit auto industry.

I turned off the engine and got out of the car.

"Hi there," I said pleasantly.

Will Sanders stood close to the door, and stared hard at me for a long moment.

"Can I ask you what you're doing here?" His tone was even and restless.

"I was just talking to Mrs. Tait. Passing the time of day. Is there some problem?"

"Is this . . ." He hesitated a little. "Was this some sort of a business matter you were talking to her about?" He tried to make his question sound unimportant.

"I actually don't think it's any of your business." I smiled disarmingly at him.

"You're probably right." He nodded his head then, and smiled at me, as if recognizing a social blunder. But he didn't move away.

"Was there something else?" I asked.

"You still haven't answered my question."

"Actually I did."

"None of my business?"

"That's right."

"It looked to me like you got Sylvie all upset back there. I was looking out the window just now."

"Well, that wasn't my doing. She got herself all upset without my help."

He relented. "I guess that does sound like something Sylvie would do." He looked at me. "I don't know you, do I?"

I shook my head. "I'm staying here for a few days with Sandy Weller."

He looked curious. "Can I ask why?"

"I'm looking at some property."

"Oh. I see." Now he affected a sheepish look. "Well. My place is for sale."

"I know that."

I really didn't like Will Sanders much, and I was pleased to think of how little a chance there was of me actually buying his house.

He looked around at the sign in his yard.

"Of course you must have noticed."

"No. I spoke to the realtor Tom Younger in Harmony yesterday."

"Ah. Tom. Yes, of course. Look," he said, making a visible show of brightening up, "what if we try and start this conversation all over again? I'm sorry if I was rude. Sylvie's kinda high-strung as you probably noticed. Excitable by nature. She brings out some kind of possessiveness and I try to look out for her. She worries a lot about her kids."

"They don't seem especially fragile."

He tried to laugh. "No. I guess they're not. Sylvie can sometimes imagine things. She manufactures her fears out of the ether."

"What kind of fears?" I asked.

"Stupid fears," he replied. "Fantasy fears. Dangerous fears. Fears that tend to leave her exposed. But she's a harmless thing. A little bird. She just cares way too much."

I said nothing.

"But this," he enthused, "this is a hell of a fine spot. Real nice folks 'round here." He was beginning to sound a little like Tom Younger.

"So why are you leaving?"

He smiled without warmth. "Maybe it's my turn to be coy. I have my own reasons."

"Which are none of my business."

"That's right."

"Is Sylvie Tait a part of it?" I asked. "You seem very protective toward her."

Something very unpleasant flashed behind Will Sanders' eyes and he punched me in the face very hard. Or at least he tried to. I took a step back and grabbed his fist as it slid off my forehead. I squeezed his hand hard and he clamped his mouth shut to stop from screaming out. Then I pulled him toward me. He stumbled over his own feet, and as his head dropped low I kicked him in the face and pulled my shoe quickly away as blood exploded out of his nose.

He felt tired as I let him go.

He spluttered, "Get the fuck away from me."

I turned away, leaving him to hold his wet but unbroken nose with his good hand.

He shouted bravely at my back. "You hear me? Leave Sylvie alone! Buy your house somewhere the fuck away from here, and leave her alone!" Another of the silver-tongued Handle residents.

"And if you come near me again, I'll sue you!"

Will Sanders was a lawyer to the end.

I wiped a stray drop of his blood from my shoe and started the car. I was late for breakfast, and very hungry.

I was also determined to talk with Sylvie Tait again very soon.

# TEN

"THERE'S A LOT more toast."

"Mmmm." My mouth was too full to say much else.

We sat in her kitchen.

I had been late, but Sandy had waited for me. Coffee had been brewed and she had carved fresh wheat bread into huge geometric chunks. French toast and sausage links had been fried in a large black skillet.

"What do you normally eat for breakfast?" She asked me.

"A low-fat muffin. Or yogurt. Something like that," I answered back.

She smiled. "Me too," she said.

"Do you get many guests?" I managed to ask her between bites.

"No. Not many. You're the first in a while. I'm a well-kept secret. I haven't even decided what I'm going to charge you yet."

"I see. Do I get some sort of discount for last night?"

She laughed. "Are you nuts? I should charge you extra."

I decided to change the subject. "You look fine."

She tossed her hair. "Yup. Just showered after a good long run. Got that all-over fresh-fucked feeling this bright sunny morning. I was very close to giving you up."

A radio was playing and I was surprised to find myself listening to public radio. I said as much. "We get very few stations in clear this far north, and I sure as fuck don't want to listen to 'Stairway to Heaven' all the livelong day," she cheerfully explained to me as Bela Bartok flooded the warm sunny room.

I got myself more coffee. I asked her if she wanted some, but she shook her head.

"You have blood on your shoe," she said.

"I was playing tennis," I said.

There was a hesitation. An eyebrow drifted upward. But she said nothing.

"Are you really here to buy a house?"

"No. Not really."

Once again she was silent.

After the string quartet, there was muted, cultivated conversation. The topic was Rush Limbaugh. Publicity-seeking blowhard or crafty capitalist iconoclast? The on-air jury was clearly still out.

"How do you feel about Mr. Limbaugh?" I asked Sandy.

"I wouldn't let him suck the fart out of my ass," she replied. "You?"

"He'd have to ask me very nicely," I said.

She snorted a little into her coffee cup at that.

At ten-thirty Sandy glanced at her watch.

"Fuck. Fuck. Fuck," she said sweetly.

She leaned across the table, kissed me hard on the forehead, grabbed a bag from the chair in the hall, and ran for the door. The bag advertised New Balance running shoes.

As she left, she shouted, "Leave the dishes in the sink. Pull the door closed when you leave. Dinner's either some horrible dried salad shit in the back of the refrigerator, or we can order a pizza. If you decide on the pizza call me and I'll pick it up on the way home. My number's on the notepad on the fridge. I can't stand olives. Anything else is fine. I'll see you around six-thirty. I can't stand little fish either."

I stood at the kitchen window and watched her as she left, as she pulled a black men's Trek 800 bike from the side of the house and jumped on, pedaling hard, cutting across the long grass of the yard, adjusting her bag on her back, then freewheeling down the hill, toward the lake, bouncing along on her own private dirt road. Once she had her bag where she wanted it she took her hands away from the handlebar and put them behind her head.

She looked just like a kid then, a carefree kid, and I imagined I could hear her laughter.

I did wonder how she could ride the bike and carry a pizza at the same time.

As I was finishing the breakfast dishes, the telephone rang. I let it ring. On the fourth ring, Sandy's mechanical voice cut in. She was to the point, and, more remarkably, she was expletive-free. When she finished, Tom Younger began to talk, and I picked up the phone.

"Say, what the hell did you say to Will Sanders?"

"He wasn't terribly friendly."

Younger laughed. "Well. He just called me and told me he wouldn't sell you pigshit on a stick."

I said nothing.

"But anyway, don't sweat it none. Truth to tell, his place was nothing fancy. Not the pick of the crop by any means. The real reason I called was to tell you to go over to Connie Alexander's house today and have yourself a look-see. I just reached her at home, and she's sitting doing nothing and would be more than happy to show you around. Connie's an honest-to-god lovely woman. Getting on some now of course. Must have been a looker at one time. Not that I'd have been looking. One-woman man. That's me. For sure. But Connie's still pretty spry and nobody's fool."

"Why is she selling?"

"Mmmm. Goddamn. I don't know. Fancy that. I should know that, shouldn't I? Well, I don't. I've no goddamn idea. You could ask her when you're there. I did tell her your name so she'll be expecting you sometime this morning."

"Thanks a lot, Tom."

"No problem, Tom. And try not to piss off any more prospective sellers." He laughed heartily at his own joke. "Say. I've just had a thought. Could you use me there? Lunch after? My treat, of course?"

"No," I probably answered too hastily. "That's all right, Tom. This is just a preliminary look for me."

If he was hurt, it didn't show. "Okay. Well. That's fine then. Good. No problem. Mar says Connie has some very fine furniture there. I wouldn't know. You might want to ask her if any of it comes with the place. Lay on the Brit charm thick. You never know. Can't hurt to ask her." I heard a whirring sound. "Look's like there's something coming in over the fax. I've gotta go. I'll call you soon, Tom. Good luck with Connie. Hope you like her place. Call me if you do. I've gotta go. Bye now."

And with that Tom Younger hung up.

On the fridge door, I found Sandy's telephone number at the health club. Underneath it was an expired coupon for a pizza place in town. Their telephone number was listed on the coupon. When I called they told me that Sandy was a regular customer who always ordered the same ingredients. I told them to make it a large one this time. I asked if they delivered. They were happy to inform me that they did, although Ms. Weller normally chose to pick it up herself. I gave them my name and my credit card particulars and requested delivery. This proved to be no problem and I was assured a pizza, hot and delicious, at the front door at seven in the evening.

I had no reason to doubt them, and I hung up smiling stupidly at the receiver.

Eventually, I reasoned, I would have to pay, but, for now, life with Ms. Weller was getting to be an awful lot of fun. I wasn't a swinger, and two greasy meals and a very fast, and quite clearly all but emotionless sexual encounter were a rare bucolic interlude. But by my hidebound standards, I was behaving like a wild man, even without taking into account my kicking an inexplicably angry man in the face, and my bizarre transformation into a private detective on a case.

I was still smiling. I thought of my wife. It didn't work. The smile remained in place.

The peach-colored paint around the windows of Connie Alexander's house was peeling. It was a fact that a real prospective buyer would, I felt, have carefully noted. The grass was long, yet, ironically, a magnolia bush was trimmed carefully. Some thought had gone into fashioning a Southern-style garden here in the northern wilds. Everything seemed to hang green and low and lush.

I rang the doorbell and Connie Alexander answered the door.

I instantly recalled the late actress Vivien Leigh. Connie was older than I ever recall seeing Ms. Leigh, but I both saw and somehow felt the resemblance. Perhaps it was the voice, when she spoke, that served as the trigger. Ms. Leigh was an Englishwoman, and worked hard on her antebellum cadences for *A Streetcar Named Desire* and *Gone With the Wind*, but Connie Alexander was clearly southern born. There was an exotic playful darkness to her voice.

She wore a short dark burgundy velvet jacket over a white silk blouse. There were beads around her neck and large exotic rings on five of her ten tiny-boned fingers. Her face was white from the kind of makeup only older women seem to use, her eyes were painted dark, yet clearly huge, even without the cosmetic augmentation. She wore wine-colored baggy, tailored slacks down to almost spike-heeled shoes made of shiny black patent leather. Without the heels she was perhaps five feet tall.

She looked dressed up for something more than house showing, but I somehow understood that this was simply everyday wear for Ms. Alexander, who was clearly determined to remain stylish and youthful indefinitely.

Her hair was long and dark, almost black, parted in the center and falling to her shoulders in a ratty fashion that would look smolderingly dangerous on a girl of twenty. It was hair a young girl would wear to play with, to twist around a finger, to puff up before a date, to tease a little, as she looked into a welcoming mirror with her supple cheeks sucked all the way in, a cosmetic weapon in her hand, just in case.

And perhaps Connie Alexander played with hers in just that way, letting the reality of the years drift away as she did.

We took our tea in her sitting room. She said little until I was seated and comfortable, serving me in a silence that was soothing.

The cups were English china, flat and tiny and decorated with elfish children skipping to and fro. As Tom Younger had noted, most of the furniture was antique, dark wood, the fabric a uniform burgundy that was close to black and which I was sure was deliberately chosen to match her clothes.

Paintings covered the walls, primitive portraits in the main, in cracked oils, strong, vivid, frightening colors, pale bodies in lace and velvet with features often subtly out of proportion. Many depicted street scenes of bucolic revelry, set in what I took to be historic New Orleans.

I stared at one, a scene in a brocaded bordello, where four effete young men sat watching a plump rouged girl dance in nothing but her black stockings.

As she watched me, a smile stole across her painted lips. When she spoke, her voice was soft yet authoritative, and I suspected that she used the trick of speaking quietly to draw her listener closer.

"I have chosen to collect primitive art from the city I was born and raised in. That particular oil was, I believe, a rendition of a famous New Orleans red light district that existed in the 1870s. The area sadly no longer exists. A terrible shame, I feel. Only a few photographs still exist. And they show such fine European-style architecture. It was surely a lawless time, yet women were sometimes the bosses as well as the slaves. Now we seem to exist purely as the latter. The hypocritical city fathers saw fit to sweep the area clean, and replace it with what eventually would become a public housing project. A misguided notion at best."

"An attempt at moral cleansing?"

She half smiled. "Hardly. But what a delightful notion. It would, I think, be an unlikely posture for them to adopt. The city is mostly famous for its corrupt politicians, its nasty outdoor drinking habits, big tasseled breasts bouncing on urine-soaked Bourbon Street, and weighty, and, I must confess, rather lovely gothic novels full of sexually adventurous vampires. My town has never shown much inclination toward moral reformation."

"And music."

"Of course. And the music. Have you ever visited the Crescent City?"

I shook my head regretfully.

"They will eventually make of it a faceless conference oasis, rife with hotels and malls. And that I fear will be the death of me. Naturally I hope to be long gone, but my experience is that progress is nothing if not both cruel and wondrously swift, thus I fully anticipate being called upon to witness the cultural abomination."

"Do you return there often?"

"I do. The few ragged remains of my once illustrious family still reside there in antiquated squalor. The rest of us are buried above ground, in one of the city's smaller but more prominent cemeteries. My family are, for better or worse, entombed in a well-traveled locale, frequented daylong by hordes of underdressed shivering tourists, who take pleasure in leaning like B-movie delinquents against my ancestors' last resting place, smoking their low-tar cigarettes and drinking their decaf lattes."

I smiled then, thinking that, if I ever got to her cherished city, I would surely go to the very same cemetery and visit, forgoing the cigarettes, naturally.

She must have guessed my thought. "I shouldn't complain I suppose. Perhaps the dead value the company of the living. Much better that than buying a loud T-shirt at a mall, or putting a dollar bill inside some poor girl's woefully meager undergarments. But enough of my decrepit southern sentimentality. Let me show you the site of my lonely exile."

And with that the tour began.

The house was quite beautiful. No. That isn't accurate. The outer shell was a ranch house on a lake, nice, if blandly unremarkable.

The inside of the house was what was special, a shrine to a bygone age and to a level of social refinement also vanished. In an austere room, chairs were padded and stiff-backed to receive callers who were expected not to slouch, nor to watch television, nor to drink their beer from cold cans. It was a room for polite conversation. And especially for books.

The spaces on the walls without art were given over instead to bookshelves. I noted from the catholic titles that Connie read widely without prejudice; and had even made a few grudging concessions to the godless present. She had mentioned vampires, and I saw that she owned several dauntingly thick works by Anne Rice, who I knew to be a New Orleans native.

"The woman's a helpless romantic," Connie informed me, as she walked through what I had at first assumed was her library. It wasn't. No room could lay singular claim to that honor, as they all boasted bursting bookshelves, and all had chairs placed just so, for the optimum light to read by.

"Have you read her?"

I confessed that I hadn't.

"Do you ever find yourself hungering for love?"

I supposed that I did. Although I couldn't really imagine how to answer her question, I tried to smile bashfully.

"I see by your painful reticence that you are uncomfortable with the question," she said. "These books display a hunger for love and companionship, as much as they take delight in the opening of rich young veins for the sensual letting of blood."

"I know little about love or vampires," I told her truthfully.

"You are far from alone in that regard."

"Are you something of a fortune teller?"

"Do I look that cheap and outlandish?" She retorted.

At the end of the tour we came to a small room in the back of the house. This was the room where Connie worked. The door was closed, and as she opened it, she peered mistrustfully in, as if expecting an ambush.

A large desk stood covered with watercolors and drawing pencils, paper, old wrinkled newspaper, paintbrushes soaking in jars of cloudy water, photographs of landscapes pinned to a notice board.

A collection of paint-splattered smocks hung on a hook behind the door.

Until we arrived at that room I had forgotten all about Connie Alexander's art career.

"I've seen many of your paintings." I told her.

She looked at me strangely, and I bit back the compliment I had planned.

"You are, I judge, a wealthy man by most standards." She spoke slowly.

I sensed that it was a question and I told her that I supposed I was.

"And are you proud of your occupation?"

I tried to laugh. "I wouldn't go that far. I'm not ashamed of it."

She nodded. "An excellent answer. I have to confess that, in my cups, I am in fact a trifle embarrassed by my occupation, which is that of landscape painter, a dabbler in singularly insipid watercolors."

"Your work sells very well."

"Yes it does." She shook her head in studied amazement. "It's a wonder, to be sure. But tell me, if you can, is that a worthy measure of success do you think? The selling of it?"

"No. I suppose not. It's an achievement though."

She all but sneered, "A singularly shallow one, I've always felt. Many years ago I discovered my love of art. And simultaneously I discovered my utter mediocrity as a practitioner of that same art. I found myself to be cast, to my abject horror, as the Salieri, rather than the Mozart, if you take my meaning."

I nodded. I had seen the movie.

"So I reviewed my options. There was the impotent cut and thrust that is the world of art criticism. There was the teaching of art. A job requiring patience, of which I have precious little. I chanced to observe the hapless simpletons sitting around the city square, painting the likenesses of delighted tourists from Instamatic snapshots and mailing the finished abominations back to trailer parks somewhere in the wilds of Iowa. That this sorry vision presented itself as a bona fide option was a lamentably sad truth."

"What did you do?"

"I postponed my fate, left my beloved city and traveled up north in search of my true muse. No, I'm teasing you. Please forgive me. I'm sadly no longer girlish enough for that particular affectation. But to answer your question, I did choose to leave New Orleans twenty years ago."

"You could have painted your watercolors there."

"Yes. I surely could have. You are quite right. But I had another reason to leave. You see I also left to be closer to my sons."

"They live near here?"

"You are a relentless little interrogator, aren't you?" She allowed herself a slight smile. "Yes. My two boys attended college here. On scholarships. They are twin boys. Or rather they were twin boys. Now they are twin men, with twin wives, and four delectable little children between them."

"Did you say twin wives?"

She laughed. "Are you in the habit of watching the vivacious Sally Jesse Raphael?"

"No. I do know who she is, though."

"Then you must have missed her finest episode, where she featured my boys and their wives. 'Twins Marrying Twins,' I believe the particular episode was entitled. I don't possess a television set. But a kind friend allowed me to watch. It was such marvelous fun."

"Did they have twin children of their own?" I couldn't help asking.

She smiled. "That would have been nice wouldn't it? But sadly, no. My grandchildren are singular creations. I naturally have a selection of adorable pictures, just like any doting grandmother. The boys settled in these parts after college, found themselves two dull yet dependable careers, and settled down for the long haul that is the upper middle class existence. I have chosen to stay here too."

"You must miss New Orleans."

She nodded. "I hope I always will. But to return there and live would probably be to shatter too many fond illusions after all this time. But you have by now doubtless found me to be a chronic complainer. And I don't wish to be viewed as such. After moving here I did find to my amazement that my pale, listless watercolors were considered to be rather fetching additions to the walls of lofts and young dentists' offices. And I am able in my lighter moments to give hesitant thanks for my gift of creation, even if it is a decidedly lesser gift. But no. I must not backslide in my gratitude to the powers that be, for I am the possessor of a genuine gift. From water and paper and soft paint shades I fashion a pretty if insubstantial pastel muzak for the less-than-discerning eye."

"A better fate than the street portrait painter?"

She smiled again in acknowledgment. "Yes," she allowed, "a much better fate."

She stopped there. The silence lengthened. I looked around nervously. In a corner of the room, six unframed canvasses were stacked against a wall. I reached a hand toward them. My eyes begged the silent question. She nodded her assent.

The first was a watercolor of the island. The second showed three forest-wrapped hills that reminded me at once of my homeland. The highest hill was crowned by a mound of standing stones: a cairn, which was a burial, a warning, or a lookout point.

The third frame held a portrait rendered in oils. It was crude and, to my feeble eye, all but talentless, resembling nothing else in the room, but I was certain that Connie Alexander had painted it.

And I recognized the model.

"But this is Keith," I blurted out in my surprise.

"Oh my goodness . . . how do . . ." She was equally bewildered.

"Where is he?"

She looked upset. "He's gone. He's gone away."

"Now I understand," she said. "Your accent. I wasn't listening before. I'm much too fond of my own voice I fear. You are his countryman I now see. Yet your voice has been filtered by years. But you have deceived me, haven't you? My house is of little interest to you. You must tell me why are you here. Please. And I would ask you to not lie to me."

"I'm looking for him."

She looked keenly at me. "But there's more than that."

"I'm running away."

"From what?"

"That's an excellent question," I said softly.

# ELEVEN

"WE OFTEN SAT HERE AT DUSK, watching the sun set on the water," Connie said. "And I must confess that I had begun to think of the place in a selfish sort of way, as our own private place."

"Do you have any idea where he went?"

She sighed. "I would surely tell you if I did," she said.

After the pretense of house showing had been rudely destroyed, Connie and I walked across the road to the beach. We had the place all to ourselves in the early afternoon heat.

I sat against a tree and watched a tight pattern of waves stroke the shore as a small yacht sailed by, far from the shore, closer to the island, soundless, almost unnoticed, the rippling aftermath the only evidence of its passing.

A Milky Way wrapper floated near the surface of the blue water.

Connie found a beach chair and brought it over to sit beside me. Her eyes were distant.

"What do they call the island?" I asked her.

She turned and smiled at me. "They call it Foolishness Island. It's really too small to justify a real name, but the locals called it that because of the distance it sits from the shore. It looks like an easy swim, but in reality it's anything but. A very good swimmer can make it, whereas a drunken fool at a beach party will quickly get himself into trouble. Each summer we have a few heroic rescues, and every few years we have ourselves a sad and silly fatality."

The sand was hot. Connie had removed her high-heeled shoes, and her feet were tiny and bare and impossibly white. I thought again of vampires.

Later we walked out onto the dock.

"The children play here after school," she said. "The young ones mostly. Their parents tend not to supervise them too closely." She shook her head sadly. "They are much older than we were, the children, when we were as young in years as they are. They are lamentably aged, by videos, and tabloid violence and earnest morality lessons from Oprah and the like. They're sometimes more like little adults with their cynicism and their premature loss of innocence. Simple nature bores them terribly. I can often observe them from my front window."

She smiled a sad smile then.

I thought of my study and the play park close by.

"They are boisterous and impossibly loud. But as the sun sets, their parents finally summon them home. The beach is a quiet and solitary place then, for a short spell, before the fires, and the marijuana, and the necking teenagers. I can usually take my turn then. I choose to sit by myself. I bring a few crackers, a slice of a red apple perhaps, read a letter, on occasion sketch out my next day's watercolor." She smiled ruefully. "Oh, I'm really such a fraud, aren't I? The simple truth is that I as often as not stare at the trees on the other side of the lake for the longest time and lose all sense of time and place. Did you notice the first fall tree over there? That one impetuous fellow has changed his color already." She pointed across the water. "A week ago it happened. The very first fall tree. If you return near the beginning of October the fall colors peak in this part of the country, and even I must confess it to be a quite lovely sight."

She lapsed into a silence. Then she spoke again.

"Keith was your friend."

"We knew each other a long time ago."

"Were you perhaps lovers at one time?"

It was an unexpected question. "That's absurd."

She stiffened at the rebuke. "I'm so sorry. I thought it was perhaps why you . . ."

"We weren't ever lovers," I interrupted her. "We knew each other very slightly."

"I never considered that Keith was homosexual." She spoke matter-of-factly. "Although I'm not especially wise in these ways. I was raised in an atmosphere of rigid discretion. I suppose he might have been."

"I really don't think that he was." I cut her off again. "And I'm not either. I haven't spoken to him in over ten years."

"He was such a sad and damaged soul." She fell silent. When she spoke again, it was almost a whisper. "He rose up from the dark water early one night as I sat here in my twilight dreaming. Thin and dripping wet and I thought then, rather a poetic figure. A little lost urchin. A waterboy. He had swum in from the island, and once out of the water he grew quickly cold. I fetched him a towel, one of the grandchildren's, a brightly colored thing. He was shivering and I wrapped it around him. Without thinking I found myself holding him. I do remember that he shivered in my arms." She looked at me. "He has the girlish look of a slightly fallen angel. Don't you think so?"

I said nothing.

She spoke softly. "I so wanted to wrap myself around him that night."

"You painted him in oils instead."

"Yes," she said dreamily. "It had been an eternity since I'd painted that way." She shook her head ruefully. "What technique I ever possessed is now very nearly evaporated. But you know? It came out much better than I expected. A labor of love, perhaps."

"Were you lovers, then?"

She shook a finger playfully at me. "Tut, tut," she scolded. "Such an impertinent question. But then I did ask you the very same question, didn't I?" She paused then. "But how shall I put it? He was young and soft and vulnerable, and I relished the perverse thought of him. I didn't know him well enough to love him as his own person. He thrilled me. But in truth I could never be less than aware that I was an emaciated shell of a woman twenty years older, and a lot less of a passionate Southern ingénue than I'd perhaps like to be."

"You very much resemble an old actress," I told her. But that wasn't quite right. "Not an old actress. An actress from the past. I faltered. "She was very pretty," I concluded somewhat lamely.

She nodded slowly. "Miss Vivien Leigh. Did you know that in one of her last films, she played an aging woman in love with the then very dashing and boyish Warren Beatty? It was a very sad film." She mused, "Perhaps it should serve as a warning to me."

"I haven't see it," I said.

"I can see that I'm giving myself superior airs. I was in truth behaving in a slightly foolish manner with Keith. Perhaps on the surface it appeared unremarkable. For a whole week I sat here, each night, at my special time of the day. That wasn't uncommon. But I was waiting for him. And each night he did come back to me. Sometimes swimming. And sometimes in the old leaky rowboat that sits on the beach. And I waited for him. I asked him once if he was hungry and he said he wasn't but I was certain that he was lying to me. I made ham and cheese sandwiches and brought them to him and he ate without pausing for breath, so I knew he was close to starving. I don't choose to cook as a rule, and sandwiches are as much as I can muster. They tend to be messy affairs. Yet he ate them up. He told me he was trying his hand at fishing on the island. He wasn't especially good at it. He had trapped some too. Rabbits, mainly. He was, he said, a little better at that. But he was still often hungry. I think he was truly terrified also."

"Did anyone else see him here?"

"I don't think so. At least not when I was there."

"Did he come to the beach at other times?"

"I really couldn't say. He came to see me, and I confess that in my mind I hoarded him most selfishly." She sounded almost proud of herself then.

"Why do you think he was terrified?"

She looked at me pityingly. "Because he was homeless and cold and hungry," she said. "Anyone would be terrified in that situation.

But I do remember now that we weren't always alone. A young child came once. It was Beth Sanders. A lovely little thing. She's my very special friend. I recall that she sat silently with us for a spell, with her little hands primly on her lap." She smiled at the recollection. "Such an adult pose. Easily the pick of the children around these parts, I've always considered her to be."

"I've met her father."

She smiled at that. "An intense experience I would imagine. Will Sanders is an overly protective man. It happens to those who come a little late to the joys of fatherhood and only produce the single offspring. He's also quite unhappy."

We sat in silence for a while.

"Where can he have gone?" She asked softly.

"I don't know," I said. "Perhaps he's just moved on."

But I didn't believe that.

She looked hard at me. "You don't need to lie for my benefit."

"I'm sorry," I said.

"I wondered about your plans," I said. "I really don't understand why you're selling your house."

"Oh that's simple. It's the two sets of twins," she said laughing. "My darling sons have found a condo close to them that they have earmarked for my forthcoming dotage; they and their better halves seemingly share a rosy vision of safe retirement-living for their dotty, frail mother in a community of similarly enfeebled crocks."

I looked at her.

Her face was deeply lined, her makeup was applied heavily, and I imagined her body beneath the dark elegant clothes would be parchment skin draped over brittle bones. She was without question physically fragile beyond her years, yet Connie Alexander's spirit struck me as youthful, and as she spoke again she pulled her dignity close to her.

"But I have a secret plan to thwart the little darlings," she grinned wickedly. "My silly boys surely don't know this yet, but I have decided to return to New Orleans. The time," she announced rather grandly, "to go home is surely come."

"Was Keith a factor in this decision?"

"I must confess that he indeed was. When he left me I felt so sorrowful, but later I came to feel some sense of relief. I was quite close to making a silly fool of myself. Even worse, an old silly fool, and I'm sure you know the saying. What he did was remind me that the years, my years, are advancing. And when he vanished . . ."

"Yes?"

"Well. I did think, if something had happened to him . . . a very bad thing . . . then this place was spoiled now for me. It sounds foolish spoken out loud. Or worse. It sounds old, and so very fearful."

"It sounds wise."

She laughed bitterly. "A polite word for fearful."

Then she turned to me. "But what of you, my noble conflicted hunter? What do you do now? Have I been a help to you?"

I spoke slowly. "I think he's dead. Nothing you've said alters that thought. I think he's dead and someplace close to here."

"And do you think he died well?"

"Does anyone die well?"

She nodded once. "Quite so. I suspect that very few do. But was he one of the lucky ones?"

I shook my head. I wanted to tell her that Keith had never been one of the lucky ones. But I didn't actually know that. I only knew the surface details of his life.

"Yet he loved." She spoke reflectively. "And he was loved."

"He had a small child," I said.

"Yes, I know."

"Do *you* have any children?" She asked me.

I told her that I didn't.

"I can see in your eyes that you regret that fact."

I said nothing.

"You are married."

"Is that a question?"

"No," she smiled. "More of an observation. I don't believe you're very happy. Can you lose yourself in Keith's misguided life?

Is that to be your intention? Perhaps you even imagine that finding out the worst about him will make your own life look brighter in comparison."

"That's really not my intention."

"I do so wonder why he came here."

"He was visiting a friend nearby."

"It's just that we're such a trivial little coven of scared suburbanites. Oh, we think ourselves a little more bohemian because we let our grass grow and we no longer commute, or have our station wagons filled with children or Tupperware. But we only fool ourselves, don't you think? Inside our timid hearts we are still so many middle-class drones. Keith was a much wilder soul than that. But perhaps he's sitting alive on Foolishness Island, watching us now, enjoying our drama."

"He could be," I told her. But I didn't believe it.

"Could it be that he came here to die?"

"Did he strike you as someone ready to die?"

"I'm being much too melodramatic and you're simply humoring me. He was surely sad and tired. But not, I think, ready for death. Not just yet."

"You don't think he's dead, do you?"

"No," she said slowly. "On balance I would have to say that I don't. But I do tend to err on the side of optimism on occasion."

It was now the middle of the afternoon.

We sat for a while longer in silence, until a child's playful scream split the stillness of the air.

"I think I want to return to my house now," she said.

The tennis court was empty as we walked across the parking lot.

A mother and her two children had pulled up in a small car. She was a young woman, baby fat, her tightly permed brown hair falling over tired eyes. Her blouse and acid-washed jeans were both a shade too tight. Her children were young, of preschool age, and utterly determined not to get out of the car.

She turned and saw us.

"Hi, Connie," she shouted with a tired smile.

"Hello Cindy," Connie replied. "Can we be of some assistance?"

"Do you have a gun with three bullets?"

"That's Cindy Clayton," Connie whispered to me. I had guessed who she was, but, not wanting to reveal the extent of the information contained in the Tom Younger dossiers, I said nothing.

I remembered that she had three children.

"Cindy's teetering on the edge of a divorce and a nervous breakdown."

I was still contemplating the chosen number of bullets. One for her? Or for the missing child?

"The other little horror must be in some schoolroom pulling the legs from a live frog. You can't really and truly want children. You might end up with something abominable like Neil Clayton, the soul and the smart mouth of a sixteen-year-old trapped in a ten-year-old's body." She shivered for effect. "He's quite revoltingly satanic."

⁂

I WALKED CONNIE back to her house, and as we parted she wished me luck. She didn't specify with what.

As I drove away, I replayed our conversation. I liked Connie Alexander very much. She was by turns mocking and melodramatic, yet, beneath her mannered façade, she was open and warm.

I did suspect, however, that she functioned on the far edges of Handle society and that if there were unpleasant things happening here, she might very well know little of them.

She clearly liked and missed Keith. Was it love? Could I even identify the affliction in others? Since I evidently wasn't capable of finding it for myself.

I thought perhaps that he had had a beneficial effect on her. She missed him now. But I wondered if love, even a thwarted love, can somehow rejuvenate, because Connie Alexander was simply far too young for her twin sons and twin daughters-in-laws to fuss over, and to lock prematurely away, for safe keeping.

All this was about as prosaic and profound as I was going to get.

I pushed the random-play button on the CD changer.

Mary-Chapin Carpenter told me to shut up and kiss her.

It sounded like good advice.

I drove away from the Handle, past the dirt road to Sandy Weller's house, and followed the edge of the lake for several miles.

I was looking for a boat.

# TWELVE

HAD I TOLD CONNIE THAT I hadn't met Keith Pringle in ten years? That wasn't strictly true. I had seen him the once. It had been five years ago. We hadn't actually spoken. But our eyes had met, and I think he knew who I was.

For seven dreary days in a February characterized by insistent cold and gentle rain my wife Patricia and I had returned to my home town to visit with my mother, who was then nearing seventy and had suddenly decided to wallow in a newfound frailty.

This was an unforeseen development as my mother had always been a physically strong and resolute woman.

We had lived out my childhood on the council estate, in a small two-bedroom house that backed onto an abandoned railway line. Occasionally children threw stones into our garden, shattering the few remaining pieces of glass in the greenhouse where my late father had puttered about during the summer.

After his death, my mother collected a pension but also worked two part-time jobs each day, as a lunch server and as a cleaning lady, at the local school, the very same school that I attended.

Her menial presence there was our painful little secret.

She got to work each day at eleven, riding on a bike with a broken bell and a basket in the front, a half hour before the ready-cooked meals were delivered. At twelve, the first lunch shift was served. And at two, when the cafeteria closed, the foil containers were washed and stacked, the tables wiped, the floors swept. At three, the catering company truck swung back, and a flirtatious yob in a stained and sleeveless T-shirt winked at the women and picked up the empties. After that she sat with the other women and smoked the third of her five allotted Silk Cut King Size cigarettes of the day, washed down with a mug of strong tea, sweetened by a dark chocolate digestive biscuit.

My mother began cleaning the classrooms from four-thirty in the afternoon, a half hour after the last period ended, until the job was done, which was usually at around seven-thirty or so, when she came home to drink the mug of strong tea I had diligently brewed. On a Monday and Wednesday she sat down to watch her favorite television show, her tea mug in hand, her last cigarette of the day glowing in a nearby ashtray. On the screen a working class soap opera played out on a cobbled street in an industrial town with bleached-blonde gossips in salt-of-the-earth workingman's pubs.

She thought it silly. Yet she watched it religiously.

We saw the most of each other in the mornings, when she got up early and made my breakfast. In the short, dark winter days we had hot porridge, with a dollop of strawberry jam in the center, the whole glutinous mass floating in the cream from the top of the milk bottle. We ate corn flakes garnished with slices of banana in the summer months.

She ate well at breakfast, tended to nibble from the lunch stuff at work, and usually made do with the biscuit with her tea in the evening.

I got a school lunch each day, and cut myself thick wedges of cheddar cheese on slices of white pan loaf for my dinner (we were sufficiently working class to refer to it as "tea").

I was always home first, and after I finished all my homework I sat down in the tiny kitchen to eat alone, a science-fiction paperback propped against a ketchup bottle, a record playing loudly on the stereo in the front room. My mother liked the Beatles, I did too, but I could never admit to that. So instead I made myself listen to the albums the other children brought to school for music appreciation class: Emerson, Lake, and Palmer and Deep Purple mostly. We forced our poor teacher, a keen classical music lover, to endure both sides of ELP's crass brutalization of *Pictures at an Exhibition*.

The man must have truly hated us.

I listened to the *White Album* at home. "While My Guitar Gently Weeps." George Harrison was my favorite Beatle, even though I knew that Eric Clapton played the best guitar parts on that song.

My strongest memories of my mother are inexplicably frozen in my mid-teen years. She naturally existed before and after that period but my sense of her then is hazy at best. She was somewhere in her forties at that time, with me an awkward fourteen or so, shy and skinny, a bookworm bound for university, which was as much her dream as it was mine.

When I dropped out to stay in America and marry Patricia, my mother was crestfallen, and would stay that way, until after Patricia's father died, until she could see that I was standing on my own two feet, without the aid of a rich man, and without the crutch of a university degree.

I think she was finally a little proud of me then.

But when I was fourteen she fretted. Were my school clothes fine enough? Did I need a new father? (She did meet men occasionally, at the pottery classes she attended at the poly, even once at a Sunday School picnic where they chatted each other up across the aisle of the bus heading home in the late afternoon, flirting and plainly oblivious to the snickering children full of fizzy pop and potato crisps, and me, silently mortified.)

Her very worst fear was that the children in my class would discover that she was a menial at the school.

Naturally we had the same surname, but it was a very common one. That alone wouldn't give us away.

To my knowledge we were never detected by the bulk of the student body. Several times I stayed behind for an after school activity, the chess club, or war games society, and she, armed with her metal bucket full of sudsy water and large mop, would enter the room, her pale blue uniform over her clothes, her red hair tied up with a white handkerchief. She was never alone. They cleaned the school in teams of three.

The other women never once let on they knew me, per her instruction.

Of course there were a handful of children who lived near me, who were close to me in age, who I knew, and who did know our secret. Each of these houses had been canvassed by my mother, who had spoken to the doubtless bemused parents, asking that her place of employment never be divulged.

Stranger still, my mother's rule of silence apparently extended to the teachers at the school, who had to know, but who never, to my knowledge, let on. My mother, a small wisp of a thing with her flaming hair, was clearly a much-feared dictator.

But that was then. On entering her seventies, her mortality seized her.

So Patricia and I were summoned home that year.

In her retirement she had moved into a small gray stone house on a busy main street. It was smaller than the council house I grew up in, if that were possible, but she owned it, or rather the building society did. An economic slump had lasted for years, and in its wake house prices were in a state of free-fall. The mortgage payments on the small house were therefore reasonable. Her savings, and her tiny pension, along with my father's pension, more than covered it and left her well provided for, especially given the frugal lifestyle that she led.

But she hadn't possessed the necessary cash for the down payment.

And I did.

She would never forgive me for lending her the money. It was never mentioned. Yet she never forgot it. It drove a wedge between us. But I was still glad I had done it, because she loved her new house, and lavished great care on it, care our council place had never received.

We sat with her the first night, in her tiny living room, as she watched her television and occasionally talked, her eyes seldom leaving the screen. She looked much the same. Yet she had aged. The world had enclosed her, and left her more fearful.

Perhaps the media was to blame. Because every mean and senseless act made tabloid headlines, and somehow lost all proportion and distance, in the transition to large black ink, or in the strident voice of the ratings-seeking investigative journalist.

So when she ventured out to the corner store, the two young men standing at the postbox would likely stab her and leave her to die if she walked past them. And a baby crying in a crib was likely an abused child. And a man buying a bottle of inexpensive wine in an off-license was in all probability a killer or rapist.

She talked that way much of the time. I found it very hard to listen, and even harder to square the vision of my new mother with the indelible model I had, proud and protective and fearless, at least for herself.

After a day or two of paranoid captivity, I had to escape, if only for a couple of hours.

As unlikely as it seems, my mother and Patricia got on well, sharing a love of afternoon talk shows. Within the genre, they even favored the same kind of show. The rule of thumb was wholesomeness: discussion groups on relationships, on tough love, crisis interventions, and self-help. The lower-grade programs, the sexist fluff with teenage transvestites and whores who were expressing impotent rage at years of suppressed abuse, were promptly turned off, and a large video library of past feel-good episodes would be ransacked for a treasured old favorite.

From her overstuffed floral print sofa my mother looked beseechingly for a beacon shining in the lurking moral darkness she was certain existed just beyond her front door. My mother monitored these shows for a sign of hope.

I never did know what Patricia saw in them. It occurs to me now that they would both have relished the warm feel-good spectacle of Connie Alexander's twin boys and their twin wives-to-be declaring their twin loves before a beaming and bespectacled Sally Jesse.

So one night I served two cups of tea, fetched my coat from the bottom of the stairs and left them to a show devoted to adopted children who had determined in later life to seek out their true birth parents and to then wallow in the subsequent cathartic release.

On an impulse I left the rented car parked outside the house and instead caught the bus into the city.

I sat in the upstairs, in the past the province of small children and unrepentant smokers. Now the buses were all smoke-free. I stared out the window, hunting for familiar landmarks as the bus left our town and slunk through the first suburbs of the city. When I was a child, a thin buffer of farmland had existed between the town and city, an unobtrusive farmhouse and a thin strip of grazing for a handful of oblivious sheep. The membrane was forever gone.

The city too had changed, offering newer and bigger supermarkets with parking for a battalion of shoppers. In general, there was much more traffic on the roads. Yet as we neared the city center, I also sensed that the heart of the place remained stubbornly unchanged. It was still gray and wet, never more than half an hour until the next gentle shower on the Georgian stone of the new town, with its monuments to dead inventors and tall imperious columns slick and shiny and green, moss-bound from the winds that blew in from the sea. The yellow glare of the streetlights reflected in the damp stone, and the smooth sheen on the cobbled streets warmed the darkness of the night that stole away fully two-thirds of the daytime in the long winter months.

It was raining as I got off the bus.

In the west end of the city center, I ducked under a wide pavement, beneath a venerable old building now housing a building society, where a fashionable wine bar now resided. Upscale yuppie chic came with a false bohemian façade. Posters of avant-garde productions hung in a near pitch-black room constructed out of what had once been a wine cellar. An arm and a leg was being charged for thin burgundy wines by the bottle or glass, or else a warm, cloudy real ale from a wooden barrel that sat on the counter beside the bored bargirl who was wearing an improbable beret set at a jaunty angle and reading *Melody Maker*.

I ordered a glass of the house red and sat in a far corner. In the early evening, the drab hours between the after-work office crowd at five and the first sightings of the night people at closer to nine, I had the place to myself.

I breathed in the solitude.

"I can turn the music up if you like," the beret girl said helpfully. "It's *Queen's Greatest Hits*."

"Would it be okay if you didn't bother?" I asked her.

"Oh sure." She smiled. "Tell the truth, I cannae stand them much either."

"Can I get something to eat?"

"Oh sure," she offered. "We do brilliant crepes."

They *were* good, if nutritionally suspect, coming drenched in grease and cheese and mushy overcooked mushrooms, with a great mound of chips on the side. The beret girl also handled waitress duties, and brought me a small loaf of warm garlic bread and another half bottle of the house red.

She also offered me her paper. I peered suspiciously at the front page. None of the names meant a damn thing to me. In my college years, I had squandered a good portion of my grant money buying limited-edition, multicolored vinyl punk singles by the very latest loudmouthed, thin-trousered collection of talentless yobs. I wondered where those yobs were now. And where my lurid green and pink 45s were for that matter. I peered at the small print. How could she read in this subterranean darkness?

I smiled and handed the paper back.

"I like your beret." I said.

She touched it, as if she had forgotten it was there. "Thanks. I got it at the January sales. Trez sheek, nez pa?" Her accent was so truly excruciating I was inclined to believe she was trying to be funny.

I smiled anyway.

Outside it had stopped raining. The wind had strengthened to a formidable northerly that left me momentarily breathless. As I zipped up my leather jacket, I looked at my watch. It was still early.

I remembered a favorite bar from somewhere in my youth, a room of dark paneled wood, a real fire with cracked brown leather bench seats close by, that had to be fought for on a cold night. The place was impossibly old, and steeped in all kinds of largely dubious history.

Even if the wool-scarved theology students from the local university dormitories had laid claim to the large table in the center of the room for their earnest alcohol-driven debates, and in the process driven all the old timers in their cloth caps supping their slow halves to moan and do their unhurried drinking elsewhere, it was still a decent enough place. But it was a long walk, up a steep curving hill into the oldest part of the city.

At the corner of the street, an old church stood in the center of a ruined cemetery where a tormented poet of questionable talent and legendary sexual prowess, a famously obese and politically connected brothel keeper, and a pioneering spirit in the field of anesthesiology were all buried under tombstones cracked and crumbling and smoothed into a uniform anonymity by the harsh undiscriminating elements.

The church was a well-known one, a gothic-towered haven of dour evangelism, past and present. It now boasted an anachronistic minister of the old order, who packed the pews with the fearful, and with a fiery retrogressive rhetoric foretold of just damnation, in a manner that brought to mind the hellfire-stoked, blinkered morality practiced in the Presbyterian churches of yesteryear.

Beneath the church was a cavernous hall, where hot satisfying meals were dispensed to the lost, where two lines of crisply folded camp beds awaited the destitute, and from which earnest young people with comforting homilies on buttons attached to the lapels of their sensible coats were dispatched, to stand on the nearby corners, in their sensible shoes, and bear loud and articulate witness to the miracle that is Our Salvation Through Christ Jesus Our Lord.

On this occasion a girl with frizzy light brown hair turned to the texture of a Brillo pad by the moist air, in a brown duffel coat, brown wool tights, and a loud scarf in the striped colors of one of the city's better private schools, was beseeching us to let The Lord Jesus Into Our Hearts.

She was a young yet wise-enough orator. Having doubtless grown up in a nice part of town, sired by tweedy, stolid parents who wordlessly loved her, and drove an expensive yet practical car, and played passable golf, and read one of the thick quality newspapers on a tranquil Sunday morning over muted strains of Vivaldi or Radio Four, she lacked the necessary credentials for a spectacular witness to her own personal redemption. There was for her no rough road traveled before her Damascus. So, clever lass that she was, she had herself a prop. A genuine downtrodden, one of the clearly fallen, a lost soul, a wretched bum at the gates, a Dickensian image sprung to life and perched at the edge of the fiery abyss.

I stood there astonished.

She had Keith Pringle by her side.

He stared sullenly at the ground. His army greatcoat was much too large for him in the body, and his thin arms stuck out from the sleeves like twigs. His hair was cut brutally short and he needed a shave. His suede shoes were old and shiny and the cuffs of his corduroy trousers dragged along the pavement.

"My friend Keith here was once lost and alone in the world."

I hoped he would look up then. But he didn't. The contrite pose he had adopted was perhaps unintentional, but it was clearly appropriate for the occasion. He was the very essence of a lost sheep.

"But Our Lord in his infinite goodness found Keith in the darkness and brought him to us."

And as I stood there listening and not listening I thought I understood the methodology. Keith might very well be saved. He might even be repentant. But more likely he was just hungry and tired, and therefore willing to perform this silly, silent mime of contrition, of abject subjugation, for a bowl of hot soup and a cup of milky tea in a bent metal mug, and a night on a metal framed single bed, with a rough blanket over him, and a thin foam pillow under his tousled head, and the company of the other ersatz repentants, all snoring and dreaming and turning fitfully in the night, sweating off their benders and gripped by the dream-state horrors that their minds, laid waste by all forms of physical and spiritual malnutrition they could fashion for themselves.

They, like Keith, were bought men. And bought cheaply.

The girl continued to speak. "That he might be saved by Christ Jesus. And that his plight might speak to us. For we should never forget, that without the grace of The Lord we are all just like Keith."

He looked up then, for the first time, at the sound of his name. Like an obedient pup. And our eyes did meet. Did he smile then for a second? And was it a smile of relief? Or was it instead a cynical smile? It was very dark. And it lasted only a second.

He pulled his coat about him. He looked at the girl as she spoke. And I knew then that he wanted her to stop. He wanted his reward, his food, his shelter. He wanted his doggy treat.

And I was certain then that he believed about as much as I believed.

Which was none at all.

"We all need to eat from the Bread of Life. To take comfort in the Presence of the Lord. To enter into the Many Mansions of his Heavenly Father." She was now unloading platitudes at a ferocious pace. Then she took his hand in hers. He looked up in surprise and I assumed the movement was unrehearsed. They stood together in silence.

There was little doubt that her witness had been effective. She relied on phrases that were not strictly biblical, but were nonetheless close enough that we outright disbelievers and Doubting Thomases could easily recognize the words.

But she was in truth much too young for the part, her words and manner altogether too stagey. And in the end she was only the soundtrack, the sympathetic commentary. Keith was the star of the show, the silent witness. And I think we all saw through his performance. He was just a starving artist. He didn't believe the words. He didn't live them. And we who watched could see this clearly.

The small crowd began to walk away as the girl scrambled to hand out her tracts. A few took them out of politeness. I refused mine.

Keith had turned away from her and the audience and shuffled slowly down a flight of steps toward his personal heaven: his soup and his sleep.

If Keith Pringle is now dead, then the stilted testimony of the evangelical girl with the rusty halo of hair in the striped scarf is the only means of benediction I have for him.

This was five years ago.

I haven't seen Keith since.

I have been back to visit my mother on two occasions. Both times Patricia chose not to accompany me, and both times my mother held me captive in her living room, her television on, her Oprah talking, the dark curtains drawn tight, the front door locked, and all the imagined demons of the world prowling at large, but, at least for the present time, restricted to the outside of her rapidly shrinking world.

# THIRTEEN

AL JR. WAS incredulous. "You don't wanna rent a jet ski?"

I was adamant. "No, I don't."

"But you wanna rent a rowboat?"

"That's correct."

He shook his head once more. "Well, for fuck's sake," he said in exasperation.

※

A MILE BEYOND the turn-off to Sandy's place stood Al's Water Sports Emporium and Live Bait Store.

Al himself wasn't available. According to his son he was in the crapper, and likely to be there awhile, on account of all the shit that was backed up inside of him, this backup being due, in Al Jr.'s view, to his father's steady diet of fried eggs, fried burgers and fried chicken. It was also the son's considered opinion that, if Al was successful in his endeavors, it was advisable to be some distance away, as the resultant aroma was likely to be, in Al Jr.'s own words, "truly fucking unpleasant."

All this information came unsolicited.

Al Jr. had shoulder-length brown hair and wore black jeans, black high-top Nike basketball shoes, a black Pearl Jam T-shirt, two leather wristbands and a small tattoo on his underdeveloped left shoulder muscle that improbably bore the legend *Daphne*.

"What do you want the rowboat for?"

"I thought I might go for a row."

"Pretty fucking slow way to travel."

"I like traveling slow."

"You're a foreigner aren't you?" It wasn't exactly an accusation. Al Jr. was just desperate to find some explanation for my odd behavior. He actually sounded relieved. "We've got a boat you can use. We use it to row out and rescue shit-for-brains tourist losers who fall off the jet skis and can't get back on." He gave me a look that silently judged me more than capable of just such a stunt.

I asked innocently. "Do you require a deposit?"

He sneered openly. "Oh yeah. Sure. You're gonna get really fucking far in that. The wood's utterly fucked and it leaks. Anyway we've got your car if you decide to make a run for it." He laughed, playing the lovable redneck for all it was worth.

We walked out to the dock, past a half-dozen shiny new Yamaha jet skis in neon colors and a rack of windsurfing boards. He pointed to the rowboat. It did look every bit as decrepit as he had indicated.

"When do you want it back?" I asked him.

"When you get yourself all tuckered out from all the excitement. If we're gone and locked up, just tie the thing back up there. I'll leave your keys in the ignition."

"And I can't pay you anything for the boat?"

He burst out laughing. "Get the fuck away from me. If anyone found out we were renting that piece of shit thing out we'd look like a pair of total fucking idiots. I'm only keeping your keys because the King of Shit will ream me out if I don't. Now go." He waved me away. "Go the fuck away. Have yourself some big fun." He laughed as he walked away.

When he had gone, I climbed carefully into the boat. The wood felt like sponge and there was an inch of warm water languishing in the bottom. As a result the boat was considerably more stable than I would have imagined.

Rowing carefully away from the dock, I headed out toward Foolishness Island.

‡‡

As a child I had taken camping trips in the countryside north of where I lived. We rowed across lakes of crystal-clear water, ice cold all year long, to set up our camps on grassy beaches and sing lewd songs and cook our sausages in the evening fires and listen to the older boys brag about beer and girls.

We would rub our smoke-filled eyes and wonder when all this would be ours.

That was the last time I had rowed a boat, almost twenty-five years ago.

The island gradually grew closer, far smaller than I had imagined, perhaps no more than five hundred yards stretching from end to end. There was no sign of a dock. But there was sand, and I could draw the boat up there. I wasn't especially worried about damaging the craft. I might even be doing Al Jr. a favor if I punched a hole in the bottom. Of course I would then have to swim back, and that would be foolishness indeed.

As I rowed to the far side of the island, I looked back at the shoreline. The Handle was still visible. I could see Connie's house, the Tait house, and Will Sanders' place. It was warm in the late afternoon and my shoulders were beginning to hurt. I tried to look for Sandy's house. Perhaps a small part of the roof peeked out from the trees. But I wasn't sure. It did look far away.

The island was perhaps half as wide as it was long, and the far shoreline boasted more flat sand. As I rowed for the nearest stretch and prepared to touch bottom, the Handle disappeared behind the island, and a sense of isolation passed over me, like a cloud across the face of the sun.

WE'RE MAKING IT BETTER FOR YOU!!!
THIS ISLAND IS CLOSED FOR RENOVATIONS
FOR THE REST OF THE SUMMER
BY ORDER OF THE HANDLE RESIDENTS ASSOCIATION

The sign was a makeshift affair hammered into the side of a tree. I wondered if it was even legal. Did the people living in the Handle actually own rights to the island?

I pulled the boat up onto the beach.

The sand gave way to ground and dense evergreen trees that hung like a canopy over the edge of the water. Under the trees, it was unnaturally dark, and a thick soft carpet of needles silenced my footsteps. A rough mud path followed the edge of the island, away from the boat.

In a small clearing stood a picnic table with a pile of dry logs underneath for a fire. A round deep pile of ashes signified the site of the fire. I dragged a stick through the ashes, which were white and fine, and I wondered how recent they were. The wind would surely soon blow them away.

There was a portable toilet, locked, and a small one-room log cabin, also locked. I picked up a stone and threw it through the cabin window, then reached carefully inside and opened the latch. I climbed through the window, avoiding the shards of glass littering the wood floor. It was airless and hot inside and, except for the glass, very tidy. Much too tidy. I expected dust but there was none. A clean sink stood in the corner. A piece of soap was still slightly damp on the underside. The cabin was clearly meant for communal use. Copious rules were Scotch taped to the back of the door, and once again the Residents Association was in evidence. I pulled a piece of paper towel from a roll and covered my hand with it. Inside an old Norge refrigerator a carton of skimmed milk was only three days past its expiration date.

The island's closure was clearly a recent development.

I wiped the window latch with the paper towel. I picked up my stone. I had been careful to touch nothing else. I pushed the door open with my shoulder and threw my stone far into the trees. Somewhere in the distance I heard the gentle hum of a motorboat moving across the water.

The rest was an airtight silence.

The density of the trees denied sound and light.

In another time I could easily have liked the island.

It could have been a peaceful place. But that day I felt sure that it wasn't.

I looked for things that were out of place, that were subtly wrong, as I walked the path. I was thinking of the traps that Keith had supposedly made. But I didn't really know what a rabbit trap looked like. My childhood camping trips hadn't gotten that rustic. I looked instead for belongings, for old clothes. But I didn't see any.

I thought of the remains of the fire, of how fine the dust was.

I kept on walking.

The path abruptly came into light, opening out, the sky a faded blue overhead. I was back at the water's edge, where the ground rose slightly, perhaps ten feet. A single tree stood on top of the rise, its labyrinth of roots exposed on the far side, where the mud slipped away to sand.

I sat down against the tree and looked out across the water.

Unlike the Handle, there was no uniformity to the dwelling places along this side of Paddle Lake. A half-million-dollar construction of glass fronting onto the water stood next to a seasonal fishing cabin or ramshackle A-frame. People had bought their summer homes here years ago, when water frontage was doubtless cheap. They had given little thought to winterizing their places, and had probably never used them much beyond a month or so in the summer, for fishing and boating, for a safe place in the country for the kids.

But lakefront access had become costly. The cottages were vanishing, and the glass palaces were taking their place. The texture of the communities had to be changing dramatically. I couldn't really tell if it was for the better. I didn't live here, and, in truth, both types of settlers were equally alien to me.

But it was without question a pretty spot.

I pulled hard at one of the roots and it came away in my hand. I could still hear the sputtering of the motorboat. It was much louder now. Much closer. My hands were dirty and my sneakers were mud and blood-splattered. I was still wearing the T-shirt and shorts from the morning tennis game with the Tait boy, and I was certain I looked like hell. I could also use a shower.

I closed my eyes and thought then of Sandy Weller, and of my wife, and of my money. I briefly considered the smattering of people who haunted the periphery of my life, haunted it because of the money. What would happen to most of the people if you subtracted money from the equation? What would happen to me if you subtracted money from the equation?

I thought about my mother then.

‡

A SILENCE STRETCHED out, and I couldn't hear the boat's motor anymore.

The first bullet hit the tree with a sharp crack. I threw myself to the ground and began to roll backwards, away from the water, away from where I thought the shot had come from.

My world slowed down as the second shot tore into the ground three feet from my left knee.

Sharp pine needles dug into my hands as I forced myself to crawl faster. I heard the engine of the boat again. It was close by now.

Whoever was shooting was doing it from the boat.

A candy wrapper lay less than an inch from my face, the paper brightly colored. I stopped crawling and lay there, my face in the dirt, paralyzed by fear, staring at the paper.

I crawled again.

My knee hit something hard, a piece of sharp metal, submerged beneath the needles and dirt. I looked back through the break in the trees. I couldn't see the boat, and I hoped, rather than reasoned, that they couldn't possibly see me.

My cheeks were salty and wet to the touch. I was still vain enough to be glad no one could see me. Could I stand up and walk? As a child my worst dreams would culminate in my legs refusing to work when I was very frightened, leaving me to crawl ignobly away from the nameless nightmare bogeyman.

I was crawling now.

This was my worst dream.

A man's loud voice. Was he laughing?

Without warning there was the sharp crack of four shots fired close together, followed by the grunt of the outboard as the boat picked up speed.

When the sound of the engine became a low drone I stood up and wiped away my tears. I took two shaky steps, before a submerged piece of metal wrapped itself around my foot, and I fell back down.

I brushed aside the needles to reveal my steel assailant. It gleamed back at me, defying its junk status, the pale metallic green of a Schwinn ladies bicycle, a basket attached to the front, a basket for Bridget Cassidy to carry her things in.

When I got back to the beach I discovered where the last four gunshots had struck. The old rowboat sported a compact quartet of leaks, each much larger than the bullet holes, as the soft, rotting wood had given way with the impact.

I was now looking at a long swim home.

I sat on the beach for a while, and waited for my body to stop shaking.

The wet wood was heavy and the old boat resisted my efforts, but eventually I succeeded in dragging it all the way up onto the beach and turning it over. It would dry out a little in the last of the day's sunlight.

I ran back to the cabin and pushed the door open, grabbing the rest of the paper towels and, from inside a medicine cabinet, a tin of Band-Aids. My hand brushed against a box of safety matches and I hesitated. The urge to torch the cabin, to destroy the whole damn island was a strong one.

Back at the beach I dried off the inside and outside of the boat as best I could, taking special care to dry the vessel's fresh wounds thoroughly. Then I packed the holes with the paper towels and secured the makeshift plugs with Band-Aids.

I had no illusions about the effectiveness of the repairs. The plugs wouldn't last much of the way across the lake. But they might get me partway, hopefully leaving a swimming distance well within the capabilities of a scared man, and a mediocre swimmer.

The boat slid slowly back into the water and I lowered myself gently in. Row fast and risk opening the repairs? Or use slow strokes that would hinder my progress but protect my handiwork for as long as possible? I opted for speed and dug the oars deep into the water. As I stroked, I watched the Band-Aids as they began to peel inexorably away from the soft wood.

I rowed all the harder.

At what seemed close to the halfway point I could no longer ignore the reality that my ship was going down. The rowing had become progressively harder, and my bandaged paper towel plugs were sodden, all but worthless. The water felt warm around my ankles.

I could see the houses of the Handle clearly.

I climbed over the side and swam toward the shore.

I learned to swim after a fashion as an eight-year-old child. The crawl had always eluded me; I never quite mastered breathing and swimming and bringing my head up above the water in an effortless sequence. But I had acquired a slow and dependable breaststroke, and this was what I employed to get me back to the beach.

I can't say how long it took. I should have checked my watch before starting. It was close to five o' clock when I reached land. I would guess I was in the water for close to an hour. I was extremely tired.

An expensive Swiss watch is about as waterproof as a thirty-dollar Timex, but ox-leather straps barely survive one good dunking, and mine certainly looked the worse for wear.

Resisting every urge to collapse for a while on the soft sand, I hurried across the beach. Paranoia was setting in. Maybe the natives were friendly, but it was also possible that the shooter on the water lived in a house close enough to be watching me now.

It wasn't a feeling for which I cared.

⚓

I WALKED FOR an hour and a half.

Al the terminally constipated and his surly son had locked up shop for the day. My car was in the parking lot, unlocked, apparently untouched, the keys as promised in the ignition.

I opened the trunk and pulled my wallet out from under the carpet. I found a piece of paper and a pen in the glove compartment and I wrote a short note, in which I apologized for the sudden demise of their rowboat. I didn't bother to sign it. Wrapping a hundred dollar bill inside the paper, I folded it up and slid it under the door of the store.

Al could buy himself a new boat, a ton of fried food, or a year's supply of laxatives.

Then I drove away.

My clothes were close to dry when I got back to Sandy's house. It would be an hour until she and our dinner showed up.

After a quick shower I put on a white cotton shirt, Timberland shoes, and a pair of Ralph Lauren jeans. There was a six-pack of Stroh's beer cold in the refrigerator. I opened one and sat on the porch with a fitness magazine I had every intention of reading. I sat instead for a long while staring at nothing.

I got the laptop down from my bedroom and fired it up, logging onto CompuServe and entering the keyword for the online version of the city newspaper. Were there developments in Keith's story about which I wasn't aware?

Searching for KEITH produced several articles about a baseball player with a cocaine problem and a low batting average. Searching for PRINGLE brought up the original article I had read, the one about tourists in trouble.

There was nothing else.

Whatever his fate, it was apparently unrecorded.

I looked for messages and found two.

Nye said little more than hi. Tom Younger had left a long rambling message. He had just gotten himself online. Wasn't it truly neat? This was his first time. This was in fact the first goddamn message he'd ever sent. Someone had told him the Vice President was online. Was that right? Maybe he'd just up and tell him what a prize putz he was. He'd figured I'd be online. Wasn't it just too goddamn neat? How was the house search going? He asked me to leave him a message. He was going to try the CB section now. He still had to think of a neat handle.

Thinking about Tom Younger speeding down the information highway made me very tired.

I cleared both messages, signed off, turned off the laptop, and sat waiting for the arrival of Sandy and the pizza.

# FOURTEEN

THE PIZZA WAS right on time. Sandy was late.

As I turned on the oven and hunted in the kitchen for a large plate, my hands began to shake, and the attack of nervous terror I had thus far managed to delay finally showed up. Despite the heat in the room, I was instantly cold. I sat down at the kitchen table before my legs gave way under me. My hands supported my head as my legs shook violently under the table.

Had I come close to death on the island?

I sat helpless, waiting for the fear to end. Sweat formed like a thin layer of ice water on my brow. Somewhere in the back of my mind I marveled at the delayed onset of panic, between then and now, between the gunshots fired in the afternoon, and the white kitchen in a big empty house in the early evening hours.

On the island, the bullets had passed close by, but I wasn't truly terrified. I had lain prone, then crawled to safety. For a moment I had wondered if the time of my death had arrived.

Now I could only sit, shaking uncontrollably, as waves of terror washed over me. All I could do was try to bend my will, push back at the waves, and make it all end soon.

The bike. I focused hard on the bike. The model and the basket and the fact that it was on the island in the first place. Was it the same bike Keith had borrowed from Bridget Cassidy? How could it possibly not be?

There was the sound of gravel under soft footsteps outside the house.

I squeezed my feet hard against the wood floor and told myself that it would just be Sandy coming home.

My fingers knotted together and I bit into my thumb hard, until the sharp pain registered.

Please let it be Sandy coming home.

The groan of the porch floorboards, then the loud retort of the screen door as it slammed open.

I set my face into the semblance of a smile.

Please don't let her see my fear.

It occurred to me then that if it wasn't her, I was utterly helpless.

"Honeybunch. I'm home." It was Sandy coming home. "I smell food. And I smell like a sick dog's shit. Let me shower fast before we eat." I heard her gym bag hit the floor, her Reeboks hit the stairs, the bathroom door slam, then the shower water hissing.

I let out a deep breath.

My teeth had drawn a little blood.

But I had finally stopped shaking.

⁑

SHE DRANK A diet Pepsi from the can and ate her pizza in large unwieldy slices with her fingers. I was still a little shaky and stuck to iced water. She was barefoot and had changed into black jeans and a cream-colored vest. Her hair was tousled and still wet from the shower.

"How was your day?" she asked.

"I went for a row on the lake," I said. "Then I had a swim. Then I took a walk."

She made a face. "That really sucks," she said. "Some of us had to work."

I laughed a little wildly and she looked hard at me.

"Are you all right? You look a little weird."

I managed to smile. "It was very hot out on the lake. I may have overdone it. Rowing the boat. Maybe I got a little too much sun. The kitchen got warm when I turned the oven on," I concluded rather lamely.

"Hmmm." She was clearly unconvinced. "The pizza's good." She glanced at my plate. "You're not very hungry?"

I looked down. She was right. I shook my head. "I guess I'm not."

"Are you tired?" She sounded concerned.

"I suppose I am. I was foolish and overdid it today. I should probably just go to bed. I'll feel much better if I just lie down for a while."

She stood up and took my plate away. I had eaten four bites.

"Oh boy, cold pizza for breakfast. It doesn't get any better than this." She cut herself another slice, put the rest back in the box, and the box into the refrigerator.

"Go get some rest," she said and kissed me on the forehead. I assumed it was clammy. "I must have been too much woman for you last night. I'm going to leave you alone tonight."

I was too far gone to respond.

As I got up to leave she spoke. "Have you been lying to me?"

"How do you mean? About what?"

"Oh, I don't know," she spoke playfully. "About your day?"

"No," I said trying to look her in the eye. "Tennis, rowing, swimming, walking. That was about it."

I dragged myself upstairs to bed. I was dog-tired. Yet as soon as my head hit the pillow I was suddenly wide awake, and quite unable to fall asleep.

For a while I did wonder if she *would* come to my room tonight. Was I exhausted or eager? I did catch myself listening for her footsteps on the landing but there was only silence, or the natural creaking, groaning, rumbling noises old houses tend to make.

I wondered if I was perhaps supposed to take charge, to announce my intentions. Should I go to her room this time? *This time?* Was I being foolish to suppose there would even be another time?

These were not the calculations of a masterful male animal, but they were unlikely to change much, even with a good night's sleep.

Wide-eyed and jittery, I now thought beyond the reading of Sandy Weller's love signs to the question of gunshots and perforated rowboats.

It was safe to assume that someone wanted me dead, or at the very least scared away from the island.

Who would that someone be?

But eventually sleep did come, deep, undisturbed, until the long-promised rain tapped hard on the window. But that was in the early hours of the morning, when I woke alert, and newly brave, and ever resourceful.

"I thought I might drive into Paddle Lake this morning," I said. "Is there anything you need?"

Sandy looked up. "Nope," she spoke with her mouth full of Rice Krispies. A selection of little cereal boxes littered the kitchen table. The overhead light was on in the kitchen. The windows were closed. It was very wet outside.

"Will you be here for lunch?"

"I don't think so."

"Can I cook you anything for breakfast?"

"You're being very dutiful this morning."

"Go fuck yourself."

"Ah," I smiled brightly. "That's much better."

"You're very cheerful. You looked bad last night."

"I overdid it."

"Humph," she said grumpily.

I reached across the table. "I'll just have one of the little boxes."

She flashed an evil grin. "I've snarfed all the good ones already."

I looked closely. "Not true. The Sugar Frosties are still left."

She raised an eyebrow. "Don't be retarded. They're just kiddie shit."

"I happen to like them," I said, as I ripped open the small box. "If it clears up, I might go down to the beach later today. I meant to ask. Is it okay for me to be using the beach?"

She nodded. "Of course. You're paying for it. It's all part of the service. I belong to the residents' association. They graciously allowed me to join and pay their yearly fee. So my guests are also extended full beach privileges."

"Did you know they have closed up the island?"

She looked up then, clearly puzzled. "No. What the hell for?"

"It says for renovations."

She shrugged. "Hmmm. News to me. It's possible." She considered. "I guess." She was clearly unconvinced and went back to her cereal.

I hadn't eaten Sugar Frosties in twenty years.

I still liked them.

Later in the morning, I drove to Paddle Lake. At the drugstore, I bought a newspaper and asked directions to the nearest car rental agency. There was apparently only one in town.

If the affable Rick at Affordable Auto Rental was curious as to why I wanted to leave an expensive German car in his parking lot and drive away in a white late-model Ford Escort, he was much too polite to show it.

As I walked out to the car, I noticed that license plates in this state were only mandatory on the rear of the car. I also located a tiny decal on the windshield that carried Affordable's name, and thus marked the vehicle as a rental. I hoped it would peel off easily. It did.

I had parked the Mercedes as close to the back of the parking lot as possible so that the car could barely be seen from the street. I had negotiated an open-ended agreement with Rick. He had taken an imprint from my platinum Amex card, which clearly impressed him.

I dimly recalled when that sort of thing had impressed me too.

Back at the Handle, I pulled into the parking lot beside the tennis court, backing in carefully, picking a spot where only the front of the car was visible to the houses. I turned off the engine and sat there.

The rain fell in a shifting pattern of rivers and tributaries, variations on a limited theme, all abruptly ending at the bottom of the windshield, grand designs dashed against the still wipers.

I had no plan beyond simply watching the houses for a while, in as anonymous a fashion as possible. A nondescript, small, inexpensive car parked in a parking lot in torrential rain. No distinguishing marks. No reason to notice.

I opened my newspaper.

I'd forgotten what day of the week it was. An inconceivable lapse for me. The top of the newspaper said Saturday, and I had no reason to doubt it.

I did want a chance to talk to the children of the Handle. It wouldn't be easy. I was a stranger, and, for a number of very good reasons, children weren't supposed to talk to strangers anymore.

The fact that it was the weekend meant that the kids might well be at home. The fact that the rain was heavy, and showing no signs of letting up, meant that they'd likely be indoors and therefore all but inaccessible to me.

⚜

IN MY MIND, I played back what I knew so far, my gossamer-thin strands of evidence. The very word "evidence" had a substantive and quite inappropriate air for, in truth, there was next to none.

Rather than there being any kind of crime actually taking place, a foreign, well-weathered, and terminally unlucky drifter was traversing across country in an untidy tangle of emotional and topographic maneuvers. Sad souls like Keith didn't leave paper trails, credit card receipts or motel reservations. He didn't jettison wives and partners and careers in his wayward wake. He shambled in and shambled out of other people's lives, littering with the detritus of dreams and expectations, but offering no resolutions.

His was a truly shambolic trajectory.

But if there wasn't evidence of what is often drolly referred to as "foul play," was there not at least some basis for suspicion? There was an abandoned bicycle on an island. There was a timid woman who drank in the morning. There was an inexplicably nervous neighbor with a hair-trigger temper. And there were people on a boat with a gun, who clearly didn't much care for me puttering about on their island.

And then there were my ethereal, unnamed instincts, uppermost of which was a sense that Connie had lost a friend who, at the very least, would have said goodbye if he could.

From the lives of those who loved him, Keith Pringle had taken a powder many times before. But this time his parents feared the worst for him.

And I did too.

Sitting in the rain, in a rented car, staking out the houses of strangers. There was a sense of liberation, or as much liberation as my hidebound persona could tolerate.

Two lonely women lived in two small towns.

It had been relatively effortless to slip into the rhythm of Sandy Weller's life, to sleep with her, at her bidding, in a slick, clean, pleasurable act that probably had as little emotional meaning as an aerobic workout, after dark, without the shiny apparatus, or the walls lined by mirrors for the buffed and vain.

And I had wanted to hold tightly to the fragile Bridget Cassidy, in the fading pastel light of her living room, at the twilight of an unseasonably chill summer's day, and to lure myself into believing that the passions she felt could be somehow appropriated by me, if I only chose to lay siege to her heart.

These were the curious notions of a married man, physically unfaithful for the first time in his ordered life, now scrambling that very same life, like a frequency on a weak radio signal, but then finding himself rather enjoying the resultant static.

As I sat up, a young girl pushed open the front door of the Sanders house and bolted across the front yard. It was Beth Sanders, Will's daughter, and she was heading for Connie's place.

The girl was wet through and shivering as she pushed the doorbell. Connie appeared quickly at the window. She smiled and waved at the girl. Then she opened the door, threw a large towel over the girl's dripping head, and the two of them went inside as the front door gently closed behind them.

I sat and watched for further developments. But the rain continued, and the facades of the houses revealed nothing more to me.

What to do now?

The maneuver of pulling away from the parking lot and driving across the street would doubtless look odd, but I hoped that the rain and the rented car would conspire to mask my identity.

I sensed myself gradually making enemies of the inhabitants of the Handle. The car might hide me from them for a little while longer.

I gunned the engine, parked at the top of Connie's driveway, jumped out of the car, and ran to her door. Standing there I was invisible, except to anyone out on the lake, and I was fairly sure no one was watching me from there today.

The front door opened and Connie stood there.

"I must assume you haven't come to make me an irresistible offer on my little domicile," she said with a slight smile. "And I notice you've lamentably moved down market in your choice of automobiles. Tut, tut. The little black Teutonic number had such unmistakable flair."

"I'm intruding," I blurted out. "I know. I'm awfully sorry. But I was hoping you might invite me in. I do think it's important."

"You really are an incorrigible snoop."

"I saw the Sanders girl arrive."

She nodded. "I did mention that we're old friends. I'm serving some hot chocolate with marshmallows and shavings of dark German chocolate on top. The weather seems to call for it. Would you perhaps care to partake?"

"That would be very nice," I said, "and I do thank you, Connie."

"We never did fully uncover your motives, did we? But my intuition tells me that somewhere a sense of honor is to be found within you. But I will warn you, don't upset my little Beth. She's my sweet angel, and my only true ally in this cultural morass."

"I'll be very good. I promise you."

"Good. That's settled. So for goodness' sake enter. That wretched rain's from the north, and is surely intent on ruining my patrician posture with lumbago and other odious infirmities reserved exclusively for those of us a little long in the tooth."

WITH THAT SHE closed the door firmly behind me.

Claiming a pan of boiling milk to attend to in the kitchen, Connie left us alone. Beth Sanders sat on a high-backed chair, her wet hair dripping on the velvet upholstery, her feet in sodden scuffed sneakers that didn't quite reach the oriental rugged floor.

"Hi," she said to me brightly. "We're going to have some cocoa now. Connie makes the best."

"Do you think she might make me some?" I asked her.

She looked at me appraisingly then shrugged. "I guess so," she said. "You have to be pretty special though." She clearly felt that I might not qualify.

"She's my friend. I have lots of friends my age at school. But Connie is my older friend."

"What about your parents?"

"Parents are fine but they aren't really like friends." She gave me a pitying look. I had clearly blundered.

"Is Tammi Tait your friend?"

Another shrug. "I guess. She's in the fifth grade. I'm only in the fourth grade. So we aren't really friends at school. But we do play at home sometimes. But when her school friends come to the beach she pretends she doesn't know me and I think that's a really gross thing to do. Don't you think?"

"Yes I do." She smiled as I spoke.

"You talk funny. Are you from another country? Is that a rude question?"

"No, it isn't rude at all. Yes, I am. But it was a long, long time ago. Why do you ask? Have you heard someone else speak just like me?"

"No. I never ever have," she answered much too abruptly. "They talk funny on television sometimes."

I laughed at that. "They certainly do. No. I meant someone real. Was there someone real?" Real versus television. I was heading into deep waters.

She hesitated. "I can't say." She looked miserable. "And I promised I would never, ever say."

Connie entered then with three steaming mugs, three spoons, and a plate piled high with chocolate chip cookies that looked suspiciously home-baked. It occurred to me that she may have deceived me on the question of her cooking skills. The marshmallows were already a solid congealed mass on the surface of each mug. Connie set them down. Beth began to slurp noisily at hers. Connie smiled at the girl and ruffled her damp hair with the towel that was draped across her small shoulders.

"Are you making friends with my Beth?" She asked me with a smile that wasn't entirely friendly.

"Of course," I said, "but she thinks I talk funny."

Connie laughed. "She thinks I do too. Don't you think he speaks much like my friend Keith? You remember Keith? You liked to sit on the beach. You were there once. This man comes from the same country as Keith. They were children together."

Beth Sanders stared at the messy inside of her mug and said nothing.

Connie spoke again. "Now no one knows what's happened to poor Keith, and a lot of people are really very worried."

Again there was silence. Connie looked across at me I tried to give her a look of encouragement.

"It's not anything serious Beth. It's just that people want to know that he's all right. If you were lost I'd surely want to know that you were okay, now wouldn't I?"

A monotone. "I suppose so." There was a long hesitation after that. Then Beth Sanders spoke again. "I'm not supposed to say, so I'll tell you because you're my friend and you did ask but you have to promise not to say anything to anyone else. I can trust you, Connie." She looked directly at me. "But can I trust you?"

She sounded so serious I almost laughed, which would have been disastrous. "I promise you can trust me Beth," I said solemnly.

"Tell us please, Beth." Connie said.

Beth Sanders sighed deeply. "All right then. But you did agree. Keith was an evil man. He took his penis out and made Tammi look at it. My dad and Mr. Tait found out, and they made him go away."

I must have looked quite dazed.

"Did you see this happen, Beth?" Connie asked her sharply.

"Yes, I did." She sounded adamant. "Tammi and me were playing on the beach."

"Are you sure he really did this?" Connie's voice was no longer quite steady.

"You don't believe me?"

"Of course I do, Darling. I just didn't expect that Keith . . ."

"Mrs. Tait says he's evil, that what he did was an evil thing. She kept saying that. Evil. Evil. She said he should be sent away."

I sat there dumbfounded.

If it were true, he was lucky not to have been lynched. *If*. I didn't have any reason to doubt the girl. I didn't have any evidence to suggest that Keith couldn't do a thing like that. But I was doubtful. There was in Beth's succinct explanation of Keith's act a clinical detachment, as if leaned by rote, or else dictated. As I looked at Connie I could see that, behind a face reflecting an anxious concern for the child, she was doubtful too.

"Mrs. Tait told us not to tell anyone."

"Was she there?" Connie asked.

"Yes. I mean no. She wasn't there. After he . . ." She hesitated. "After he did that to Tammi, we ran to her house. Her mother was there. We told her what happened. She said it was an evil thing. That he was an evil man to do it. She told us that Tammi's dad would take care of it. She gave us Cherry Cokes and cookies and we watched Bugs Bunny cartoons on their big screen television."

"Did he take care of it?" I spoke then, more to myself, in truth not really expecting an answer.

She nodded. "I bet he did. Tammi told me that her dad and my dad beat him up and sent him far away. I never saw him again. Tammi said her mother made her promise not to say anything about it. And that I was to do the same. Not even to my dad. Even though he knew all about it later when Tammi's dad told him. I wanted to tell my dad, too. But I promised I wouldn't. So I didn't. I'm only telling you now because Connie asked me." Her tone turned petulant.

Connie asked. "Are you glad they sent him away?"

"I suppose. But it made you sad didn't it? And I liked him before that. Before he did the evil thing. When we all sat on the beach it was fun. But Mrs. Tait's been nice to me ever since. And she can be weird and mean to me sometimes. I don't like having a secret thing from my dad though."

"Maybe you should talk to him," I said.

"Oh no. I can't. I promised. I'd get into big trouble."

"How would you get into trouble?" Connie asked.

"I don't know. I just would." She spoke snappishly. "Can you stop asking me all these questions? I shouldn't have told you anything. I need to go to the bathroom now."

She got up and left the room.

Connie and I looked at each other.

"I know Beth very well. She's not telling us the exact truth," Connie said.

"I know," I said.

"Is it possible she's being made to lie?" Connie said.

"It's possible," I said.

We both sipped at our hot chocolates, which had cooled but which were still potentially delicious.

Mine tasted like mud in my mouth.

# FIFTEEN

WHEN BETH SANDERS RETURNED from the bathroom, she asked for a spoon and proceeded to dig out the marshmallow remains from the bottom of her cup. When she was finished, she had chocolate encircling her mouth, but she did look extremely pleased with herself.

"I have to go now," she said suddenly and jumped to her feet. Connie's cheek was kissed, transferring a little chocolate, and for a long second she regarded me quizzically. Did I rate a kiss? A handshake perhaps? Finally she settled for a shy smile.

After the girl had gone, Connie wiped absently at the dark chocolate stain on her milk-white cheek.

"I simply can't believe any of it," she spoke gently into the silence.

I couldn't either.

She took my hand and squeezed it. She shook her head back and forth emphatically.

I left Connie a little later, when our mutual silence had become a dark and overbearing presence. We held each other's hand as we walked to her front door.

The rain was still heavy as I got behind the wheel of my rented Ford Escort. I started the car and drove carefully away, following the beach road. The rain was loud and too much for the windshield wipers. If they beat fast, they cleared the water but distracted me. When I slowed them down, they merely swept the rain listlessly in waves across the windshield and temporarily left me unable to see the road.

I slowed the car down and watched for the side road that led to Sandy's house.

Before I could turn the engine off, the phone rang and startled me. I had unthinkingly pulled the mobile unit from the Mercedes before changing cars. More to deter theft, in truth, than to keep in touch.

I hadn't been especially effective at keeping in touch lately.

"Hello, Tom." Patricia's voice was barely audible. The reception was very poor, and the rain splattered loudly on the roof of the car.

"Hello," I said.

"Why do you sound so odd?"

"No. I'm fine. It's difficult to hear you."

"Are you driving right now?" She spoke louder.

It struck me as an odd question. "No, I'm not. I'm parked. There's very heavy rain." I sounded slightly asinine.

"Are you alone in the car?"

"Yes, I am. Of course I am."

"I wanted to talk to you."

"I called you the other day."

"Yes. I did get your message."

There was an uneasy quiet to my wife then, an anxiousness, and in that daunting silence, the next line of the conversation came to me a long time before it was spoken.

"This might seem terribly sudden, but I would like us to divorce very soon." The words were like gunshots.

"I see," I said finally, stupidly, throwing words into the silence.

After that I said nothing, waiting for the arrival of the appropriate emotion, knowing it wouldn't be surprise and equally certain that it wouldn't be sadness.

"I think we've grown too far apart," she said finally.

I blurted out, "Don't you think that's a somewhat trite line?"

So there was the emotion. At last. With a veritable cornucopia of noble attitudes open to me, I had, in all cowardice, opted for petulance.

"Yes," she said it thoughtfully. "I suppose it is trite. Do you deny that it's true?"

"No. If you imagine it to be so then it clearly is. I never really noticed."

I thought she might be smiling ironically then.

"This would perhaps be one of those situations, Tom, where, if you possessed a strong opinion you might care to actually voice it. To tell me I'm wrong for example, that our love can endure, something along these lines might be called for."

I didn't say anything.

"No? Well then. Our lives are really quite insular. I have talked with Jeff." Jeffrey was our lawyer. "And he tells me that our money is a simple matter. You own your store and your car and your investments. And I apparently own everything else, as per your very specific instructions, which were never to my knowledge ever discussed."

"Was that something wrong?" I asked.

"No. Perhaps not. Certainly it was secretive, and presumptive, and quite possibly rather arrogant."

"You're very wealthy."

"How nice for me. Would you care to deny that it was a little cold-blooded?"

"Perhaps it was."

"But as you say, I am now rich. And as Jeff says, the cut will be a clean, straight, uncomplicated one. One might almost imagine you had planned for this . . . as if you foresaw . . . did you think we would eventually split apart?"

"No. I just thought . . . it made sense to me then. It was simple. Straightforward. I thought it best."

"Do you know I took a walk around the house this morning? There's virtually nothing here of you. Oh, I didn't expect to find your spirit haunting the place; that would be quite absurd. But physically there's nothing. In the kitchen there's the coffee you like. A few shirts and things you bought for yourself hang in the bedroom closet. There's nothing anyone else has ever given you that you've cared for . . . even the things we bought in the beginning. Standing in the cutesy stores together on Sunday afternoons, nodding your head. You must have hated it all."

"I do need to get some things. Computer files and some other things. I can send Nye over, if he doesn't mind. He can take everything off the hard drive. It's an old machine. Maybe you'd like to have it."

As I sat in the rain and arranged the exchange and retrieval of the detritus of my marriage, all I could think was that I would miss my empty office and my bay window and the children playing in the park across the street.

"Thank you. I suppose I should be relieved that we're not going to have one of these difficult divorces. We aren't, are we Tom?"

"I don't suppose so."

"I suspect I haven't been very warm to you."

"I'm not altogether sure that I need very much warmth."

"Oh I think you're quite wrong there. I think that we all need warmth. You and I either pretended that we didn't, or else came to realize that the other couldn't or wouldn't provide it. I think we gave each other to believe we were such strong and independent people. But I suspect that we're in reality anything but. But these are simply my little theories, and I'll stop now because, as we speak, I have to wonder if you truthfully care one way or another. You sound as you always do. Polite and a little bit distracted. I should, I think, be a little offended that this particular conversation isn't capturing your attention."

"That's unfair. I am listening. Do I care about you? Is that what you're asking me? Do I care that my marriage is ending?"

"Don't, Tom. You're going to endeavor to produce a decent facsimile of emotion and care, and it's simply not worth the bother. We are in the process of splitting up. Your wife of fifteen years and you, and this conversation is a messy little chore you have to get through, before you can move on to the next piece of ordered, all-consuming business."

"I'm truly very sorry, Patricia."

"About?"

"About everything. About not making you happy. About not paying attention. I should have let you buy me some nice shirts."

"I did buy you some nice shirts."

"Then I should have worn the bloody things more often."

"You hated them. You tried them on, and you looked as if you were choking to death. You might want to consider living alone, Tom."

"Is this something you've planned for a while?" I asked her. "Or is this a sudden thing?"

"No."

"You've thought this out then?"

"Yes."

"And I never even noticed."

"No. You never did."

"Is there someone else?"

"Now it's your turn to be trite."

I paused in acknowledgement. "I do want to know."

"But do you truthfully care?"

"I don't know," I said.

"Why do you want to know?"

"I can't really say. Isn't it something people always want to know? A precursor to the inevitable jealous rage."

"That would be a falsehood on your part. You've no such emotion. But there isn't anyone else, although I must admit that I do find myself thinking about it sometimes. Perhaps even wishing that there were, but purely in the abstract form. For the company, I expect."

I said nothing then.

"And have you started to stray yourself?"

I thought briefly about lying, but it seemed an idiotic option at this stage. "I have a little. Only of late."

"Does it mean terribly much to you?"

I almost laughed. "Actually it seems to mean a great deal to me. But for reasons that don't have very much to do with the other person."

"You're perhaps finally letting your guard down."

"Perhaps. I'm getting more than a little tangled up in myself."

"You should take that as a positive sign. You might actually find yourself in the process."

"But then again, I might simply stay lost for a while in what could well be my midlife crisis."

"Is she a young and terribly pretty creature?" Her voice grew very quiet then. Patricia was a proud woman, and, for a split second, I thought that if she was going to cry it would be then. "But I shouldn't really ask." Her voice grew distant. "I don't suppose it matters that much."

Then there was a long quiet.

"Is your computer's fax modem operational?" She asked abruptly.

"Yes it is."

"Then the customary papers will be coming your way in the near future. You will have to sign a great many of them. You should speak with Jeff first. And please send Nye over any time. I did tell my mother, by the way. She sat and cried for hours and hours. She's always been a silly romantic woman with little grasp of reality. But I do have to go now. We should talk when you return. Have you managed to locate your lost friend yet?"

I told her that I hadn't.

It occurred to me that Patricia might even doubt the existence of Keith. She might think that this was all for sport.

She said goodbye.

As she hung up, all I could think of was that this had been the longest conversation I could remember us having in a great while.

I switched the phone off, climbed out of the car, and walked through the rain into the house of the woman with whom I had been unfaithful.

For lunch I picked listlessly at a slice of cold pizza and tried to kickstart some sort of cathartic reaction to the news that my empty structure of a marriage was close to collapsing. But nothing much came. I drank the last of the milk from the carton in the fridge and noticed the note attached to the door, held in place by a plastic toy girl in a skimpy blue leotard.

*Tom, Don't wait up. Chance of a killer date with young nubile town stud currently between bleached bimbos. Us oldsters can't afford to wait. Might pan out. Might be a total bust. Really wish I'd shaved my pits this morning. Hope he likes it natural! Forage for scraps or else dine out. See ya!*

The note wasn't signed.

This wasn't turning out to be an especially great day.

I put the remains of the pizza back in the fridge, finished the milk, and left the plate to loll in the sink in warm soapy water, an uncharacteristically sloppy gesture on my part.

Outside, the rain had finally stopped, and the air felt dense and tropical.

I stopped the car at the bottom of the dirt road, at the intersection where the shore road crosses over, and waited as a Corvette sped past. A man sat behind the wheel, a little cramped inside a performance car designed for smaller men with the sporting blood. The T-top roof was optimistically open. The car was white, a mid-seventies vintage. I knew this from a session in the sports club sauna barely listening to a Corvette owner with a soggy cigar and a protruding gut discuss his life's passion for close to an hour.

I didn't recognize the driver but the car was the one I had seen inside the Taits' garage. The one the teenage Tait fiercely coveted, the one his older brother drove when he hadn't displeased his father. I couldn't think of the older boy's name for a moment. Then it came to me. Chip. Chip Tait. Greg and Chip. Such all-American names. They should be Beach Boys, or else distant heirs to the Kennedy fortune.

But that hadn't been a boy behind the wheel. By a simple process of elimination the driver had to be their father, George Tait.

Without thinking, I spun the wheel, turned the Escort in a deep puddle, and, spraying brown water, followed the trail of the Corvette.

Norm's Nook was a rundown bar squatting in an empty
space between two small towns. The place was bigger than profit
margins might have reasonably allowed. Perhaps once it had been a
roadhouse full of happy revelers, on a road that had maybe been the
shortest distance between two places people actually wanted to get to
and from.

The parking lot was weeds winning out over cracked concrete.
The words in the window flashed FIRE BREWED STROHS ON
TAP. The building was weathered wood that had been once a rich
red color, now fading fast to nothing at all.

I parked beside the Corvette and locked the car door. We had
the lot to ourselves. I assumed that the bar would be close to empty,
that there would be no Norm in living memory, and that none of the
customers would care much what a nook is or was.

I pushed the door open and was blasted with stale beery air and
near total darkness.

Gradually my eyes made the adjustment.

George Tait evidently liked to drink fast. He was in the act of
pushing an empty beer glass across the bar toward a pale woman
in a man's white cotton shirt and black jeans standing in front of
him. His glass was still frosty. I sat down at the stool beside him and
waited for my eyes to adjust to the gloom and my body to get used to
the chill.

The floor was cheap wood-patterned parquet. The walls were a
darker paneled wood punctuated by fake knots, posters of girls with
blue eye makeup and cutoff jeans and yellowed paper advertising events
long past. The bar had once boasted its own softball team. They had
even won a trophy, which now stood dust-covered beside the television
set mounted behind the bar. An old Beatles movie was playing, and an
unnaturally innocent looking John Lennon was singing an acoustic song
to a girl with long dark hair in unbecoming pigtails.

George Tait picked up his fresh drink without saying anything.
He looked at the glass. "This is a ways off the tourist map, pal. You
must be seriously fucking lost." He spoke loudly.

"Not really," I said.

"Get you something?" The woman behind the bar spoke quickly.

"A beer sounds fine," I said.

"Light or regular?"

"Regular." It truthfully didn't much matter.

"That rain. It let up at last. I thought it never would. Figured the day was shot all to hell." She spoke between us as she poured the beer.

Tait stared straight ahead, his eyes tracking the dusty bottles on the shelves behind the bar.

"Can I buy you one?" I asked him on impulse.

He snorted. "Do I need to buy you one back?"

I shook my head. He laughed once. It wasn't a nice laugh.

"I'll take a draft then." His last was close to empty.

A minute later, the woman placed the drinks on the bar. When I gave her a ten and told her to keep the change, she smiled sweetly at me.

"Well, check out Mister Money." His smile was ugly and I heard a threat in his voice for the first time.

George Tait was a tall man shaped like a pair of scissors. Sitting down, he looked squat, short in the arms and torso, but standing up the long legs knotted beneath the barstool would telescope out beneath him. There wasn't much hair left on the top of his head—what there was had once been blonde and was now swept back in hair-creamed strands that left a widow's peak but did a respectable job of covering the spot in back. You wouldn't actually call him bald yet.

He wore old Levi's jeans and new basketball shoes and a red T-shirt from a crab cafe in the Florida Keys, that was too small for him. He didn't have a gut but his chest was shapeless, like a young kid's, the muscle slack and undefined. He was probably lucky not to be fat.

His third beer was fast becoming a thing of the past. He paused before drinking the last inch.

When it was empty he spoke. "So now what happens, pal? You followed me here. You pissed my lovely wife off. And you've got that sensitive fuck of a neighbor of mine Will Sanders all fired up." He turned toward me and spat the last words out. "So what the fuck is it you want from me?"

"I'm looking for someone."

"The tramp."

"He's a friend."

"That's nice. He's still a tramp. And a pervert."

"I don't believe that."

"No? Why should you? Like you say. He's your friend. He tried to show his dick to my daughter."

"You believe that?"

He smiled. "Maybe. My kids don't lie in general. Not if they figure they'll get caught. Who knows? I really get off on beating the piss out of weak people, so I don't truthfully give much of a fuck one way or another. I wasn't real thrilled to have him hanging around our place, that's for sure."

"He wasn't doing any harm."

"True. He wasn't doing any harm. That's very true. But then, so fucking what? He made the place look real shitty."

I sensed that the barmaid was no longer close by. I heard a voice on the TV set murmur a weather forecast. More rain was apologetically promised. The cooler behind the bar kicked in loudly. A car driving fast on the wet road outside came and went.

"You sent him away."

He shrugged. "It's a free country. He chose to vacate the premises before we kicked his sorry ass."

"We?"

"The townspeople and I." He laughed.

"He's missing now."

"That so? Fuck of a shame." The fresh beer in his hand, number four, vanished in one long swallow.

"Listen. You've got as much out of me as one beer entitles you to. I understand you got the jump on Will. Big fucking deal. That's no big thing. Will's damn good with his mouth. Fucking worthless with his fists."

"You hurt Keith?"

"A little. We told him to kindly get the fuck away from our lake. Maybe we had to hit him gently a few times to make our point. He was soft. We did nothing real unpleasant. He's pretty much a worthless runt. He ran like hell away from the place. I never saw him again."

"Did the police ever ask you about it?"

He tried to look bored and amazed at the same time. "A missing tramp and a sicko? Pal, you're clearly unaware how law enforcement works around here. We form committees here, we eat pancake breakfasts, we dig each other out of the snow in a storm. We're one big happy fucking family. The police chief's name is Andy Borland, okay? His daughter Maggie goes to school with my Tammi. We ice fish the lake in the winter. He stops by here sometimes. He'd shoot you straight through the fucking head if I asked him quietly. You're pretty much all alone here, pal, asking your smart questions, getting your ashes hauled by the Weller woman cause you've got a fancy car that for some weird reason you ain't driving right now, baby-smooth skin, and no dick to speak of. Now get the fuck out of here because that's all I'm saying to you."

I swung my fist at him. He saw it coming. He smirked and moved to one side. He was supposed to. The real punch came a split-second later and caught him hard in the cheek. He tried to laugh through it.

"Very fucking clever."

"That's for shooting at me."

He made a weak effort to look surprised. "Oh yeah? Heard the shots out on the water. That was you? Gotta be more careful out there, pal. That's our own personal island. You must have been trespassing on private property."

Then he pushed himself off his stool and charged at me.

We fell awkwardly onto the floor. As he rolled on top of me I grabbed the remains of his hair and smashed his head into the bottom of the bar. He hit it hard. I did it again. And again. When he had all but passed out I got to my feet. The room was still empty.

I reached behind the bar and found a sharp wooden handled knife still wet from slicing limes for mixed drinks that no one would ever order in this shithole of a place.

It was time to leave.

In the parking lot, I slashed the tires of his Corvette. The sky blue leather seats were pristine, baby-soft leather, and the blade went through them like wet tissue paper. I left the knife embedded in the driver's seat about where his dick would be.

My bid for anonymity was drawing to an end, and my list of enemies was getting a little out of hand.

I drove away from Norm's on a road still slick and wet, the heat forming a thin mist that rose a foot above the surface. I headed back into town in the rented Escort, which cornered like a plate of rice pudding on an ice rink.

The rental office was closed. I parked in back and left the keys in the ignition. The gas tank was half empty. I would be charged for a full tank of gas. It was a truly shabby business practice.

Snug inside the Mercedes, I let out the breath I felt like I had been holding since I was still inside the bar, and I started the engine. The car purred reassuringly. Like an addict I stabbed my finger at the CD changer and Bruce Cockburn began to sing.

I gave in to a mad impulse and picked up the mobile phone. Information got me the number of the bar. It rang three times before someone picked it up.

"Yes."

"Is he coming around yet?"

"Oh, no. It's you, isn't it? You can't actually be calling here. This is just way too wild." Was she laughing a little or just scared silly?

"So?"

"He's in the can."

"Put him on when he gets out."

"Listen to me. He's not a nice man. That tip you gave me is more than I've gotten out of him in five years. You should be real careful."

"I'm afraid it's much too late for that."

"Here he comes now."

There was a rustling sound. Tait didn't say anything. Still, I could sense him there. Holding the phone. Silent. And hating up a storm.

"How's the head?"

Still he was silent.

"You shot at me. I think you hurt a friend of mine. Maybe you even did worse. You think you're a hard man. You're not. You're just an inbred, white-trash fucker used to dealing with people nearly as retarded as you."

Then he hung up on me.

The tarmac on the parking lot and the tennis court was almost dry, and the rain clouds had rolled out across the sky and far away to the west. Paddle Lake lay mirror flat, and everything looked safe and welcoming.

I wasn't fooled for a second.

I risked the radio and found an all-oldies station playing Badfinger's "Baby Blue." I turned up the volume tentatively. Oldies stations were always dangerous. Let down your guard for a second, and old clunkers by bands like Kansas and Styx are suddenly ravaging your ears.

Power-pop guitars jangled and suddenly mid-period David Bowie was hollowly lamenting the endless pitfalls of "Fame."

So far, so good. I had Victoria Williams ready on the CD changer in case things turned ugly.

The inside of the car was warm, and I rolled the window down. I thought about turning the music up louder. Bowie's voice was sliding the word *fame* through several octaves using fancy studio technology.

I chanted quietly along until Bowie got too low for me.

My soon-to-be ex-wife had hinted at the inherent selfishness of my trip up north and she was no doubt accurate.

I had pursued Keith Pringle to, I now felt certain, his last spot on this earth, always knowing that he was dead, even from the outset of my travels.

He had been on the island. The bike borrowed from Bridget Cassidy proved that. He had sat on this beach. My talking to Connie Alexander had authenticated that.

I was certain things had gone badly here for Keith from the reactions of Will Sanders, George Tait and his flighty wife, Sylvie. They had expressed fear and anger and terror, respectively.

It was the terror aspect that was perhaps the most frightening of the three.

Bowie was done and Free was singing "All Right Now." It wasn't much of a favorite of mine, but I hung on, praying that the station would have the long version on the turntable, and that they wouldn't cut short the guitar solo by the late Paul Kossoff in the middle of the song.

My prayers were answered. They had, and they didn't.

Keith stood accused of exposing himself to the Taits' young daughter Tammi. I wasn't especially keen on giving credence to George Tait's accusations. Sylvie Tait wasn't believable, either, and a brief exposure to Oprah and her talky ilk had given me a strong sense that children could be rather easily tutored in deception.

Yet Will Sanders had struck me as an essentially honest man. His side of the story would be worth hearing.

I would never get to hear Keith's own side of the story.

But the trip was for myself as much as it was for Keith. And in that regard it had produced results. How else to explain the discovery of my flair for violence and for tenacity? There was also the fact of my fundamental loneliness, witnessed in the desperate emotional reactions unknowingly elicited by Sandy Weller and Bridget Cassidy. It was clear I was in serious danger of falling in love with every woman I met. At the same time, the one woman already in my life was very close to becoming a total stranger.

Awaiting my longed-for moment of epiphany, I sat and looked out across the water toward the island.

But there was nothing more.

On the radio, my fears soon proved to be founded as Bachman-Turner Overdrive commenced singing. I quickly turned them off and started the engine.

My vigil hadn't produced dramatic results. George Tait hadn't come home. But he would drink off his pain at Norm's and come looking for me sooner or later. He would come with friends, or he would come in secret. Perhaps he would come at night. He would only come in such a way that he would have some sort of sneaky advantage. He wouldn't freely choose to play on a level ground.

There was no sign of life in the Tait household. There was no sign of life in the Sanders homestead. Yet I felt scared eyes behind the blinds, watching me, as I, in turn, watched them.

On the beach, the rain and wind had conspired to manufacture a fake tide line, washing a slick film of green dirt up onto the soft sand.

I was wasting my time.

I pushed the gearshift into drive and pulled away.

⚌

I FOUND A neglected piece of pizza still sulking in the back of Sandy's fridge and resuscitated it in the microwave. It tasted like playdough. Nevertheless, I was very hungry. I sat on the porch and ate it.

When the pizza was all gone, I sat back in the chair, checked my wristwatch (it was close to six-thirty), and shut my eyes for a second. When I opened them again, two-and-a-half hours had passed, and darkness had wrapped itself around the house. All my remaining energy was expended climbing the stairs, brushing my teeth, pulling the white sheets back on the bed and falling face down into the pillow.

A series of explicit and frenzied grunts from the floor below woke me later, where Sandy had apparently succeeded in capturing the young hunk of her dreams, and was putting her aerobic expertise to good use.

It was for me a sad and apt end to a hard day, and I felt the multitude of ironies crashing down on me like ocean waves as I once again closed my eyes.

It was with both the squeals of the pummeled bedsprings below, and the stray and unmistakably country-song corny thought that I was definitely giving my heart away too cheaply, that I fell asleep again.

# SIXTEEN

THE SUN SOAKED THE BILLOWING lace curtains as I got out of bed, bug-eyed, far from rested, with a marked absence of pep and a great deal of apprehension. Perhaps the weather should have appeased me, as outside it was sunny and freshly dry; quite impossible to guess that the day before had been so wet and stormy.

I had half expected George Tait and a posse of sheepish cretins to show during the night with a rope and a reservation at the nearest hanging tree, and while it hadn't actually happened, I wasn't out of the fire just yet.

The house was almost soundless except for the breeze poking through the open windows, gentle against the wind chimes that hung on the back porch, making them tinkle like a bad noir movie scene, softly hissing through the leaves on the tall trees that circled the unkempt backyard.

Sandy and her young man were doubtless resting the sheet-defiled sleep of the young and the fit and the wicked, which I naturally envied them very badly.

But instead of wallowing in self-pity and thwarted lust, I showered quickly, packed my one bag with my customary efficiency, and found myself feeling much better with the careful placement of each folded shirt and compartmentalized personal accessory.

After putting my bag at the bottom of the stairs, I made instant coffee in the microwave and poked around in the kitchen. In a drawer in the kitchen table, I found the machine used for credit card transactions. I ran my card through the machine, signed at the bottom and left most of the boxes blank. I didn't know the exact rate, or the tax in this state offhand. I wrote what I thought was a ludicrously large amount in the box designated for tips and used the leotard girl magnet to attach the invoice prominently to the center of the refrigerator door.

Sandy Weller would only charge me what was fair. I was utterly certain of that. I briefly considered appending the invoice with a short note. Either petty, or else fawning, or more likely a schizophrenically deranged blend of both.

I hastily abandoned that idea.

So there had been a brief and pleasing attraction between us. Anything else, anything beyond that, had existed only inside my head, or inside whatever warped portion of my fevered body was claiming responsibility. She had never hinted at or promised more.

There had been no betrayal, only an absurd amplification, my misguided notion of where our relationship was headed. It hadn't reached anywhere. And it never would. I was quite certain she would tell me all this if I asked her, her face no doubt smiling uncertainly, embarrassed, quizzical at the patent absurdity of my romantic projections.

There wasn't any room for subterfuge in her well-disciplined body and spirited mind.

I pulled the screen door gently shut behind me, breathed in a balmy lungful of the fresh new day's air, and climbed into the car with an unforced jauntiness that made little kind of sense at all.

Driving away, I activated the Victoria Williams CD I had kept in reserve yesterday. She sang to me sweetly. There was no sense risking the likely pitfalls of oldies FM radio on a fine day like this.

I wound down the window and sped down the dirt road.

It was a good day for a kidnapping.

As I drove into Paddle Lake, I dialed the Taits' number on the mobile phone. It rang three times before a woman's voice answered.

"Yes?" It was Sylvie Tait. Hesitant. Suspicious. I imagined it to be a permanent condition—a symptom or manifestation from a life spent shackled to the tempestuous George Tait. I shivered a little inwardly at the thought.

But then we do get to choose our own hell.

"George in?" I affected a gruff, no nonsense bluster.

"No . . . he . . . Greg's playing at a tennis tournament. George and Chip went over to watch."

Even in a state of perpetual nervousness, she would remain at her very core a trusting mother living in a well-to-do small town, in a place removed from tabloid violence, so that nameless voices on the telephone were above suspicion, and instantly made privy to everything.

I wondered how George had explained his bruised face to his family. I wondered if they even thought to ask. Perhaps his was the kind of family where the man of the house wasn't required to explain anything.

"But they should be back real soon," she added lamely. A defensive untruth. She had no doubt suddenly realized she had no idea to whom she was talking.

Then she said, "Who is this?" Which, by rights, ought to have been the very first words out of her mouth.

"It's Bill. At the supermarket. The meat counter. George swung by a little earlier. Must have been before the game. He ordered a rib roast. It's all trimmed and ready. Does he want it delivered or will he pick it up?"

"A rib roast?" She said uncomprehendingly.

"Yup. A real nice one too. We don't have a driver available right now . . . it being the weekend," I trailed off.

"George ordered this?" George clearly wasn't much of an impulse meat shopper.

"Sure did. Picked out the cut himself. Paid for it and everything."

"Did you serve him?"

"No, ma'am. I believe one of the girls did. You know, it might be easier if you picked it up yourself. The meat, that is. Stays nice and fresh that way. Saves me sticking it in the freezer. A real nice cut of meat."

"Was it expensive? I mean . . ."

"It's already paid for, Mrs. Tait. I did mention that, didn't I?"

"I'm sorry. Yes. You did." She was thinking. There was a short silence. Then she spoke again. "I'll be right over. It's really not like him. Are you positive?"

I recited her husband's name, her address, and her phone number.

"No, that's us all right. Well. I'll come over right now. I guess I need a few things. Will you be there?"

"Should be. If I'm not I'll leave it up front for you. Just ask for it. Thank you, Mrs. Tait. I'm sorry to have bothered you. And real sorry if I ruined George's surprise."

I hung up on her quickly, marveling at the impromptu weirdness I had manufactured, how slick a liar I could be, and how willing Sylvie Tait was to believe that her creep of a husband could still do an impulsively nice thing once in a great while.

Love is truly blind. Or at least severely blinkered.

I pulled into the supermarket parking lot and parked behind a white Jeep Cherokee that offered the best available cover. From several angles my own car was close to invisible.

I had spotted the supermarket across the street from the car rental office and I prayed it was the only one in town. I also prayed that the Taits did their shopping there. Both seemed like reasonable possibilities. I did wonder at how much attention Sylvie Tait had paid to my car as her son was drooling over it. She had seemed more concerned with corralling her unruly brood.

But it seemed like a prissy, halfhearted kind of maneuver. I'd now been shot at, I'd given George Tait a bruised face, and I'd delivered one solid whack to the already paper-thin membrane of his psyche.

The cute time was over.

Now I was going to abduct his wife, a flighty housewife, in broad daylight and drive off in a conspicuously expensive car with no clear destination in mind. Perhaps a better plan would present itself. In the meantime I slunk my head down below the dash in the textbook furtive manner, and peered out across the parking lot for the arrival of my prey.

Sylvie Tait arrived ten minutes later.

She pulled into a parking place close to the store and ran inside. Less than five minutes later she was back at the front door, accompanied by a young man sporting a severe haircut and a blindingly white short-sleeved shirt whom I took to be at least the store's assistant manager. They both gazed out across the lot as they spoke. I hunkered further down, rendering myself, I hoped, all but invisible.

When I looked again the young man was shaking his head and smiling in a comforting manner. Sylvie clearly wasn't convinced. She spoke to him once more. He continued to shake his head as the smile gradually evaporated.

She didn't have any shopping bags. The other items she had intended to buy were no doubt forgotten in the unfolding mystery of the missing meat.

Please don't walk her to her car, I whispered to myself. And he didn't. But perhaps he offered, because she shook her head a last time and took off across the hot summer concrete. He turned away from her, heading back to his pressing duties inside the store.

I put the key in the ignition and hesitated, as the cruelty of what I was about to do suddenly manifested itself. The woman would be scared half to death. But I didn't have a better plan, and in the back of my mind was the resounding suspicion that Sylvie Tait was clearly guilty of something.

The engine started.

I drove slowly toward her car. She was ten feet from her car door. She didn't reach for her keys. The door still had to be unlocked. She turned toward the soft noise of my engine, but the sun shone bright and low and dazzling in the morning sky and the windshield glass was tinted secretively dark and she didn't register either me or the machine. There were cars parked nearby but thankfully no one was getting in or out. I pulled in beside her as she opened her car door. I climbed out with the engine still running, called her name, reached for her arm, then I pulled her roughly toward me.

She turned. She was a little puzzled at first. Then slowly she grew fearful. Then a series of other emotions that were fleeting, nebulous. Stoic? Accepting? Acquiescent? Even perhaps mildly relieved?

Incredibly, the beauty of her dark hair struck me then, for an idiotic, inopportune split-second.

She was wasted on the strutting moron Tait, I thought to my asinine self.

Maybe I would fall in love with her too.

After all, why should she be any different from any of the other women I had met in the past few days? The emotional link between kidnapper and kidnapped was well documented.

Then I remembered what I was about to do.

My voice was harsh. "Get inside the car now, Mrs. Tait."

I must have sounded convincing to her. My words were ragged and pitched low. Threatening. As if I meant business. Even if, at that very same moment, I felt wretched and indescribably worthless.

Yet she climbed unaided into the car. I had anticipated some sort of struggle. But she was almost demure, like a young girl on a prom date with a boy she liked. If she'd been wearing a skirt she'd have perhaps primly adjusted the hemline as she gingerly sat down.

She wore cut-off faded jeans, white generic sneakers, and a pale blue T-shirt that mirrored the color of her eyes and advertised a public radio station. She looked around the inside of the car, her eyes never looking directly at me.

"As if my George would buy a rib roast," she said simply, a bemused whisper, shaking her head a little as she spoke.

Then she fastened her seat belt, settled into the seat, and we drove out of the parking lot in an enveloping silence that grew to be almost comfortable. As I drove she began to sneak looks at me. But she said nothing for a while.

She broke the silence finally.

"You're the one who hit my husband, aren't you?" Her voice was soft, without accusation. "The one playing tennis with Greg the other morning? The one who's been nosing around?"

I nodded.

"Why have you come for me like this? Why have you come after my family? We can't help you. What is it that you want from us? I just don't understand what this is about."

"I'm looking for my friend."

"Your friend?"

"Yes. His name is Keith Pringle. He was living on the island. He was on the beach. He was at the Handle. Now he's missing."

She changed the subject. "Why did you hit George?"

"He asked for it. Did he tell you I hit him?"

She shook her head. "He's come home with his face messed up before. People like to hit him. I also know you gave Will a hard time. I thought maybe you did the same with George."

"I also spoke with Beth Sanders. She says Keith exposed himself to your daughter. Is that what really happened?"

"This isn't any of your damn business," she snapped quickly, then relented. "But that's exactly what did happen. Tammi and Beth both told us the same story, about what he went and did to Tammi. George and Will got real angry when they heard. And they sent your friend packing after that. That's all I know about it. Now you can go away too."

"Do you know where he went?"

"No. No I don't." She sounded adamant. "He went away. Someplace. He just went away. Please let me go now."

"I really don't think Keith did anything to your daughter, Mrs. Tait," I said then.

But she said nothing more and stared pointedly out the window.

When we were ten miles further out of town, and had the road to ourselves, I turned down an unmarked dirt track for a mile or two, and then turned again, onto what was clearly a bike and hiking trail in the summer, and a ski trail in the winter months.

The path was heavily shaded, still wet and puddled from yesterday's rain.

I hoped we would have the place to ourselves for a while.

I turned off the engine. And we sat. She tried to smile.

"I'm not scared of you," she said.

I turned to her. "I could be a vicious killer for all you know. I did abduct you. When I met you outside your house you were quite clearly scared of me. I was curious about that. I still am."

She looked appraisingly at me. "Yeah. So you abducted me. In this fancy car. And I was scared of you. And you could be evil and mean and be planning to do me all kinds of harm. But I've been watching you driving, and thinking about all this, and about what it is that you want from me, and I'll just bet you're not any kind of a killer. You're much too refined for that. Your accent is real pretty. Like I say, I've been watching you."

"I hurt George," I said.

She snorted at that. "George likes to play tough with people, and it blows up in his face sometimes. It's happened to him before. I don't doubt he deserved what you did to him. You might even have been merciful."

She spoke softly then. "And if nothing else he deserves it for how it's been for me and the children all these years."

"Does he abuse you?"

She smiled slowly. "That would be real simple, wouldn't it? So now you could get my whole sob story of a life. But it would be a lie because he doesn't abuse me. Not in the sense that you mean. Oh, he's bad enough in his own way. But we're not all bruised and beat up like on a TV movie. Not bruised on the outside anyway where it shows, and well-meaning folks can feel all sorry for you. He's what you'd call a mean man is George Tait. Always has been a mean man. Pissed off royally most of the time at everyone. Especially folks with more fancy stuff than he has. Folks he thinks got their stuff the easy way. Not hard workers like he is, which is a crock, but he still manages to believe it himself, which is truly sad, if you ask me.

With men he'll lash out likely as not. Me and the kids he just bitches and moans at most times. He tries to make us feel small, and the hard thing, especially for the kids, is that he never lets up, like he feels small himself, and figures he has to make us feel the same way. Leveling the playing field. He can't help himself, I guess. Low self-worth, the shrinks would say. Low self-esteem. Plenty of that old self-loathing in the mental mix too, I'd guess. He's very tough on the boys. Chip's never going to amount to much, because his self-esteem is all up and gone, and he's destined to screw up all the time, and he needn't have turned out that way. Greg's real good at tennis. So he has a slim chance. But he's clearly no prodigy. There's no fancy scholarship or Nike guy out there with the big bucks, so if that slim chance doesn't pan out for him, then he's back to where Chip is already headed. Which is where his dad's already at. Which is a sad mess heading into a real bad mistake that's pretty much just waiting to happen. Tammi might just make it because she's tougher than the rest of us, but she'll likely screw up too in her own way, because she's never going to do anything the right way, she's always taking the short cut. Like I say she might make it, but she might just fall even further by being a cheat. You can easily love my boys soft as they are, but Tammi's a good ways harder to like."

As she spoke I wondered why she'd married. Why she still was married. Perhaps in my face she could read the silent questions.

"You're getting my life story in all its white-trash glory."

I smiled at her. "That's okay. You're going to talk about what I need to know later."

"I really don't know what happened to your friend after Will and George saw him."

"But you do know what he really did that day on the beach."

And on her face then was an admission. That what I'd just said was the truth. She did know something I needed to know. But I would have to hear her story first. That was understood. That would be the nature of the compromise.

"Do you know Detroit?" she asked me.

I shook my head.

"We lived there after we got married. My folks both worked for Ford in the Dearborn plant. George's father was Liam Tait, and he owned a tavern in the neighborhood where I grew up, a place full of Polish immigrants, even though the Taits were a solid Irish family. So Liam owned a bar with nothing but dumb Pollacks for customers and no one seemed to care one way or another. "Red Liam," everyone called him. On the surface, he was a lovely man. The whole neighborhood adored him. But he was a bad bartender and a bad businessman. For all I know, a bad father too. George has never said much, but sometimes I get a hint or two. People did love Liam's place though. Cabbage and corned beef and wild beer nights and the singing of Irish and Polish songs. His wife, Mary, George's mother, did most of the cooking and she was a fine woman. George's dad was also a falling-down drunk, a boozing legend for the greater part of his adult life. Not a mean drunk, or one of these sad drunks, but a truly joyful drunk, one that always drew others to him, made you forget the shambles that his place was, made you even forget that he was an Irishman surrounded by all us stupid Pollacks doing the grunt work for the high-and-mighty Ford family and seeing the best parts of our town vanish before our eyes. Because Detroit was on the way to turning black then. Now it's a pure black city. The first one in the country. Maybe it's a bold new experiment. Maybe it's just a hell of a mess and well on the way to becoming one gigantic ghetto. Maybe the blacks, they deserve a city of their own. I kind of feel that they do, to tell you the truth. But the old neighborhood folks took it real badly. Guys were laid off in the city as businesses, the white businesses that is, went under or moved out to the suburbs. The car plants always needed bodies and, to be fair, didn't much care what color they were buying cheap. But the tax base in the city went down the toilet as the wealthy folks fled in droves. Our neighborhood struggled on for a while. But poor Liam wasn't doing the business he was used to, and he took to drinking harder and being less of a joy. Then he up and died. And Mary amazed everyone by telling us she was sick and tired of life in America. So she moved back to Ireland and lived out her last few years there. George and me had gotten married by then and I was pregnant. George had got his big stupid hands on the bar by now and figured to make a go of it on his own. To his credit he did try awfully hard. But his dad was a well-liked kind of a drunk and George was a loud, bullying one, and neither one of them had any idea how to run a business. One day George got an offer from a smart black businessman looking to open a fancy department store in the neighborhood for the black folks that would surely be taking over the place any day now. He was right of course. George was close to going broke, but that didn't stop us Poles from telling George not to take the offer, which was a very good one. Maybe if they'd voted with their thirst instead of their voices he might have listened, because God knows George sure did like owning that bar, pissing off his customers royally, and drinking his way steadily through his stock."

"You sold up."

"Yup. Took the money and ran up north. Came up here and bought the house we're in now with the money, which turned out to be the best thing we ever did, because we never had any real money to our name again."

"How do you manage to live?"

"Oh, we live cheaply, by necessity, and George is a master at laying his hands on stuff. People always need work done. George is good at landscaping. He does dry-walling. He likes not to take money in payment but saves up favors and carts off stuff he can use. He likes cars and is actually real good at fixing them up. He takes beaters and works on them. And people always seem to owe George something. He collects favors and cashes them in when he needs something. It's about the only gift he possesses. I sometimes wonder if he is actually owed anything, or if he just threatens people into giving. I've never asked him about it."

"Were you the first of the Handle settlers?"

"The first of the new folks. The old timers lived in their summer cottages around the lake but we were the first folks in the Handle, which always feels like a suburb type of place to me. We were the first of the year-rounders. We couldn't have afforded to move here now, or even a few years after we did. The place really took off. The house values began to climb and the old timers began to vanish. When we came here it seemed like the best kind of luck at the time."

"Not now?"

"No," she said. "Definitely not now."

"You listen real well," she said.

"Thank you."

"No. I mean it. You do."

"Well. Thank you again."

She asked suddenly, "Are you married?"

She caught me by surprise. "Yes I am. At the moment."

"Things going badly for you there?"

"I'm inching ever closer to a divorce."

"A man who listens real well should be more appreciated."

"I'll certainly pass on your opinions."

"I don't believe I'll ever divorce George," she said.

"Perhaps you should consider it."

She smiled. "Oh there's no question that I'd be happier."

"But you're scared?"

"I'd have nothing then. Pathetic, isn't it? The kids and me. All alone. We'd be homeless. I've never worked outside the house. None of what they call the marketable skills. Never even used a computer. It scares me to think about it sometimes. I'm just a total housewife. A nearly worthless thing in the modern world."

"You could learn," I said weakly.

She shook her head. "It's too late for that. George has won, you see? Beaten us all down. We're left with nothing. I'm more scared of living without him, than I am of living with him. And that's sad."

"What do you do with your time?" I asked her.

She tried to smile. "I try to make it pass a little faster. I like to drink, and I find that that makes the hours fade to nothing. George is even nastier after he drinks. I've no idea what I'm like, but I know it makes the time go fast and I'm real grateful for that." She paused then spoke coyly. "I also like some company when I can get it."

She caught me by surprise. "Company?" I asked stupidly.

She smiled. "I'm still pretty. Don't you think?"

Once again she caught me unawares. "Yes," I said. "I think you are."

"Other men think so too. I try not to talk them out of that impression."

"Did Keith think so?"

Her smile turned nasty then.

"You've been patient. So maybe you deserve to hear what happened. You ask if your friend liked me? Well I was certainly working hard at it. You see. I had his dick in my mouth when Tammi and Beth came wandering out of the bushes and caught us that damned night."

I must have looked strange.

"That shook you up," she said.

"George was out someplace and the boys were, too, and Tammi was God knows where, and the air conditioner just wasn't cutting it so I had a couple of gin and tonics and then I walked across the beach in my bare feet and let the water cool me down at the end of the day. But it wasn't doing it."

She stared straight ahead as she spoke, her eyes locked on the events of that day, which were tied fast in her memory. I held my breath. She spoke again. "Your friend came out of the water as I stood there. Like I had wished him. So slow. The water was still and the sun was setting fast right behind him. His skin was wet and real pale. Some kind of male mermaid. I saw he was very tired because he almost tripped and fell down. He had swum all the way from the island to the beach so he should have been tired. I can swim pretty well and that would be beyond me. He wore just an old pair of raggedy swim shorts that looked like they might almost fall down. He must have weighed less than me. Thin as a stick. All skin and bones. Like a teenage boy. He must have been pretty once. Was he very pretty?" She asked.

I nodded.

"He could never have been a powerful man. Now he was just ragged. And ghostly white, whiter than anyone should be in the heat of the summer we get here. I watched him walk out of the water and stand dripping on the sand. I told him I could get him a towel if he wanted, but he smiled and shook his head. His breathing was hard and forced. I don't think he could even manage to speak yet. His eyes were red and watery and his thin shoulders shook a little. I asked him why he didn't just row the old boat in from the island. I knew he was living there. Everyone did. He shrugged for an answer and then just smiled that boy's smile again. His hair was a mess and it fell into his eyes. I just wanted to push it away for him and before I could think about it I had. He didn't even look real surprised. Then I just kissed him as hard as I could. He kissed me back at first, not as hard as me, then he started to draw away from me. He said he was tired, that this wasn't a good idea, that this was wrong, that he was very sorry, that I was pretty, that I might have been a little bit drunk." She smiled then. "He thought I was pretty. At least he said he did."

"You are pretty," I told her again in reply.

"He said I didn't know what I was doing. But I sure did. I was right in the middle of a fantasy that was a hell of a lot of fun. It did cross my mind that we might be seen, but I didn't care by then. I put my hand inside his shorts. He tried to pull it away gently. He was a little hard down there by then. I did notice that. So I got down on my knees, pulled his shorts down and started to suck him off right there on the beach."

And then Sylvie Tait laughed loud and laughed dangerously.

"His face was all lit up by the last of the sun as he stood there. I liked looking up at his face. And then there was something, a movement in the bushes. He really pulled away from me then, and his pretty face got even whiter and the two kids were suddenly right there beside us. Jesus Christ, I got a hell of a fright. Of course my little darling Tammi was smirking like the know-it-all she is, and poor Beth was looking at both of us with the strangest look on her face, like she didn't have a clue what it was she was seeing, which was probably about right, because her parents protect her to death, and sex is something that she's likely never even heard about, which is pretty weird because her father and I have certainly had our moments. But my Tammi is a gutter-mouthed little punk from way back, with two degenerate older brothers, who will probably get her first sexual experience long before I did. And I wasn't exactly a wilting flower when I was a teenage kid."

"What did Keith do then?" I asked.

She smiled. "He ran like all hell back into the water. Then he swam back to the island and all that tiredness had magically gone by then because he was going faster than Mark Spitz."

"And you?"

"Got myself sober in a real hurry. And now I was kind off scared, wondering what George would say if the kids told him what they'd just seem. So I told Tammi to lie. That wasn't a hard thing for her. An extra big allowance for a week or so would do it. Then we worked on Beth who was still standing there with her eyes bugging out of her little head. That was easy too. We could have told her the Loch Ness monster was kissing me on the ass and she'd have believed us. Naturally Tammi couldn't wait to tell her dad about the bad man who had done a very bad thing to her. She's watched a bunch of talk shows where kids wreck grownups' lives by telling all kind of lies about sexual stuff. She thought it was a lot of fun and she's a real clever little liar. That's my little girl."

"Beth must have told her father what really happened."

"She swore blind that she wouldn't. Tammi told her father. George went to Will and together they went out to the island and chased your friend away."

"You got Keith into a lot of trouble."

"Don't be stupid. His dick got him into trouble."

"You started it."

"So what? He could have stopped it. He was having his fun. Just like I was."

"Your husband beat him up. Maybe he did much worse."

"He's a big boy. Anyway, you took George easy enough. He's not that tough."

I stared hard at her.

"What?" She nearly screamed at me.

I stared some more.

"You want me to be sorry! Is that it? I'm very sorry then. I did get him into trouble. Then I got my daughter to lie to save myself. But . . ."

"But what?"

"George would have killed me."

"What? He thinks you're so pure?"

She laughed. "Hardly. No. He sure doesn't. But he knows and then he doesn't know. He doesn't ever want to know for sure. But, you see, this happened here. On his beloved beach. In front of his daughter. In plain view of the other folks, the ones he sucks up to, the same ones who think he's the lowest kind of white trash, behind his back. That would have been too much for George to deal with. He would have killed me for sure. I had to do something. So I did that."

I couldn't think of anything else to say.

"You must hate me," she said.

"No."

"You must think I'm a coward?"

"You are a coward."

"I just wanted to stay alive. Even if my life is pretty much shit by any standards, I still want to have it."

"I could tell George now."

"You could. I doubt he'd believe you. And I doubt if you really would tell him. You're an honorable man."

But I wondered if I was.

"Why do you think that?" I asked.

"Look what you're doing for your friend," she replied.

There was no answer to that.

Keith had let Sylvie Tait seduce him to his death in this alien place that night. She had been understandably scared, after being discovered by her daughter, and she had lied her way to safety. Lots of people would have done the same. Perhaps not with the same lie. But with some other lie. I would have done the same. I wasn't even close to being honorable.

I asked her. "Where's George now?"

"The tournament's probably over. For Greg anyway. Could be in a bar. Still pissed off about you I'd guess."

"Do you know which one?"

"It's probably only one out of a possible three. He isn't real adventurous by nature."

I handed her the phone.

"You want me to call him now?" She asked in alarm.

"Later," I said. "I want you to call Will Sanders first. Have him meet me at the beach now. Tell him it's very important. Tell him he helped kill a man for the wrong reason."

Without a word she took the phone in her shaking hand and began to dial a number as I started the car.

# SEVENTEEN

IT WAS EARLY IN THE AFTERNOON, and we were back on the beach.

Overhead, two lost seagulls dipped and shrieked, their sound catapulting me back to my childhood vacations, usually spent all alone, running barefoot and fearless across seaweed-slick rocks to the deep saltwater pools left by the retreating tide, small frantic crabs exposed between home shells, jelly-like anemones waving their blazing colors, and always the tide waiting to turn, a menacing presence behind the last still-wet rocks.

Sylvie Tait dragged a stick listlessly across the wet sand in a curving pattern that resembled the movements of sine waves. I stood apart from her, watching her for a while, then turning away, choosing instead to throw a succession of small flat stones across the surface of the water. Counting the bounces. A solitary child once again.

Our backs were to each other. She faced the houses that stretched in a line along the beach road, while I looked out across the lake, toward the island. As I had requested, she had issued the urgent summons, and now we waited for Will Sanders to show up.

When he walked across the sand, his face was drawn taut and the skin-shrouded bone that remained was working at a study in determined expressionlessness. It was a would-be poker face, or else a good lawyer's demeanor, prior to the onset of earnest bargaining.

But up close he looked instead to be simply fearful. When he forgot to grip his jawbone tight shut, his chin broke loose and shook uncontrollably.

He said nothing at first. He looked at Sylvie, then pointed a finger at me. When he spoke he sounded flustered.

"God. I can't believe I'm here. I just can't believe all this." His head shook from side to side. "This is about him? Isn't it? The homeless guy who was here? Jesus. This is all getting so tiresome."

Sylvie didn't speak. I didn't either.

"It is about him. That guy." He looked at me and sneered. "Your deadbeat sleaze of a buddy. The one who's taking a fucking powder and no one gives much of a fuck about and shouldn't anyway."

"You don't usually swear like that, Will," Sylvie said.

"Have you quite finished?" I asked him coldly.

He looked at me defiantly. "I'm just getting started. You were lucky before. This time you won't get to sneak up on me."

"I don't want to fight you." I said.

Then Sylvie spoke.

"He knows, Will."

He looked bewildered. "Huh? About us? About you and me? What does that have to do with anything?"

Did she smile then for a second? "Nothing, Will. It meant nothing. It means nothing, except maybe to your trusting better half. And even then . . ." her voice trailed off.

She spoke to me. "Will and I had ourselves a fling once."

I spoke to Will. "I want to know about you and George and Keith Pringle. After your children lied about what Keith did."

"My daughter doesn't tell lies, Mister."

"She does if enough people tell her to," I said.

Will Sanders' petulant notion of bravado was wilting fast in the afternoon heat. He turned again to Sylvie. "Why did you ask me to come here? What's so important? I really don't want to talk to him."

"He knows all about us," she tried again. "And he knows about me and his friend. About me and Keith. Not the story George told you."

"His buddy exposed himself to Tammi and Beth, didn't he? He needed to be taught a lesson for that."

"By you and George?" I asked.

He hesitated. "That's damn right. By me and George. Because of what he did to the girls."

Could this really be an expert legal mind in full flight? It seemed unlikely. Will Sanders sounded more like a blustering fool hell-bent on holding fast to the flimsiest of self delusions.

"He knows, Will," Sylvie said.

"About what? For God's sake."

She sighed. "About me," she whispered in a tired voice. "Because . . . me and Keith. When the two girls saw us. That night . . ."

He looked bewildered. "What! What are you saying to me?"

And then Sylvie was almost shouting at him. "I was with him. His friend, Keith. That day. That night. On the beach that night. It wasn't the girls seeing him there. It wasn't Tammi. It was just me and him. We were caught in the act. The girls came along. And they saw some things that they shouldn't have. And, oh God, don't you just see? I had to lie then. I had to."

"My Beth doesn't lie." He was almost speaking a mantra to himself.

"No," Sylvie said, her voice soft again, almost kindly. "She doesn't. But she did then. Because she didn't really know what was happening. And we told her what to say. And she said it."

"This can't be true," Will said quietly.

"It is," Sylvie said in a whisper.

He looked at me. I nodded. There was a silence then.

Her words had punched a series of little holes in Will Sanders, bleeding him of everything, and leaving him empty. His eyes were cast down toward the sand, staring deep inside a sad void.

Then the screaming began. A wordless cacophony of sound. He ran at me in a senseless assault, waving his fists, and striking wildly at my face.

His first blow, guided by sheer luck, landed lightly on my forehead. I grabbed him by the forearms then, while he howled and tried to pull his arms away. But I held on tight. His face was dirt-streaked by his tears, his wet eyes soaking up pain like a dry sponge. The fight left him as quickly as it began, and as I let him go he sank to his knees in the sand, throwing his face to the ground, rocking and keening, the silent sobbing shaking his body, as I looked on, in a mixture of pity and embarrassment.

Minutes passed and then he began to talk. I sat down beside him. I was very tired. The sun was hot. The sand was every bit as soft and inviting as Tom Younger, the blustering real estate salesman, had told me it was, in a conversation that seemed to have taken place about a million years in the past.

The story was drawing to a close now. My search. My noble quest. My idiotic folly. All I would find out from here on in would be sad and ugly, but I was determined to miss none of it, to back off from nothing.

Will talked softly at first, his face downturned, his eyes focused but unseeing.

"George battered on my door that night very late, howling about the son of a bitch, the fucking psycho, was how he put it, and what he would do to him for showing his fucking cock to our kids. We should take care of this ourselves. This was our goddamn place wasn't it? This was our turf. He kept on talking that way."

"You knew what he was talking about by then?"

"Not really. Beth had been quiet and upset at bedtime as I read to her but I didn't know why."

"Did George tell you about it?"

"He ranted on about something, about the guy, and his cock, and the girls. He kept shouting as he dragged me out across the road to the dock and onto his boat. He kept talking about the sheer nerve of the fucker and his being right there on our island."

"What do you think of George Tait?"

He shook his head slowly. "The same as most everyone, I guess. He's loud and he's essentially stupid. You could argue that he means well. He certainly loves this place more than most of us do. But I've never much liked him, although I've always tried not to let him know that because he's a bully and he's a little intimidating. He's always scared me some. He certainly scared me to death that night."

"You took the boat across the lake to the island?"

He nodded. "Yeah. We cut the engine a ways from the island and drifted up onto the sandbar where everyone ties up. The old rowboat from the beach was there. It was carefully tied to a tree branch. Both oars were inside it. It had recently been missing from the beach a lot. The kids always used it to play in. Pringle was using it sometimes to get to and from the island. Other times I guess he swam instead.

"Was Keith there?"

"I didn't see him then. George jumped off the boat and into the water as I was still tying up. He grabbed an oar out of the rowboat. Then he stopped."

I waited for Sanders to continue.

"Did I want to take the other one? He wanted to know that. I didn't really understand. Was I going to help him? He was going to take care of the fucker here and now, he said. And was I going to help him? He wanted to know."

"Did you help him?"

He shook his head. "No. I was too scared to move. So I just sat on the boat and tied knots in the line. They were knots I thought I didn't know how to tie. I'm not really much of a sailor. That kind of thing comes easy to a lot of people 'round here but I have to work hard at it."

"What did George do?"

"Called me a fucking coward and left me sitting there on the boat. He walked across the beach with the oar in his hands. He called me a fucking sissy too, as I recall."

"What happened then?"

"Like I said. I just sat there. For a long while. I can't say how long. I don't think I was wearing my watch, but I'm honestly not sure. I didn't hear anything. But much later George returned." Will Sanders paused. "And he was dragging a man's body behind him."

"It was Keith, wasn't it?"

He nodded once. "There wasn't much of him left. George had beaten his head into almost nothing. The oar was shattered in pieces and all bloody and other stuff hung from it. All pink and soft. Pieces of bone and brain tissue. George threw him into the old rowboat. He pulled the anchor out of the sand and wrapped it tightly around the body. The body wasn't moving. I thought he had to be dead. I remember hoping he was. Then George pushed the boat out into the water. He pushed us out, then fired up the engine on his boat and got behind the rowboat. He nudged it out into the middle of the lake like we were pushing a stalled car down a road. When he'd found a place he thought was right he picked up the oar and smashed it into the rowboat. The wood was all rotten and waterlogged and it was like poking holes in a wet bag. The old boat filled with water quickly and the body went under with it. There was blood on the surface of the lake for a moment. The boat sank quickly."

"How deep is the lake?"

"At that point? I don't really know for sure. Perhaps forty feet. The wood was badly rotted and would break up very fast."

"And the body?"

"If it stays down the fish will get to it, until the winter, when the lake usually freezes solid and by the next spring there won't be much left."

"They could still identify the body."

"Who are *they*? And anyway the flesh will be all gone and George had destroyed the teeth inside the man's mouth. George is a real stupid man but he managed to blunder into committing a pretty effective murder."

"And what about you?"

"I'm just like George said I was. The fucking sissy he said I was. I sat on the boat and said nothing and let George beat a man to death for a stupid lie I only partly believed in the first place. I'm not even sure George was convinced either. And since then I've lied to myself about it."

"How?"

"I wanted to believe it. The lie. To think that your friend was some kind of pervert, but truthfully the story never did make much sense. You have to consider the sources. Tammi is a wild kid who likes to make things up and get people into trouble. George is a brutal man who would kill you for a wrong word if he got the drop on you. I didn't know the truth and I didn't try real hard to find out. I never asked Beth about it because I knew she'd crumble in a second and tell me everything. She's not soft, she's just an extremely truthful person."

A big fresh tear attached itself to the sand on Will Sanders' blood-drained face and carried some of it downstream.

"I'm sorry about your friend," he said. "I just sat and let him die there."

"There was no trace of Keith on the island when I got there," I said. "Except for his bicycle."

He looked up. "Did I leave that behind? That was a stupid thing to do. I went back to the island a couple of days later, afterwards, to tidy up. I got a fire going and found his clothes and stuff. There wasn't very much. His life had to have been pretty empty."

"Only if you judge a life on the accumulation of possessions," I said, instantly realizing my own dubious position with regard to that pompous statement.

"He had a few photographs. One was of a young child. Was it his?" He asked me suddenly.

I supposed it was. I had forgotten about the child until now.

"On colder nights, he must have sneaked into the cabin on the island. He'd never taken anything. He'd left the place as tidy as he'd found it."

He began to cry again. "We killed a good person, didn't we?"

"He wasn't a perfect man by any means."

"But he wasn't an evil man either?"

And as I thought back through the years that I had known Keith Pringle, nothing inherently vicious did spring to mind.

"No," I said. "He wasn't evil."

"What happened afterward?" I asked.

"What do you mean afterward?"

"When I went out to the island that afternoon. When you shot at me."

"No. That wasn't me." He looked genuinely surprised.

"There were two men on a boat."

"Are you sure about that?"

"Yes . . ." But suddenly I wasn't.

"It could have been George," he said. "It could easily have been George. But it could just as easily have been half a dozen other God-fearing folk who live nearby and who take a dim view of trespassers."

"That sign isn't close to legal. The island isn't your private property."

He paused to consider. "No. It probably isn't. But the law tends to get more flexible in rural parts. Much more open to interpretation. You see, everyone here knows everybody else. We owe each other all kinds of favors."

I remembered that George Tait had said something very similar.

I couldn't think of anything else to say then. Most of my questions now had answers. Few of them were good ones. Few were especially likable. But they all made a sad kind of sense.

Will had stopped crying. I looked around and realized that Sylvie Tait was nowhere to be seen. Somewhere in the conversation she had left the beach. Had the truth about George been too much to bear? It didn't seem very likely. He was a known tyrant. But now he was a known killing tyrant. Had she balked at the newly exposed far limits of his brutality? Maybe she had.

I glanced back at her house and noticed that the garage door was closed. Had it been closed before? I didn't remember.

"Would it surprise you to learn that I was a very good lawyer?" he suddenly asked.

"No," I said. "It wouldn't."

"What if I told you that I loved my daughter very much, that I always have loved my daughter very much. Would that surprise you?" His voice was odd, coming from a great emotional distance.

I realized that these were questions that didn't require answers.

At least, not from me.

"I had an impressive list of clients who relied on me to look after their best interests. I got some bad press for the high-profile cases that I won. Certain liberal journalists thought I never took the side of the little guy, that I always represented the gray-suited demons of corporate America. You know a little about my work?"

I told him that I did.

"I simply did my job. I did the best I could for my clients. It was as simple as that. I gave them my best work. That was what I did. That defined my work. The company man. My own politics are as liberal as the newspapers who went after me. That's the ironic part. Let me tell you about one case. Actually it was after the case was settled. This is what happened. The father of a boy who died in a car crash sent me a box in the mail. The burnt remains of a cat were inside that box. His boy had died when his car caught fire. His family had sued the car manufacturer and they had lost. I had won the case for the company. The tires on the kid's car were found to be nearly bald. He skidded on a wet road with a couple of beers inside him, in the middle of the night, in god-awful visibility, and slammed into a truck full of inflammable material parked on the side of a road while the driver took a crap in a gas-station toilet. The kid was enrolled in a community college. He didn't have the money for a set of new tires. His family didn't have the money either, I guess. A sad story. There was no bad guy, just all kinds of bad luck. But I got the fried cat in the box and the old man's blame because their son died. I got to be the villain."

"Transference."

"Correct. But it doesn't make it any easier."

"I slept with Sylvie," he said suddenly.

"I know that."

"That was my one unfaithful act."

One apiece. We were even in that regard.

He asked, "Are you a married man?"

I told him that I was.

"A model of ceaseless fidelity no doubt."

"No. Not really. We're close to separated."

"As I say. I slipped just the once. With Sylvie. In my defense I would mention that she possesses a certain earthy charm."

"You're making fun of her."

"No. I'm spinelessly attempting to alleviate some of my guilt. She made it all very easy. She demanded virtually nothing from me. I'm inclined to believe I wasn't her only conquest."

I suspected that he was correct.

"But once again, I'm trying to wriggle loose from under my own conscience. A gutless reaction. I should know better. I told my wife about it. That was stupid. The noble and selfless act. She elected to show great understanding and compassion and took me back into the bosom of the family. A pitiable mistake there. Viewed with the luxury of retrospect. We never were the same. That was when we decided to put our house on the market. A fresh start someplace else seemed like the best thing for us."

It occurred to me then that while four houses were currently for sale in the Handle, none of the sales actually had anything to do with Keith.

"I'm like the repentant drunk on the wagon," he said. "I'm eternally watched by eyes that continually expect to be disappointed at any moment, that expect to be failed. I'm pitied more than a little. You see, I'm of the opinion that in order to be fully loved you also have to be admired at the same time. I think that ideally the two should go hand in hand. I'm still loved, I think I am. I'm just not admired any more. And it isn't quite enough. And when you factor in the absence of trust, the equation gets very much worse. A terrible mistake to wander. Trust me on this. And an even worse mistake to admit to the wandering. I need to know what kind of man we murdered that night."

"It's not important."

"Oh. But it is to me. I want to know. Is the world a sadder place for losing him? Do you think?"

"I couldn't say. I knew him a long time ago."

"As young boys?"

"Yes. We came from the same town. We lost touch over the years."

"I assume you're a wealthy man now."

"I'm doing fine."

"You're being a trifle modest."

"I have more money than I know what to do with," I said truthfully.

"That must be a pleasant way to live."

"It's essentially meaningless."

"Only to you. To a poor man it would mean everything."

"He'd very soon realize it didn't."

"Your friend was a poor man?"

I nodded.

"But perhaps a richer man than you in essence? In your estimation?"

"You're becoming something of a sage."

He smiled a beatific smile at me then.

"Oh yes. You see, as my life is about to end, I can afford to be of a philosophical bent."

"You expect George Tait to come after you?"

He smiled again. "I hadn't thought about that. It's certainly likely. It would certainly be his style. Oh gosh yes, that would be George all right. But no. I'm going to beat him to the punch. I let him take charge before. And a stupid death occurred. This time I'm going to be master of my own destiny." His laugh was hollow. "For what it's worth."

I didn't understand what he meant. His voice had retreated far into himself. He was smiling a kind of dazzled grin, shell-shocked, blissed out. I worried about him then. Tait's revenge might be the least of his worries.

"Can I ask you to do something for me?" he asked.

"What?"

"Nothing."

"I don't understand."

"I'm asking you to do nothing," he said.

"I still don't understand."

A child's toy surfboard was pulled up from the edge of the water. Made out of white polystyrene, it had been dragged clear, then left sprawled on the beach. A tiny frog poked his head out from under the board, then it shot across the hot sand and into the darkness of the evergreen trees that surrounded the fine powdered ashes that had once and would once again be the scene of merry campfires. A charred log stood sentinel. It had rolled too close to the fire once and was doubtless sorry for itself now. On a wooden swing, a toy car lay abandoned, pale blue paint fading in the sunlight. A model of a Ford Mustang convertible, dating from the middle of the dragster sixties.

The wind shifted and caught the branches of the trees close to the water. Out across the lake a speedboat full of brightly undressed adolescents brutalized the soft silence, their iced beer and their hormones flowing in tandem.

Will Sanders pulled off his shirt and walked barefoot toward the edge of the water. The sound of the kids on the boat faded. Idiotically I could think only of the scene in the first version of *A Star is Born*, where the doomed movie star, played by Fredric March, his fame eclipsed by the fast arc of his young wife's career, walked into the ocean water to end his torment and the rivalry that had suffocated their once-pure love.

It was a memorable scene.

Will reached the water's edge. Did his pace then falter for a split second? Did he question his actions for a moment? He walked forward again, with unmistakable purpose. The water seemed to rise up and meet him, like a welcoming friend. He walked out. When he was submerged to chest height, he began to swim, a measured breaststroke, his arms barely stirring the water. His technique was awkward, his head ridiculously high out of the water, his swan neck stiff, aloof, rigid.

I watched him, detached and horrified at the same time.

His strokes slowed after a short while. He was still relatively close to the shore but I sensed that the water was already deeper than head height, and that he had reached what he felt to be an appropriate distance from the shore, and from safety. He stroked one last time but there was next to no momentum.

The top of his head went under.

Then nothing moved.

It had all the sleek movement and implied symbolism of an elegy, and I watched, now breathless, fascinated by the melodramatic, almost celluloid image.

But of course life is seldom that prosaic and Will Sanders' lungs choose to rebel from the hushed tranquility of the moment. He broke to the surface, spluttering and thrashing around wildly, as one part of his body chose to render up a violent protest at his clear and awful intention.

But he was still far enough out to drown easily.

As I kicked off my shoes and ran for the water, in my mind was the simple thought that I could still save him.

But as I ran, I sensed movement. Another person. Another running body heading for the water. I would have some help now. We would pull Will Sanders safely to the shore. We would force the lake water from his lungs. Despite his intentions, we would save his life. These thoughts were with me as I ran. Sustaining thoughts.

I jettisoned these noble intentions as the second body veered and crashed into me, knocking the wind out from me, forcing me to the ground a foot or so short of the water. Now I was trying instead to lift my head, to spit out the sand that had gathered in my mouth, the sand George Tait was forcing me to eat as he straddled my back.

When I tried to wriggle out from under him I couldn't. He held me fast. I lay still and tried to think.

"You fuck." He was out of breath, twisting his body to pull something from his trouser pocket.

"You clever fuck."

Please don't let it be a gun. Please. I managed to turn my head half around. He pulled it out finally, and twisted it around in his hand. I saw that it was a gun.

Then he called me a stupid, nosy yuppie fuck and smashed the handle of the gun once into the back of my head with a sickening force that only registered for a split second.

I woke up to George Tait's words hissing close to my ear.

"You just missed yourself a drowning," he said.

I sat up. My head hurt. He stood before me. Over me. He had the gun in his hand. His hand was steady. The gun was pointed at my face.

Behind him the lake stretched out toward the island in a calm, unbroken mirror that reflected the sky full of gathering clouds at the close of the day.

I sat up and the quick motion made my head hurt. There was no sign of Will Sanders in the water. How long had I been out?

"You left him to die," I said.

George Tait smiled unpleasantly. "No sense stopping a man doing what he wants to do, is there?"

He put the gun closer to my face.

"You've been a real fucking pain these last few days," he said. "You should probably be made to die now."

I started to talk. "How long do you think you can do this kind of thing before the real law comes after you? You think you're safe? You're not. I'm not a tramp. And Will was a well-known lawyer. We're not nobodies. We can't just vanish away."

He pretended to look confused. "Will killed himself. What in the fuck does that have to do with me?"

"I'll say you drove him to it."

He smiled. "But you'll be dead, too."

"Then they'll get you for killing me."

"A fat lot of fucking good that'll do you."

"I'll be past caring. On the other hand, you'll be getting your asshole reconfigured in prison for the rest of your sorry life."

He sneered. "Big fucking talk. But I could maybe let you live. Then it'll be my word against yours. They'll never find your friend out there and Will isn't going to say much of anything now." He pulled himself up proudly. "I'm a respected man around these parts. Folk will take my side for sure."

"You're seriously deluding yourself. Most of the folk think you're a bully and a moron. Even your wife won't back you up."

He laughed at me. "My wife? I married myself the town pump. Didn't know it then. Pretty little thing she was. Still is. I guess. For what that's worth. She hasn't even the guts to leave. Just drinks and fucks anything that moves when I'm not around and pretends she likes me when I am."

"You mean like Will Sanders?" I said.

He shrugged. "Whatever. She only picked herself losers. And usually she did it away from the lake where no one I knew could see her. Will was her first real serious fuckup, and blowing your little pal in front of the kids was just too fucking much."

"You knew." It wasn't a question.

He shook his head in fake sorrow. "It was a lame fucking story from the start, and getting Tammi to talk wasn't what you'd call real hard. I maybe didn't go to college, but I'm no fucking idiot. After I've taken care of you, me and Sylvie will be having a good long talk. But until then, she's still scared enough of me to say what I want her to say. So there'll be two of us against just the one of you and anyway, you're forgetting the most important part. As far as folks are concerned your friend was nothing but a pervert, and he died just like he deserved to do, and at least four people are gonna testify to that."

I shook my head. "We know that's not right. Eventually the truth will come out. One of the children will break down and say that it was just a story. That Keith was getting his dick sucked by your tramp wife."

He grinned nastily. "But that's nothing but a fucking lie. That didn't happen. Why, there's just no way that could have happened, your honor." He was almost laughing now. "Face it, pal. You're seriously fucked."

I shook my head.

He pushed the gun closer. His voice grew soft. "Now I want you to take back what you said about my wife."

"You just said it yourself."

The words came very slowly. "What I can say and what you can say are two different fucking things. I want you to take it back."

I shook my head.

"Then you're going to have to die."

"You keep forgetting. If you kill me it isn't going to be handled by the local police yahoo you suck up to at church rummage sales. Big time professional cops from the big city will be all over you. And even if Sylvie takes your side at the start, she'll break down after a while, and then you'll be finished.

His eyes shifted out across the water to the island. "I still haven't heard you take it back."

"She had an affair with Will Sanders."

"Maybe Will led her astray."

"Get real."

But I was wasting my breath.

George Tait's notions of reality shifted like soft sand underfoot.

"You don't understand this place. Any of this stuff. This is a community, out here. A private place. We live away from the big cities and the rules you slick urban fucks have to follow. We don't have drugs and we don't have sex perverts walking the streets. We all know each other's names. We all go to the same church. We're all white and we all tan easy. Hell, I'm no racist, but you can't deny that life's a whole hell of a lot easier if we're all the same color and stuff like that. We all dress the same. Buy the same piece-of-shit Madras shirts from the spring sale at the place in town right on Main street. We're a bunch of lily-white fucking clones. Tomorrow we all go to the town meeting where we all vote the same way and elect the same dumbass mayor we been electing for the last fifteen years. He's a jackass but we all like him. Saturday we all go to the school soccer game. They lose every fucking game. Afterward, there's a church corn boil in the afternoon if the weather holds up. It's my turn to bring the Kool-Aid for the kids, the cheap jug white wine for the pastor's prissy wife, and the beer for the rest of us. Sylvie's in charge of bringing bread and hot dog buns which is about the easiest fucking thing in the world to do but that's about her speed, especially after she's had a few drinks."

"It sounds just like heaven."

"Don't try and be fucking clever. We're all the same here. That's what I'm trying to say. There's some safety in numbers. That's what I'm talking about. We're safe here. You come up here and stir things up, and we close ranks on you. That's the way it works. You can't get in our way. Pervert or not, your little friend didn't belong. Simple as that. And maybe that's all the reason we need to kill him. He was trespassing on private property. Our private property."

He seemed to have finally arrived at what to him was a logical conclusion.

"Will Sanders might have argued with some of that."

"Will hadn't the balls to do things right. He was a big talker with a big space where his spine should have been attached. A good family man mostly, when his dick wasn't twitching at the sight of my wife, but still a sorry-assed piece of shit for all the fancy cases he won and the big companies he saved from all these little hurt guys with their little pinhead lawyers who couldn't talk the way Will could for the big retainers from the car company guys in the good suits."

"Why are you telling me all this?"

He smiled almost ruefully. "How the fuck should I know? I guess maybe I wanted to get things a little clearer in my head. It's surely helped. It might make you feel better too."

"About what?"

He smiled. "About dying," he said. "Now would you care to say something sweet about my wife?"

"Would it really make any difference?"

He pretended to mull it over. "I guess not," he finally said.

When he placed the gun in the middle of my forehead he sighed, like it was a distasteful chore someone had to perform. When he began to squeeze the trigger I closed my eyes.

There was no epiphany. I didn't hear soothing voices or see a warm white light reaching out for me through a tunnel of soft clouds. I waited to die. Maybe I thought of Keith. Maybe I didn't. Maybe I wanted to hold him responsible for my eminent demise. But then again, maybe I didn't.

"Hey?"

He suddenly pulled the gun away. I opened my eyes. He was looking with some confusion somewhere past my head.

"No," he said. "Please, Hon. NO."

There was a sharp sound.

George turned his head away at the last moment, and the bullet from the gun Sylvie Tait was holding ripped away half his skull and sent blood and brain matter oozing onto the sand like rich red wine onto a pristine white tablecloth.

Sylvie walked barefoot across the burning sand and dropped the gun at the feet of her clearly dead husband.

"He keeps a lot of guns around our house," she said. "And I've never much cared for the habit."

Her dark tanned foot touched his blood. She pulled it away, then stared down, her face curious, as if unsure what it was, and how it got there.

I was still sitting.

She sat down beside me.

"Maybe I should run away. Start myself a new life in a new town far away from here. Would you like to start a new life with me? With a killer woman? We could live on an empty beach somewhere. You have plenty of money, don't you? I could dye my hair and change my name. Maybe they wouldn't come looking for me. Why should they bother with me?"

"You know that they will."

"But why should they? That's not fair. It's not like he was a good man. Everyone knows he wasn't. He killed your friend didn't he? He drove Will to kill himself. He'd have surely killed you."

She was feverishly intent on establishing her self-justification.

I wanted to tell her that if she hadn't lied to George he wouldn't have killed Keith. But I wasn't sure of that anymore. If she hadn't stayed with him none of this would have happened. If she hadn't been so fearful. But there were too many improbables, too many ifs.

The reasons weren't important.

It was possible for George Tait to have killed Keith for no good reason at all. Or simply for trespassing. Or for borrowing the old rowboat. Or for sitting and talking to Connie on the beach. Even just for being on the beach, his beach, for being an unwanted stranger, and for stumbling uninvited into the superficially ordered world of George Tait, which was at heart a false world, that didn't cotton much to the presence of strangers, of random patterns that disrupted the smooth surface.

"So. If I don't run away with you," Sylvie asked, "what will happen to me next?"

I didn't have a good answer, or one that she would have been delighted to hear. I could have told her that she'd rid the world of a nasty presence. It would have been the truth. But I could also have told her that the world wasn't going to show her any great expression of gratitude for her action. That also would have been the truth. I hoped the legal system would go soft on her.

She had, after all, saved my life.

But I was saved from having to answer her.

Perhaps George Tait was fundamentally right. In these parts, he was the law, and strangers like Keith and I were the outlaws. Perhaps my death would have been as unnoticed as Keith's was. And perhaps the local townspeople would have closed ranks, and left George to administer his border-town justice.

But in this instance, he was mistaken, or at least he was overoptimistic. Because, at the sound of the gun, someone nearby had done their duty, and had thought to call the police.

The siren grew shrill and loud as the marked car skidded into the parking lot beside the beach, its roof lights pulsing.

George's good buddy, whose name completely escaped me for a moment, got out of the squad car and slowly approached us. Idiotically, his handgun was drawn.

Unknowingly, he was the first of the townspeople to pay his last respects to his good neighbor.

# EIGHTEEN

IT WAS TWO HOURS LATER when I was able to leave the beach. I had told my story to local police chief Andy Borland, who obligingly gave me his name.

My story took close to half an hour, told straight through, then Sylvie Tait told hers for a second half-hour. The time in between was occupied by Borland and the ambulance crew checking the body, photographing the body, using the traditional yellow tape to seal the death area off.

It surprised me that Borland allowed Sylvie and me to eavesdrop on much of each other's stories, but, as a result, I can attest that there were few discrepancies between the two tales.

It became increasingly obvious that Andy Borland had hated George Tait. He never came out and said it, but I soon realized as he gently coaxed Sylvie through the events that he was anxious for us to collaborate, to present a united front.

He was hell-bent on serving up George Tait as the one and only villain, and short of outright lying, we were being silently encouraged to aid in this endeavor.

I should mention at this point that we were more than willing to oblige.

A share of the blame for the whole sad business had to belong to Sylvie Tait, her scene on the beach with Keith, and her clumsy attempt to cover it up, which, for all her hard work, had come to be believed by virtually no one. She had primed and loaded her husband like a gun and he had come out firing wildly. But that was slightly unfair. George Tait was an incendiary device all by himself, and Keith and Will Sanders were dead at his hands, one directly, the other, indirectly.

Sylvie had been married to a brutal man for a long time and most of her natural defenses no longer functioned. She wasn't a criminal. She wasn't a killer. She had saved my life, for without any doubt George Tait would have killed me.

So as I spoke to Borland I managed to recall every detail of George's cruelty, every dark aspect of Keith's death, as it had been related to me by Will Sanders. Did I embellish? Not really. But who would know or care if I did? All three men were now silent.

I didn't choose to relate the nature of Keith and Sylvie's encounter on the beach that night. I rather let it be known that George killed Keith for stepping into the Handle and upsetting George's unofficial reign as unelected tyrant and psychotic town booster. Sylvie too said nothing on the subject. It would be her secret. The cop was more than happy to nod along, more than willing to believe the tale as we related it to him. He didn't need any another reason. George was George. And that was clearly reason enough.

As he sent us on our way, he asked if we would like to think about what we had said and submit something to him in writing. We both agreed. It was surprising the way the cop was handling the investigation, but the chance to think about what had happened, and put it down in black and white, was welcome.

The cop, I'm quite sure, was hoping for an additional nail or two for the Tait coffin, and was also intent on making the whole business look as official as possible.

Sylvie walked away. I turned to do the same, as the two-man ambulance team got into a hasty conference with the police chief. Before I could leave, I was called over.

It transpired that one ambulance attendant was unable to swim. This was sheepishly admitted. The other one could. But the police chief also couldn't. This fact was relayed in a forceful manner meant to discourage any adverse comment. Borland wanted Will Sanders' body out of the water fast, and, incredibly to me, was more than willing to hand the chore over to the one orderly and me.

Equally strange was my ready agreement.

We both waded gingerly into the water. The body wasn't too far out. Not floating on the surface. Not sunk to the sand below. Will Sanders lay in a shallow parody of purgatory a foot or so beneath the surface, his face upturned, a pale and pasty white, his eyes bugged, staring in vain, his mouth futilely wide open.

We pulled him to the shore and the non-swimming orderly took over from me to help load the corpse into the ambulance, after a flurry of triplicate forms were signed and divided between the two caring arms of the public service.

After Will's body was examined in vain for signs that he had died in any way other than drowning the cop began a slow methodical walk around George Tait. He stopped and made short notes. He bent down to bag George's gun, the one that had been in his hand, the one he had used to hit me with. He had taken the other gun earlier, the one dropped by Sylvie. He had taken a blood sample. He had photographed from several positions. Yet he kept on walking, around and around, as the two orderlies leaned against their ambulance, waiting, watching impassively.

"You should get going now." He spoke to me softly.

"I wanted to ask you something," I said.

"Go on." It was a noncommittal answer.

"Where was George hiding?"

He smiled. "Inside his garage with the door closed. I guess there's a peephole. He must have been watching you for a while. When it got to a good part he opened the garage door and came out. You must have been too busy to see or hear him coming. Sylvie was hiding in the house and heard the door open. She watched George walk toward the beach, then she turned away and shook for a while longer, 'till she got up the nerve to come out with one of George's guns in her hand. Her timing was pretty good for you. So was her shot. Jesus Christ. She couldn't have killed him faster if she'd tried."

One of the orderlies had recommended an inexpensive motel close to town that, in his own words, "wasn't the biggest shithole on the face of the planet." I told him I would be happy to pay more. He laughed at this foolishness and told me it was also the only decent motel in town, cheap, shitty, or otherwise.

I asked the chief if he needed me for anything else.

"You leaving town tonight?" he asked me curtly.

I told him I would leave tomorrow morning.

"Fine. We have your address. Write up your statement, and be careful with it. Very careful. Get everything in it. Don't forget any stuff." At that point he looked at me meaningfully. "Then drop it off when you leave. The station's on the main road out of town. There's no way you can miss it."

I told him I could fax it to him.

He laughed at that. "Too fancy for us," he said.

As I left the beach, I watched him. He continued to circle the body. Did I imagine him edging closer and closer? Zeroing in on a metaphysical second kill, this one beyond flesh and blood, this one going after the reputation, the sights set on the personality.

It was open season on George Tait now, and I didn't care.

I did find the Shady Nook Motel easily. It was where the orderly said it would be. Not terribly far from the car rental office, or the supermarket, where I had daringly abducted Sylvie Tait.

It was as plain, as cheaply anonymous, and as ill-named as I expected it to be. A bored girl named Jeanette, with hair like Reba McEntire, took my credit card at the front desk and handed me a key without a smile. She was watching a sitcom on a tiny television beneath the desk, and I was fortunate enough to have approached her during a commercial break.

"Is ordering dinner a possibility?" I asked. It was still early, not yet eight, still light outside, still warm, but I felt I had lived several lives inside the trappings of the last few hours and I was tired, soaking wet, and my head was sore and liberally covered with dried blood where the late George Tait had hit me.

But for some odd reason the prospect of room service was an inviting one.

It was also clearly an unrealistic one. Jeanette looked at me oddly. Perhaps I had spoken in Farsi or more likely she had finally noticed my appearance. There was no room service available at any time. There was a burger place across the road.

"It's real good food they got there." Jeanette spoke without much enthusiasm. As she handed me a copy of my credit card receipt a flurry of canned laughter signaled that *Rosanne* was about to begin again, and that I could no longer count on her undivided attention.

Laid out across the soft queen-size bed and facing a washed-out print of what I took to be Mount Fuji enveloped in suggestive mist, I licked the remains of a cheeseburger from my fingers and fired up the laptop. When I logged onto CompuServe, I found a three-page message from Nye.

He was as always succinct and ruthlessly efficient. Patricia had called, and he had been apprised of my marital situation. As always I had no secrets from Nye. With a shock I realized how little I knew of his life away from ArtWorks. With another shock I realized how little I had thought about ArtWorks in the past few days.

But we all need to get away sometimes.

He was, he informed me, swinging over to my house in the morning to remove all traces of my presence from the property. Neither he nor Patricia thought the process would take terribly long. He would pick up some clothes for me there, and at the stores he knew I was partial to, if it was required.

He knew my size. He knew my taste. He knew my budget.

He had also, he added, found me a place to stay.

As a past master of subtly shaded nuance within the emotional confines of electronic mail, Nye was able to inform me of all this with evident hesitation. Aiding me in leaving my wife smacked of emotional territory, was, by nature, uncharted waters for Nye and I.

He had always liked Patricia very much. I knew this. And the feeling was, I think, firmly reciprocated. How could they not have found common ground? They were painstakingly precise people occupying key positions in my life. As it transpired, it was Nye who actually occupied the key position, while poor Patricia had been unknowingly been benched a while back.

But in one other way, they differed markedly. I felt sure that Nye was fulfilled. And Patricia clearly wasn't.

At the moment, however, I felt a little sorry for him.

He would not like being placed in the position of aiding and abetting our marital destruction. On the other hand he was brutally organized, and my life would have to be placed on an even keel as quickly as possible. I needed a place to stay. Ergo, Nye had found me one.

I was now in possession of a short-term rental, a small, sparsely furnished loft a stone's throw from my business. My clothes would be there, a computer would be up and working, the hard drive freshly loaded with the programs and files that had once resided in the machine back in my old study.

My new domicile would boast a table and a chair and a bed. There would be gleaming white walls and pale, stripped wood. Patricia had filled a box with my few knickknacks—a handful of the modern history books I professed to love but seldom found time to read; the computer manuals I loathed but read, rather than admit my ignorance to Nye; and a good coffee machine.

In a pathetically short time, my gossamer-thin life would be effortlessly crated and unpacked, just as it was before.

Contact had been made with my lawyer and my broker, and faxes had been brandished and exchanged. Things were moving quickly and efficiently. Between Nye and Patricia there would be scant room for sentiment or indecision. If I would activate WinFax Pro on my laptop, Nye would divert the waters and begin to send them on with all due haste.

I knew better than to argue, and did as I was instructed.

In conclusion, Nye said, my art-framing business was ticking along uneventfully, although Tye, my most wayward of employees, had threatened to seek employment elsewhere. There had been a tearful delegation of my female workers before Nye, begging him for a softer attitude from the management (Nye, in other words) toward tardiness and sloppy framing work. Nye decided on a policy of appeasement and we were thus still in possession of Tye the terminally tardy.

Nye ended by referring to our recent conversation and his plans for squeezing a little more money out of ArtWorks. I sensed trepidation. But he would try. Perhaps he thought I would soon be that particular American sub-species, the alimony-paying man, and that I would need ready cash by the bucketful from here on in.

I sent a short note back, thanking Nye for everything, and asking him to continue to shamelessly mother me. I knew he would read it within the half hour, as he could only keep his hands away from a keyboard for so long. I also raised the possibility of my taking a little more time off, knowing he would be happy to see the back of me, but would probably not choose to phrase it exactly that way.

I switched to Word Pro and began to write my statement for the police. It went quickly and remained mostly true to my verbal version on the beach. It would have gone faster, but the faxes began to pile up in the background. I was soon faxing back, restating that the title to the house was in my wife's name only, moving sums of money from me to her, instructing lawyers to expedite the divorce proceedings, pleading no contest. The lease for the loft even showed up. Nye had thought of everything. The papers were beginning to blur, but I was still aware enough to recognize a rental agreement when I saw one.

I left the room to find more ice for the large Diet Pepsi that had come gratis with the burger, which I had anticipated barely touching, but which was already half gone. When I returned after a successful sortie, the incoming faxes had finally ended.

With Nye's expert help, I was well on the way to casting myself adrift.

When the statement was finished, I read it over carefully, spellchecked it, saved it, sensibly made a backup on a floppy disk, switched WinFax from download to upload, and prepared to unleash an electronic blitzkrieg.

I used my memory, and media databases, and when all else failed I called directory assistance. I faxed and e-mailed my version of Keith Pringle's death to seven major newspapers, two in Chicago, one in Detroit, one in New York, one in Washington, one in Los Angeles, and one in London. I made sure to send one of the Chicago copies to the woman who had written the original piece on dying tourists in America, the one that had mentioned Keith by name.

Would the story be of any interest to them? I suspected that it might, especially in Detroit and Chicago. But truthfully, I wasn't sure.

It was to be a paper trail, an electronic burr that would ensure that Keith's death wouldn't remain the sole property of one strange cop in a small town.

But I wanted a little more insurance on that score.

So next came the authorities, the Chicago and Detroit police, the British Consulate, the Department of Immigration and Naturalization. I even toyed with the White House.

In the case of the consulate fax, I once again fine-tuned the direction of my communication, this time singling out Phoebe Chalmers, the woman I had spoken to on the phone.

When I had finished, I closed WinFax and kicked the burger wrappers off the bed. The soda was empty and the ice in the bottom of the plastic cup had melted to a warm, pale brown. My stomach felt obscenely full and my mouth tasted horrible. When I looked at my watch it was almost ten thirty.

On an impulse I checked CompuServe for messages before turning off the computer.

There was one.

It was from Nye, and it simply said—good luck.

I woke at 1:37 in the morning, pulled on dry clothes, and drove back to the Handle for no good reason. The yellow crime tape had claimed more ground, the bodies were gone, and it was too dark to see the blood.

The dock remained accessible.

The nighttime view was odd, or it seemed that way, given the frame of mind I was in. There were lights across the water, unblinking, static, house lights no doubt. Except for one area that was completely black. I was initially confused. Then I understood. Foolishness Island was blotting out a part of the other side of Paddle Lake like a blanket of dense fog.

I watched the stationary lights. Every once in a while, a pair of vehicle headlights moved like a shooting star on the coast road. Or at least it looked that way. The darkness was sufficient to obscure the demarcation between land and sky.

What was I doing here?

I turned back toward the beach. The Handle was dark, except for a dim light in Connie Alexander's front room. I thought of ringing her doorbell.

It was a foolish thought.

I drove back to the motel in silence.

Sonny Landreth's loud delta guitar filled the interior of the Mercedes early in the morning, as I pumped gas at an Amoco station perched on the far edge of town.

I had handed my statement in at the police station earlier. The office had been open but empty. Perhaps the chief was stuffing his face with doughnuts at a nearby diner. Perhaps not. He wasn't an especially fat man.

Much more likely he was up and already investigating the murder-suicide that took place yesterday out at the Handle, the murder-suicide that would surely make him a famous man in these parts, for a little while at least.

I signed the document in the empty office, dated it, added my address, then scored my address out, added my work address and phone number, and then quickly left.

If there was only one cop in town and he was otherwise occupied with the solving of a murder, then it followed that I was free to speed. Examining the argument for flaws, I detected none, and gunned the black convertible out of the gas station and onto an open road just as a ferocious guitar instrumental began.

I opened both passenger windows and resisted the urge to shout some form of childish obscenity at the proverbial dust of the town as I endeavored to quickly shake it off.

My feeling of euphoria prevailed. I was glad to be leaving Paddle Lake. My less-than-noble quest was over. My joy didn't extend as far as my going home. It hadn't been much of a home I had left behind, and it had been further eroded in my absence. But I was able to take pleasure in leaving. At the Handle a rock was lifted, and I had watched with some fascination as the creatures underneath froze, then scurried about in the harsh sunlight, frantic to reclaim their shelter, angered and aroused and exposed. There were people like Connie that I had liked, people like Sandy that I had lusted after, people like Will that I hadn't fully understood, people like Sylvie that made me nervous and sympathetic at the same time, and people like George Tait who just plain terrified me. As I drove they all resonated inside me. They surely would for a while. But I knew I would carry the memory of George Tait for a lot longer than the rest.

Driving fast, it took less than an hour to reach the exit for Harmony, the town where Bridget Cassidy resided. I slowed down. A mile and a half to go. I thought about her tanned arms, thin and sinewy inside the sleeve of her faded shirt, the bleached hairs like soft down, the smoothness of her legs as she sat, the leafy pattern of the fabric on the small couch, and the yellow/white sunlight applied like a balm to the living room in her compact, comfortable house, set halfway up the sand-sprinkled road that bottomed out onto a stretch of seldom-used beach.

She had formed an indelible image. Or at least her aspect and her topographic location had.

But now, more fully aware of the skittish nature my emotions had adopted in these past few days, I hesitated. In my present state, untold legions of women were capable of laying claim to my loyalties simply by breathing loudly in the same room. It was almost sitcom funny. I was clearly in classic rebound mode. The ironic aspect of this was that I had been in this state before being fully aware that I had anything from which to rebound.

But now I could more easily identify my malaise. The next step would be getting a firm grip on it before I became a leering midlife buffoon. I already had the sports car, after all.

Descending toward reality was made easier by the growing suspicion that I had barely registered with Bridget; she saw a friendly man perhaps, a concerned man, chasing after her missing quasi-relative for good and loyal reasons. Had she totally missed the personal agenda, the purely selfish rationale?

I didn't for a moment believe that she saw a likely lover, any more than Sandy Weller did. Sandy saw availability, horniness, and a chance for fun. She could probably locate horniness with her eyes closed and her hands tied behind her back. And she had never promised me anything but fun.

Bridget had been quietly focused on a missing man, the one she herself might have fallen a little in love with, while, just possibly, on the far periphery of her vision, I lurked, a would-be good knight anxious to find his own personal grail.

She had feared the worst about Keith when I had seen her. Like a parent knowing something, but not knowing it for sure. She would find out soon, as this was the heartland, and bad news was seldom slow in coming.

And she would grieve in the soft, understated manner in which I suspected she did everything.

She would remain an indelible image.

As Sonny Landreth's slide guitar spluttered and died, the exit for Harmony came and went.

The next five days and four nights limped past. I had my new place and my few possessions were geometrically arranged in it.

On the fifth night, I yielded to the demands of the traffic, and opened the large bay window to the mega-bass radio of passing cars that boomed their multicultural rap up at me. Once, bizarrely, I even heard Beethoven's Ninth Symphony.

I stood motionless in the milk-white room, my face pressed against the screen that filtered the humid, city-stained air that occasionally hitched a ride on a stray breeze coming westward from the lake.

I had lived my married life in climate-controlled rooms, in germ-destroying environments, chilled to a frigid state by silent running air-conditioning, and now I wanted it hot and natural.

The previous tenant had attached potted plants to the metal bars that ran waist-high outside the window, denying me a fast three-floor descent and a squashed impact on the parking lot below. They were mostly sunflowers and they were dying slowly and beautifully, their long petals intact and stiff, dry and turning brown around the edges.

One floor above me, the roof of the building housed a dozen lounge chairs and a scrupulously clean pool that got energetic if sporadic use from the hundred or so affluent young people who, for whatever perverse or practical reason, were doggedly determined to rent rather than own.

On the fifth night, I was alone, as I had been on the previous four. A sound system would have been nice, but it had remained in the house with Patricia. I had borrowed a CD boombox from the office, and Joan Osborne was singing. I had brewed coffee. I had also guiltily wolfed down a chili dog with onions from a hot dog stand a block away, so life was therefore not altogether wretched, even if my breath was.

Connie Alexander had written me a letter that had arrived care of ArtWorks. I hadn't opened it until now. I sipped my coffee and began to read.

The case of the Paddle Lake suicide-murder was moving along nicely. The death of Keith Pringle, an indigent foreigner, was being attributed to George Tait, a local handyman. Will Sanders' death was to be ruled a misadventure. No charges were being brought against Sylvie Tait for the shooting of her husband.

Sylvie was quietly assuming the aura of martyr. She was still in her house, and the neighbors, even Connie herself, were beating a path to her door with casserole dishes and offers of babysitting. As I had expected, the case had been large and brutal enough to draw the legal big guns, and the local police chief had been suitably praised for his diligence, but then forced to give up the case. Federal agents and hardened urban cops had descended en masse.

Two houses away, Will's wife, Chloe, was distraught and heavily sedated. His daughter Beth was doing okay, and there Connie was at her most helpful, as the youngster had begged to be allowed to stay with Connie, and Connie was more than happy to oblige. They gardened and walked the beach and played board games indoors when the rain or the photographers drove them inside. The Handle had fast become a mecca for the media. Al and Al Jr. at the jet-ski store were in clover, as was Sandy Weller, whose house was full of newspaper sharks with easily padded expense accounts. Sandy was also busy with a handsome local man much younger than herself, and poor Connie had trouble keeping the scent of naked envy off the pages. Tom Younger had strongly advised his four Handle clients to hold out for a higher price, in light of the area's newfound notoriety. I was powerless to decide if this was a wise or foolish strategy.

For the sake of Beth, Connie had told her two well-meaning identical sons and her well-meaning identical daughter-in-laws to take her house off the market. She would stay on for a while, and keep little Beth company, until things died down. And if she ever moved from the Handle, it would definitely be back to her beloved New Orleans, either under her own steam, to a small vine-shrouded house in the Garden District, or else in a watertight box, bound for the family vault in the elegantly decrepit grounds of the Lafayette Cemetery.

She ended by wishing me well with my life. And she hoped we would meet again soon. She hoped too that I would visit New Orleans in the near future. She didn't remember if I had been there (I hadn't, in fact).

I finished her letter. She was a lovely person. And she'd got me thinking about a trip.

Later that same night I sat in the semi-darkness and listened to the traffic. At two o'clock I picked up the phone and dialed an international number. I had been putting off calling Jimmy Tait for five days, but somehow, a little of Connie's natural resilience seemed to be all I needed. I waited. When he at last answered I spoke.

It wasn't much fun for either of us.

Nye poured the wine and handed me a glass.

"The apartment is . . . ?" he cautiously ventured.

"Very nice indeed," I said. "And thank you."

We sat in my office.

The store sound system was louder than usual, and I was fairly certain we were listening to the Canadian pianist Glenn Gould playing Bach's *Goldberg Variations*. I wasn't terribly strong on classical music. Nye was. As was Patricia. They both liked Bach, although Nye's position was in truth closer to an outright addiction.

"Bach?" I gingerly ventured.

He nodded slowly and sipped his wine.

"Early or late?" I was faintly aware that Gould had recorded the piece as a child prodigy, and then again much later, toward the end of his singularly odd and unhappy life.

"Late."

I suspected that knowing which version he had chosen to listen to should provide some valuable insight into the hidden and controlled personality of my stalwart Nye, but I was as usual powerless to go anywhere with the information.

ArtWorks had been closed to the public for a full twelve minutes, and we had had the place to ourselves for two of them. Nye had closed up shop and I had found glasses, plates and whatnot. We had ordered two Caesar salads from a local restaurant and Nye had wordlessly produced a bottle of Napa Valley Cabernet from some secret hidey-hole of his.

"It's not really suitable for salad," he said apologetically.

I had ordered the salads, knowing that Nye liked them. Nye had produced the wine, knowing my fondness for red wine. As was often the case, we were very subtly at cross-purposes.

"Are we celebrating?" I asked hesitantly.

"Your return," he said with a rare faint smile. "It's been a week now."

"I wasn't gone especially long."

"No." He paused with some significance.

I spoke. "I know. It felt like a long time for me too."

He carefully put his glass down. "Was it satisfying? Your trip?"

I shrugged helplessly. "I don't know quite what I expected. It certainly felt as if a lot happened. I didn't expect to come back to my own divorce."

Nye nodded but said nothing.

I asked, "You've been to the house?"

Was his look slightly sheepish? "I've helped Patricia with the computer you left her. I took all your programs off the hard drive and loaded Novell's PerfectWorks instead. I also helped her with Quicken, and showed her where Solitaire was."

I smiled. "She'll like that last part. But don't for God's sake treat her like an idiot."

He smiled. "I'll try not to. She's a much faster learner than you were."

"I see."

He hesitated.

"Can I say something?"

"We're drinking your wine."

"Actually . . . it's two things."

"Okay. What's the first?"

"I would just like to say that I strongly suspect that your marriage is salvageable."

"By me?"

"Oh by both of you, I think. But perhaps by you first."

"The proverbial first move?"

"Correct. It does fall within your province. But if you do make it, I think she will be willing to listen."

"Did Patricia say anything?"

"No."

"Then you're simply guessing."

"Partly. But I still think I'm right."

"Is this advice from an agony aunt?"

"No. It's simply an observation."

"But one you think I should act on?"

"Are you at all interested in resurrecting your marriage?"

I paused. "I don't know. I don't think so. But I don't know."

"I see."

"Do you know that I often feel a lot like Captain Kirk when we talk?" I said suddenly.

"Captain James Tiberius Kirk of the Enterprise?" Nye was gazing quizzically at me.

"The very same," I replied.

"I presume I have the part of Spock in this scenario?"

"That would be correct," I said, smirking.

"Well then," Nye said, "I should admit that the thought has also occurred to me on occasion."

"You mentioned something about a second question?"

"Yes." He paused. "It's a little trickier." And I knew that it would be about money and not love. Personal money that is, not business money, because the flow and ebb of ArtWorks money is largely Nye's domain.

"In the past ArtWorks has just about broken even."

"I'm aware of that."

"And you were happy enough with that?"

"Correct. I was."

"Am I right in assuming that we have to do better than that now?"

"I don't quite follow."

He spoke carefully. "You're very possibly getting divorced in the near future."

"It would certainly seem that way."

"And by way of settlement Patricia is receiving . . ."

"Ah, I think I can see where this conversation is going."

"Surely this places a new onus on the store to generate more money."

"No. Oh, it would be nice. But let me ask you, could we make more money?"

Nye shook his head slowly at that.

"Perhaps the tiniest little bit more profit?"

"That's a possibility." He paused. "But you could always sell. The business. The property. Both. The property is certainly valuable."

I cut him off. "I know it is. But the truth is I like ArtWorks. I even like pretending that I run it. After my divorce, I will still have plenty of money by any standards. I'll have less than I did, I'll admit that, but since you're bluntly asking, I'll bluntly state that much of what Patricia and I jointly owned was more Patricia's, or her father's, than mine, and I was never especially comfortable with my name attached to it. Perhaps that statement exemplifies the problematic nature of my marriage. I can't argue. So now all of that will return to Patricia, and ArtWorks will be wholly mine. I know you know the mechanics of our ownership, but very little about the actual profits everything generates. Patricia is destined to die a very rich woman, and if I keep my nose relatively clean and don't do anything earth-shatteringly stupid, I should survive to live well and long without the need of Medicare."

"We could do something else with the property?" Nye ventured.

"We could. Any thoughts on that?"

"No." Nye said. "I'll start thinking."

"Good. I'd also like you to start thinking about being my equal partner."

"Suppose I don't come up with a good idea."

"Then you can still be my partner in poor old ArtWorks, and we'll share in the poverty. Tell me, would firing Tye help to turn a tiny profit?"

"It's a nice thought, but I would have to say no."

"Oh well," I shrugged. "It was just a thought." I sipped my wine. There was a silence.

"I would very much like to stay here." Nye spoke quietly. "And I'd be honored to be your partner."

I smiled. "That's a tremendous relief, because otherwise I'd actually have to do some work. Speaking of which, is my presence required for the next few days?"

He sighed audibly. "Another trip?"

"I thought perhaps New Orleans."

"A very nice town." He said.

"You've been there?"

"Once. A while ago. Are you taking the laptop?"

I made a very quick decision. "Nope," I said. "It's a real holiday."

"We will miss you," he said dutifully.

"I seriously doubt that," I scoffed.

At that point, we stopped.

The pitch of the conversation had been on a personal level several floors removed from the place where we were most comfortable, and we were both acutely aware of it. Yet we'd truthfully only said what needed to be said. But now, seized with mild embarrassment, we both picked up our forks and ate our salads in silence, as the older but very possibly no wiser Gould played on.

Three large television sets were mounted to the walls and squawked at the endless cavalcade of tired travelers. I had unwittingly picked a seat equidistant from all three, and was being relentlessly assaulted by two channels of dueling news broadcasts and a rerun of *Cheers*. Inexplicably, the public address system was equally strident, and we were being treated to the later works of Bruce Springsteen, who had apparently made the sorry descent to elevator, or in this case, train station muzak.

I had called the airlines in the morning and received the sad news that all the day's flights to New Orleans were overbooked. There was no explanation tendered.

At Amtrak, however, no such problems existed, and I was quickly booked a coach seat for that same night. I was asked by an extremely courteous woman if I wanted a pillow. I told her that I certainly did. I was also informed that for a pittance more I could indulge in three months of unlimited travel up and down and across the Midwest, with only minor restrictions applied. I was sorely tempted, but I thought of Nye and declined her kind offer.

My train was scheduled to leave early in the evening and arrive in New Orleans in the middle of the next day. I was proudly informed by the woman on the phone that the seats were more comfortable and spaced further apart than those found on a plane. I hoped she was right, since I'd never sat on a plane for eighteen straight hours.

But first there was the train station to endure.

My packing had largely consisted of consolidating the items of new clothing Nye had procured for me into my one larger bag. It didn't appear as though anything had been overlooked, but I was being uncharacteristically blasé about the whole affair. I could always buy there, and then give Nye grief when I returned.

I had nothing to read, as I was unable to muster the necessary enthusiasm for a large and doubtless very dry history book. At the train station, I bought an Anne Rice paperback and a guidebook of the city on impulse.

I read the first paragraph of the novel. Then I read it again. The noise was brutal. In stereo, a prominent city official was reputed to be being fired and indicted, in that order, and Sam was making a botch of babysitting Frasier and Lilith's son, Frederick.

A preschool child sat down three seats away from me, and listened to Ringo Starr loudly narrate the adventures of a train, on a cheap cassette recorder that didn't appear to have headphones.

I opened my guidebook instead, locating the Garden District on the map, the cemetery, even Anne Rice's own house. I had already found a room in a house offering bed and breakfast that faced a park beside a zoo, that was close to the university, and right on the streetcar line.

It all sounded both intimate and convenient.

Was the city really that small? It appeared that it was. I rejected the idea of renting a car, reasoning that between the streetcar and a lot of walking I could surely reach all the places I wanted to explore.

I would sip cafe au lait and eat beignets till they poured out of my ears. I would gaze at hidden courtyards and flowered gardens till my eyes glazed over with horticultural and architectural overload. I would devour seafood possibly three times a day, and I would forget myself, even if I chanced to wander onto the hormonal war-zones of Bourbon Street, where a red-faced teenager from Wisconsin would doubtless chose to relieve himself of a stomach full of sickly sweet hurricanes all over my fresh new trousers.

I *would* forget myself.

It would be dishonest of me not to remark that, as passengers, we were a decidedly scruffier crew than the airlines normally attract. We were on the whole younger. We looked much more tired. Our tiny children fell more often and cried louder. Our bags were more mismatched and not one of us possessed the wheeled suitcases mandatory to flight attendants. A few of us had reached a fashion plateau somewhere in the late seventies or early eighties, and were seemingly content to stay there in acid-washed purgatory.

This might seem a cruel series of observations, as a few of us were no doubt wearing the best clothes that we owned, and traveling the only way we could afford to travel.

Bruce no longer sang for the lonely (or was it Roy Orbison who sang for Bruce who, in those days, was one of the lonely himself?), and a new voice silenced the cathode trio, announcing the imminent departure of our train.

The window seat proved to be initially less of a godsend, as the southern half of the city opened up its industrial innards to the glow of the red dusk, which did little to soften the decades of industrial decay that lay there.

But eventually we passed beyond the edge of the city and found the flat green-gold of the traditional Midwest.

In a college town further downstate, a tall, tanned girl dressed sensibly for hiking took the empty seat next to me. She looked obscenely healthy and practical, her hair tied up with a frilly knot that did double duty as a fluffy bracelet, her knapsack stowed away, her travel bag unpacked; thick brown-bread sandwiches, domestic bottled water, cassette tapes and letters with foreign stamps rubber banded neatly together.

She told me her name was Kate Carmichael. She was twenty-seven and the recipient of a postgraduate degree in business studies. She was traveling to New Orleans to meet a close friend. They were hostelling to conserve their money. She pulled the bracelet away as she spoke and her hair exploded in brown-red curls that flopped down beneath her shoulders. I tried not to look impressed.

Later she removed her hiking boots and her thick wool socks and slipped on ropey sandals that looked inelegant yet very comfortable. She wore a plain white T-shirt and old jeans cut off for walking comfort, rather than for sex-bomb effect.

Even allowing for the truly berserk wanderings my romance-fixated heart was currently doing, Kate was quite breathlessly beautiful.

We talked until late about college years and I tried to sound as young and impressionable as a man a full decade older, and almost twenty years away from campus life, could. If I had had it in me to blush and be altogether winsome, I would have cheerfully done it.

But I suspected that I would only register as truly desperate, and after a while I found it impossible to deny the passage of the years, as all my jaded nonchalance escaped to the surface. I hoped that it somehow masqueraded as heroic world-weariness rather than chronic trepidation, but I wasn't especially confident on that score.

Across the border into Tennessee, the train abruptly went dark, a movie was offered, the dining car was declared closed, and the snack car put their ham and Swiss cheese sandwiches with potato chips and a soft drink, on special until midnight.

I offered to buy her something (I had previously suggested dinner and been smilingly turned down, as she waved one of her sandwiches at me) and was again gently rebuffed.

I returned to my seat much later, having in my ignorance been made to eat my food purchases in the snack car, and not to return to my seat, *until* I'd damn well finished every bite.

Kate was asleep and half smiling by then. She no longer wore lipstick, I noticed. She had her own blanket wrapped tightly around her. She had received a pillow, and mine was sitting on my seat, waiting patiently for me.

So I edged past her and sat down, pushing the handles and buttons that flattened the seat out, positioned the leg rests, turned out the reading light, and pulled down the window shade.

Then I lay wide-eyed and a million miles away from sleep close to an inch from her face and gazed under the curls at the half smile that was still shimmering on her innocent and pretty young face.

Much later, our train was inexplicably motionless.

The riverfront lights of newly restored downtown Memphis woke me for a second, and I looked at my watch. Almost three in the morning. The dark car was lit by lonely streetlights outside freshly built condos and restaurants. The train slowly inched forward.

I had traveled some during the night. Now I was lost inside her hair. I smelled her shampoo. I moved my hand gingerly and found her face, her cheek. I stroked her skin, then I leaned forward and kissed her softly on the forehead. Kate smiled and her eyes opened and we sat without moving, not knowing what on earth to do next.

I touched her hair, terrified of squandering the moment, and she put her head on my shoulder and I kissed the top of her head again and she spoke softly.

"I think they called this 'bundling' in a Bette Davis film I once watched. She plays a spinster, who was once fat and unlovely, in love with a married man she can never have. He was the same man who played Lazlo in *Casablanca*. I don't remember his name, but Ingrid Bergman called him 'Veek-tor' all the time. He always lights two cigarettes for them both to smoke. I don't remember where they are, or why they're there, but they're together and alone, and it's dark, and they can't get back to wherever they're supposed to be, so they bundle together, beside a fire, and nothing else happens all night, and she tells him that 'bundling' is an honorable thing to do, or something like that. It's all very romantic in a repressed kind of way. Have you seen the film?"

I shook my head.

"He wakes up in the night and looks into her face while she sleeps and then he pulls the blanket around her. That's all that happens."

I told her that I hadn't seen the film. She smiled and told me that I should.

Later I fell asleep again.

When I woke up again it was in the whole new world of Mississippi in the white of the morning sunshine.

PETER ROBERTSON is a native of Edinburgh, Scotland, and currently lives near Chicago.